THE CHANGEOVER
MARGARET MAHY
Orion

ORION CHILDREN'S BOOKS

First published in Great Britain in 1984 by J. M. Dent & Sons Limited
This edition published in Great Britain in 2018 by Hodder and Stoughton

1 3 5 7 9 10 8 6 4 2

Cover design by Christabella Designs
Cover photograph courtesy of Trevillion Images
Author photograph courtesy of Fairfax media NZ / The Press

A CIP catalogue record for this book
is available from the British Library.

ISBN 978-1-5101-0505-8

Printed and bound in Great Britain by Clays Ltd, St Ives plc

The paper and board used in this book are made
from wood from responsible sources.

Little, Brown Books for Young Readers
An imprint of
Hachette Children's Group
Part of Hodder and Stoughton
Carmelite House
50 Victoria Embankment
London EC4Y 0DZ

An Hachette UK Company
www.hachette.co.uk

www.hachettechildrens.co.uk

To Bridget and other midnight visitors –
Governor's Bay, 1983

Contents

Introduction

by Elizabeth Knox

I read *The Changeover* a mere day after my first ever encounter with Margaret Mahy's work. I'd picked up *The Haunting* on a Saturday at my weekend bookshop job, read it overnight, then borrowed a copy of the newly published *Changeover* on the Sunday. I was twenty-five and hadn't the decades-deep reading experience I needed to thoroughly understand what it was in my first reading that seized me in a grip that's never failed.

I did know I was thrilled by the appearance of the local in a book of fantasy. In my reading till then the enchanted wardrobes, history-haunted country manors, and moors where Black Riders arrive when the mist rolls in were all Britain, or in Britishy shires. But when *The Changeover*'s protagonist, Laura Chant, sets out to find the witches whose help she needs, taking a night walk from her down-at-heel suburb, through a raw subdivision, once a farm, to *Janua Caeli*, an old house sunk in great trees, I recognised everything she noticed on her walk. I was a Hutt Valley (then a Wadestown and Paremata) girl, and I too had walked at night through new subdivisions to quiet roads with old gardens and hidden houses, streets where the tallest tree wasn't a fast-growing sycamore, but a slow-growing oak. My childhood was full of *The Changeover*'s swampland reserves, kingfishers, and co-ed schools with unflattering uniforms. This familiarity delighted me, but what I now understand I responded to with greatest excitement was the effortlessness with which the mythical and commonplace blended to make the story.

Laura Chant is the put-upon daughter of harried solo mother Kate, and sister of a much younger Jacko. This is Jacko, happy and well:

> On seeing Laura he did not so much run as bounce across the lawn in little jumps as if he were made of rubber and someone had cheerfully tossed him in her direction. First he hugged her and then pretended to growl and bite her.

Laura is regularly asked to cover for her mother. Though she loves Jacko deeply Laura would sometimes rather be with her friends—or alone with her thoughts, because she's that kind of girl and because there are less-everyday things about her existence that need thinking about. The first is something she accepts as natural, if not normal. She has hallucinations of herself, a Laura who's a little older, warning her of danger. This alarms her, but she's used to it. She pays her warnings attention, or puts them aside if she has no time for them. The other odd thing in Laura's life is a boy at her school—very well behaved, but in the habit of smirking at her as if they share a secret—a boy she somehow knows is a witch. Most novels for young people would have Laura keep this to herself, but she discusses it with her mother, in a wonderfully practical conversation full of arguments about why it would be implausibly out of character for such a boy to be a witch.

Laura is warned, and ignores it. Then, on her mother's next late-night Thursday, when she has charge of Jacko, desperately wanting to entertain and soothe him, she takes him into a new shop in her local mall, a store full of toys, and very attractive to children. Till this moment Laura's troubles have been pretty much everyday, or treated as such: a grizzling child, no funds, having to push-start her mother's car, having to put herself last. And then:

> . . . once in this enchanting shop, all Laura wanted was to get out again for it was full of the stale, sweet smell, laced with peppermint, that had assailed her in the morning – the smell of something very wrong and unable to conceal its wrongness.

Carmody Braque, proprietor of Brique à Braque, is possibly the best villain in New Zealand fiction: a desperately over-eager, wittering, clammy man, who latches onto Jacko. Laura is quickly able to recognise that he's not just a creep who is rather too attentive to a sweet young child. Not just someone to avoid, but fatally dangerous.

There are countless versions of this story. A sister, daughter, lover or friend single-handedly braves great danger to save a loved one from a monster. Its ancestry encompasses Hans Christian Andersen's *The Snow Queen*, *Beauty and the Beast*, Christina Rossetti's *The Goblin Market*, with lineages running all the way back to Persephone and Demeter, and Inanna and Gilgamesh. Margaret Mahy's knowledge of myths, and feeling for them, was vast and impeccable. She understood that no matter how you coloured and configured those ancient stories, their energy would stay with them. There are no difficulties or dissonances between *The Changeover*'s everyday, and its world of witches and legendary monsters. Even Laura can recognise that she is somehow living the reality of an ancient myth, so that, instead of hovering by her brother's hospital bed, she chooses to be guided by the sort of things that happen in stories, and goes to find a witch to help her.

The Changeover could be a realist book about a girl who lets her brother down then has to go to extraordinary lengths to save him. There'd be enough jeopardy in that. But there's additional jeopardy in the rules, conditions and complications of the discipline of magic. Margaret Mahy loved and was utterly convincing about magic in stories—what it would mean, how it might work if it worked. She had a curious, scientific mind, so her magic is always systematic and logical. Like science, it requires an exercise of imagination, as well as a mastery of information.

In order to help Jacko, Laura must gain knowledge and change herself. To save her family she has to enter into the life and rules of another family. *The Changeover* is a coming-of-age story, but a wise Mahy sort, where the young person doesn't leave childhood and become an adult, but gains adult power and responsibility by carrying her family and her childhood self across the rift of a crisis, a crisis which looks to most of the world like a mysterious illness, but to those who know is something much worse.

The Carlisle witches are Laura's kind of people, a family beside her everyday one. But of course they have their own problems, and they want things from her in return for their help, in true fairytale fashion. Laura's stern quest is the heart of the novel, but the romance between her and Sorry Carlisle is the blood pumping through that heart. *The Changeover*—subtitled in the edition I first read 'a supernatural romance'—is, I think, the mother of contemporary supernatural romances. It is also, in itself, a powerful coming-of-age story, a deeply original quest and transformation tale, and a pleasingly fraught, satisfying love story.

1

Warnings

Although the label on the hair shampoo said *Paris* and had a picture of a beautiful girl with the Eiffel Tower behind her bare shoulder, it was forced to tell the truth in tiny print under the picture. *Made in New Zealand,* it said, *Wisdom Laboratories, Paraparaumu.*

Just for a moment Laura had had a dream of washing her hair and coming out from under the shower to find she was not only marvellously beautiful but also transported to Paris. However, there was no point in washing her hair if she were only going to be moved as far as Paraparaumu. Besides, she knew her hair would not dry in time for school, and she would spend half the morning with chilly ears. These were facts of everyday life, and being made in New Zealand was another. You couldn't really think your way into being another person with a different morning ahead of you, or shampoo yourself into a beautiful city full of artists drinking wine and eating pancakes cooked in brandy.

Outside in the kitchen the kettle screamed furiously, begging to be taken off the stove. Laura, startled, emerged from under the shower only to discover there was no towel on the rail. She could hear Kate, her mother, moving about in the room next door, putting the kettle out of its misery, and tried to shake herself dry as a dog does though she knew it could never work.

'There's no towel, Mum,' she called fretfully, but as she spoke she saw a towel in a heap by the door and grabbed it eagerly. 'It's all right! I've got one. Oh blast! It's damp.'

'First one in gets the driest towel,' Kate shouted back from the kitchen.

The mirror had been placed in the steamiest part of the bathroom and showed her a blurred ghost. However, its vagueness suited her, for she was uncertain about her reflection and often preferred it misty rather than distinct. No matter how hard she tried to take her face by surprise, she could never quite manage it, and found it hard to be sure what she looked like when she wasn't trying, but her body was easy to know about and filled her with a tentative optimism.

'You're beginning to look all right from a distance,' her school friend Nicky had told her. 'Only seeing you close up spoils it. You're too simple. Get your mother to let you have a really trendy hair cut, or a blond streak in the front or something.'

Laura did not want a blond streak. Mostly she was happy being simple and living simply at home with her mother and her little brother Jacko. Yet sometimes, confronting the mirror, Nicky's remark came back like a compliment, suggesting that changes were now possible for her if ever she wanted them.

Out in the big room across the narrow hall it was Kate's turn to complain.

'I can't have driven home in just one,' she was saying. 'I'd have noticed everytime I changed gear.'

'Lost shoe!' announced Jacko as Laura, the towel wrapped clammily around her, ran past him into her bedroom.

Once through the door she stopped. Just for a moment something had frightened her, though she had seen and heard absolutely nothing special. Yet, even as she stood there, she felt it again, like the vibration of a plucked string.

'I've looked absolutely everywhere,' Kate said, a familiar note of morning panic creeping into her voice. Laura, shrugging away that inexplicable tremble in her blood, began to scramble into her school uniform – all regulation clothes except for the underpants, because it was a point of honour with all the girls at school never to wear school underpants. It was a stricter rule than any the school could invent.

'It's going to happen,' said a voice.

'What's going to happen?' Laura asked before she realized that the voice had spoken inside her, not outside in the room.

It's a warning, Laura thought with a sinking heart. She had had them before, not often, but in such a way that she had never forgotten them. It always seemed to her afterwards that, once she had been warned, she should be able to do something to alter things, but the warning always turned out to be beyond her control. The warning was simply so that she could prepare to be strong about something.

'Still no shoe!' said Jacko, standing in the doorway to report progress.

Laura picked up her hair brush, looking into the mirror in her room, the best one in the house because the light from a window fell directly on to it. She stared at herself intently.

I don't look so childish, she thought, turning her attention from the warning, hoping it might give up and go away.

But her reflection was treacherous. Looking at it, she became more than uneasy; she became frightened.

Sometimes small alterations are more alarming than big ones. If Laura had been asked how she knew this reflection was not hers she could not have pointed out any alien feature. The hair was hers, and the eyes were hers, hedged around with the sooty lashes of which she was particularly proud. However, for all that, the face was not her face for it knew something that she did not. It looked back at her from some mysterious place alive with fears and pleasures she could not entirely recognize. There was no doubt about it. The future was not only warning her, but enticing her as it did so.

'Stop it!' said Laura aloud, for she was frightened and when she was frightened she often grew fierce. She blinked and shook her head, and when she looked back, there she was as usual: woolly, brown hair, dark eyes, and olive skin, marked off from her blonde mother and brother because her genes were paying a random tribute to the Polynesian warrior among her eight great-great-grandfathers.

'Help!' she said, and bolted across the narrow hall into the room her mother shared with Jacko, which looked empty at first because Kate was on her hands and knees scrabbling under the bed, in case the shoe had hidden itself there during the night. 'Mum!' she said. 'No fooling! I've had a real warning.'

'What do you mean?' Kate's irritated voice struggled up through the mattress.

'It's happened again,' Laura said.

'I know it's happened again,' Kate said, but she was talking about something different. 'It's the second morning running. Just tell me how a perfectly ordinary – no, a nice, rather expensive – shoe can walk away overnight, and I'll give you a reward.'

'I looked in the mirror and my reflection went older all of a sudden,' Laura said.

'Wait until you're my age and that will happen every morning,' Kate declared, her voice still muffled. 'There's nothing here but dust.'

Jacko stood in the doorway, holding his Ruggie and watching them as if they were doing a circus trick for his amusement.

'The world's gone funny,' Laura complained. 'It would be dangerous for me to go out today. I'm staying at home in a good, strong bed. Could you write a note?'

'Write a note on Thursday?' cried Kate coming out from under the bed, brushing dust from her palms. 'You must be crazy, Laura! I need you much too much on Thursdays. It's late-night tonight, and who'd collect Jacko, take him home, give him his supper and read him a story? No notes on Thursdays and that's final.'

'I can't choose the day,' Laura said. Her voice was already giving in. 'It chooses me.'

'Thursday isn't allowed to choose you,' said Kate firmly, as if she could control destiny simply by refusing to take any nonsense from it. 'Be very careful, that's all! Look both ways! Keep out of sight of the teachers!'

'Oh Mum, it just isn't like that!' Laura protested. 'It's a warning about something serious. You don't know what it's like.'

'Tell me later,' said Kate, but Laura knew she could not tell. It was a condition that could not be described. People had to have faith in her, and somehow this was asking too much of them, especially in the morning, when life ran in three different directions and only one of them was hers.

Kate was seized with a memory that became an inspiration and hobbled into the big room where she found her shoe on the mantelpiece. Standing by the empty fireplace last night she had absentmindedly put her shoe there while she looked at a drawing of Jacko's – a happy, family drawing, for that was all he could draw. There they were – Laura, Jacko and Kate, wild yet geometrical, with huge heads and little legs and smiles so wide that they extended beyond their faces on to the paper around them. Under the influence of these smiles, Kate relaxed once more and began to walk evenly. Her shoe had come to heel and she forgave it at once.

But for Laura, who had come apart from the world, reconciliations were not easy. She looked at the soft sky. Only a few minutes before, it had been simple, clear and beautiful, but now she felt all summer leaning its weight against the house, breathing a hot and wolfish breath at her.

'Where's your basket, Jacko?' asked Kate and Jacko ran to get his basket which held a clean jersey, clean underpants, his library books, his special tiger book, and Rosebud, a pink, smiling crocodile made of felt. He carefully folded his Ruggie and put it on top of all these valuable possessions.

'Come on!' Kate said. 'Let's get this show on the road, shall we? I do hope you're feeling strong, Lolly, because I have a feeling the car might be difficult to start this morning.'

'Just for a change?' Laura asked, politely sarcastic because the car had been difficult to start for weeks without exception.

'It needs its battery recharged; probably needs a new one,' Kate said. 'They're so expensive.' She gritted her teeth in financial agony. 'Never mind, once we get going it will be all right. You keep an eye on Jacko, Lolly. Then I'll be sure where he is.'

Laura admired Kate's heroic appearance as she leaned her weight against the car doorway, forcing it to inch forward. Even pushing a car she managed to look graceful and pretty, smiling fiercely to herself, her fair hair boiling around her head. The road sloped away, slightly at first and then more steeply. The trick was to get the car rolling, jump into it and shock-start it on the steep part, and this Kate did, as she had done many times before. Across the road, Laura's next-door friend, Sally, stood waiting for her father to come out of their family garage and drive her to a private school on the other side of town.

'We won't be living in this place all our lives,' Sally had once said scornfully, but Laura liked the Gardendale subdivision for she had just spent a wonderfully happy year there and was trying to lead the sort of life that would encourage a replay with interesting variations.

Sally waved again as, a little further down the slope, the car coughed and then settled to a steady, hoarse grumbling.

'There she goes, mate!' said Laura to Jacko. 'Run, run as fast as you can – you can't catch me, I'm the gingerbread man.'

'Gingerbread running, eaten by fox,' said Jacko and seized his Ruggie to comfort himself in case a fox came by.

'I wish I had a Ruggie,' Laura said. 'I need one more than you do right at this moment.'

They hastened to catch up with Kate, piling in, brother, sister, basket, pink crocodile, school pack and all. The car shuddered with welcome.

'Don't worry!' Kate said to Laura. 'I've done it so many times before.'

'Not on a day with warnings!' Laura said. 'Just for a moment I thought you might fall under the wheels and get mashed up.'

'You and your warnings!' Kate said affectionately, but almost as if she were speaking to Jacko instead of Laura, who was fourteen and deserved a different voice.

'All right! Don't believe!' said Laura. 'I don't really blame you, but it's true, that's all. Everything lights up as if I were playing Space Invaders and says, *Warning! Warning! Warning!*'

'Have you been into that place again?' Kate said, gladly talking about something else, real without superstition. 'I wish you'd keep clear of it. There are a lot of rough types there and I don't want you getting into any trouble you can't handle.'

She was talking of the Gardendale Video Parlour where the Space Invaders machines peeped and sang all day. It was always alive with young men who couldn't get work and had to kill time, as well as children playing truant from school.

'Warning!' insisted Laura refusing to be diverted. 'First the look of everything changes . . . things stop flowing into each other and stand separate, a bit silly-looking but scary. The world gets all accidental. It's as if you had a house which seemed to stay up by being propped against itself and suddenly you realized nothing was really touching after all.' She slowed her voice down. 'The weekend Dad left with his girlfriend I had warnings. That's why I didn't get more upset. You said I was very brave but actually I was frightened it might be worse. I thought one of you was going to be killed or something.'

'Julia's his wife now, not his girlfriend,' said Kate, fastening on the least important thing. 'You might as well learn to use her name. They're happier together than we ever were.' But Kate meant that he was happier than he had been with her; he had always been very happy with Laura who looked like him.

Laura did not let herself be distracted by tired, sad, family recollections.

'And the next time it happened, that is in the last few years,' she went on, 'was when Sorry Carlisle came to school.'

'Sorensen Carlisle!' Kate said and gave a little yelp of laughter. She sounded knowing and amused. 'What on earth is there about that boy that you need to be warned about? It's like being warned about Red Riding Hood instead of the wolf . . . Isn't he the school's model boy – clean, quiet, hardworking, going around with an expensive camera photographing birds – the feathered kind, of course. A bit dull, really!'

Kate was being unfair but she was not to blame. She had only Laura's descriptions to go on.

Sorensen Carlisle had appeared at Gardendale Secondary School eighteen months ago, although his mother had lived there since she was a little girl. She had a place in local history; had belonged there before the name Gardendale had appeared on the city maps, before the city had stretched and flowed between the spurs thrust out from the main range of hills to form this sudden suburb, an instant village within the city's wider boundaries. Friends who had known the family for years said Miryam Carlisle had never been married, and she did not explain Sorensen in any way except to say that he was her son, sixteen years old, apparently studious, and marked out by a terrible stammer which had, however, grown steadily better over the last year and a half and was now barely noticeable. He had done all the average school things, played cricket in the summer, and rugby in the winter, and won a special prize for photographs of estuary birds in the Secondary School Science Fair, winning a book about birds of New Zealand for the school library. In class he did well, but not so well that he bothered himself or others. His unfortunate characteristic from the point of view of teachers was that he couldn't resist a smart answer, but this did not worry Laura who had never exchanged more than half a dozen words with him. On these occasions he had spoken in a soft, hesitant voice, simply a prefect instructing a younger pupil. What was impossible to describe was the remarkable smile accompanying his instruction – a smile directed at her alone. Laura had never mentioned this smile to Kate or the reason for it.

Even now she hesitated, and as she did so Kate was moved to say, 'If you're never warned against anything more threatening than Sorensen Carlisle you've got nothing to worry about.'

Outside, Kingsford Drive unreeled as long and straight as the surveyor's string that had laid it down only a few years earlier. However, road repairers were already struggling with something subterranean, and Laura, Kate and Jacko progressed crookedly, driving between giant pre-historic monsters, earth-moving machines making an island of Silurian time in the twentieth-century streets. The Gardendale subdivision reeled past and though all the houses were not exactly similar they were at least cousins, or maybe members of the same team. Laura and Kate were coming close to the gates of the Gardendale Secondary School and the footpaths began to teem with school uniforms all moving in the same direction. Taller than almost anything else in this flattened-out area of a flat city, the Gardendale Shopping Complex reared up ahead, a cross between the Giant Supermarket from Outer Space and an Industries Fair, for it had been designed to look jolly, and succeeded in its own way. *Kiwi Car Sales,* said a confident sign, and the salesman was already out whisking the night's dust from mudguards closest to the ground. Laura knew a lot of people despised the Gardendale subdivision, but she had grown fond of it and sometimes loved it for the very things that other people criticized it for – because it was new and raw and rough and filled with vandals who wrote strange things on walls with spray cans of paint. At night its streets became dangerous, but she frequently enjoyed this razor-edge of risk waiting outside their comfortable, family door. Laura thought about all these things in a single second while she prepared to tell her mother something she had known for a long time, but had never told anyone else before.

'Sorry Carlisle is a witch!' she said. 'No one knows but me.'

Kate did not laugh or tell her not to be silly. She knew when things were serious even when she was driving around a fairy ring of oildrums standing in the middle of the road.

'Lolly, if you'd thought all day I don't know if you could have come up with an unlikelier witch than poor Sorry Carlisle,' she said at last. 'He's the wrong sex for one thing, which in these non-sexist days shouldn't matter much, but from what I can make out he's about the best-behaved boy in the school. You're always complaining about him because of it, and you can't have it both ways. Now,' said Kate, starting to sound really enthusiastic, 'if you'd mentioned his grandmother, Winter, or even his mother. Quite a different story – witches to a man – a woman that is . . . They've got the sort of craziness that gives them class!' Kate added. 'Mind you,' she went on before Laura could say anything, 'I can't imagine them bringing up a boy of seventeen or eighteen between them. Old Winter gets madder day by day and Miryam floats around staring into space as if she saw only tomorrow or the next day. But the boy seems as normal as the rest of you . . . with a slight edge towards good behaviour, perhaps.'

'Have you finished?' asked Laura. 'Listen – I know all about Sorry Carlisle! No one notices but me. Mum, can't you see he's like a TV advertisement – matched up with an idea people have in their minds, not with real life. Even when he does something wrong you can feel him ticking it off on a sort of desk diary – '20 November – *Please Note* – think of something wrong to do!' And no one notices except me. He knows I notice, mind you!'

'You've never mentioned anything of this before,' said Kate. 'You can't blame me for being doubtful.'

'I've always known!' said Laura, 'but I know he doesn't mean any harm. He's hiding. He just wants to be left alone. He's never done anything really witchy. Just wants to be left alone. He just *is*, he never *does*.'

Kate never let herself be confused by statements like this. She was sometimes capable of making them herself.

'I remember him buying two really sentimental love stories one day,' she said thoughtfully. 'He read the ends of them in the shop, looking really puzzled, and then bought them both.'

'He reads them himself,' Laura said scornfully. 'I saw him reading one once in the Mall teashop. He doesn't behave like a witch but I know he is one.' There were many other things she did not add about Sorry Carlisle because they were too uncertain to describe, including the fact that sometimes, knowing himself recognized, he let her see another face – not the mild everyday school face but one which she found very exciting because it looked dangerous.

'Well, I know he rides a motorbike, not a broomstick,' Kate remarked, giving her long, curly grin.

'A Vespa!' Laura said with a sigh. 'I knew you wouldn't believe me.'

'Lolly, how can I?' Kate asked, stopping the car outside the school. 'I've never understood your warnings – and be fair – until now you only mentioned them *after* something has happened, not before. But I do know this: I'm going to have to go because I'll be late for work, and what if I arrive to find Mr Bradley on the doorstep, fuming because I haven't opened the shop in time? But Lolly, be careful with yourself, and later on be careful with Jacko . . . just in case.' She gave Laura a quick, warm kiss.

'Kissing tigers!' said Jacko from the backseat, turning them into animals just for fun, for he particularly liked tigers. Laura undid her seat-belt reluctantly and walked towards school while Kate and Jacko drove on to Jacko's babysitter and Kate's work.

Laura was alone with the day. It panted at her with a stale sweetness on its breath, with a faint, used-peppermint smell that made her want to be sick in the gutter, but she shut her mouth tightly and walked on.

'Hurry up, Chant!' said the prefect at the gate. It was Sorry Carlisle himself, checking that people riding bikes were doing so in a sober fashion, not doing wheelies or riding on the footpath. 'First bell's gone!'

He had grey eyes with the curious trick of turning silver if you looked at them from the side. Some people thought they looked dependable, but to Laura there was nothing safe about them. They were tricky, looking-glass eyes with quicksilver surfaces, and tunnels, staircases and mirror mazes hidden behind them, none of them leading anywhere that was recognizable.

Laura and Sorensen looked at each other now, smiling but not in friendship. They smiled out of cunning, and a shared secret flicked from eye to eye. Laura walked past him in at the school gates, bravely turning right into the mouth of the day, right into its open jaws which she must enter despite all warnings. She felt the jaws snap down behind her and knew she had been swallowed up. The day spread its strangeness before her resigned eyes, its horror growing thin and wispy as it sank away. The flow came back into the world once more, and the warning became a memory, eagerly forgotten because it was useless to remember it. The warning had come. She had ignored it. There was nothing more to be said.

2

The Jack-in-the-Box Man

Every evening Kate would ask Laura, 'Well, what happened at school today?' and Laura usually said, 'Nothing!' meaning nothing she could be bothered to talk about. There was always school work, of course, somehow taking the interest out of quite interesting things, and then there was her school friend, Nicky, who was busy at present with a boyfriend. She was trying to find a boyfriend for Laura too, so that they could all go out together and she could tell her mother that she was going out with Laura without totally lying.

'You're a bit dreamy,' Nicky said at break. 'Don't be such a dead loss! I'm trying to arrange your future happiness.'

'It's Thursday, you know, Thursday! Late night!' said Laura. 'It's my day for domestic responsibility, not future happiness.'

'Couldn't you have domestic responsibility towards Barry Hamilton?' pestered Nicky, smiling triumphantly. 'He likes you.'

'I'll bet you're just making that up,' Laura replied, but felt flattered because Barry was quite handsome and was allowed to drive his mother's car to school some days.

'I'm not,' said Nicky. 'He asked my brother to ask me if you liked him and I said you did.'

'I do quite like him,' Laura replied, looking around the school grounds to see if she could see Barry, and imagining how it might feel to go out with him. 'I mean, he's not outstanding, but he's quite nice.'

'You've got big ideas,' said Nicky, rather annoyed, for she thought she had presented Laura with a jewel. 'If you don't want him, can I have him?'

'But you like Simon,' Laura said, and Nicky grinned.

'Nothing wrong with two,' she said. 'I've got two best dresses. Shall I get Jason to tell Barry to ring you up?'

'I'm not on the phone,' Laura said with regret and relief. She thought she liked the idea of going out with Barry more than she would enjoy actually going out with him and, besides, she knew Kate would not let her go. So after school she found herself walking to collect Jacko from the baby-sitter, alone and watchful, ready to hide from any car that looked as if it might escape from its driver's control and climb up on to the footpath, ravening after helpless pedestrians.

Laura liked collecting names that ran opposite to the people who owned them. Her collection had started with her own name, Laura Chant, when she found she could not sing in tune. However the best in the whole collection so far was Jacko's baby-sitter, Mrs Fangboner, who sounded as if she should drink blood instead of tea and sleep in a coffin rather than a 'Duchess' luxury bed with matching flowery sheets and pillowcases. She was a little, thin woman with very pretty, brown hair which she was proud of and which she had set once a week at 'Hair Today', the salon in the Gardendale Mall. Laura had never seen her without lipstick, had never seen her naked smile.

'I've been married ten years and I've never let myself go,' Laura had once heard her tell a friend, and had thought that, even if Mrs Fangboner did let herself go, she probably would not go far. She defended herself with lipstick, her garden, and cups of tea, and enjoyed her defences too much to leave them behind her.

On this particular day she was punishing the grass edges with some instrument of gardening torture. The front step, laid out with secateurs, shears, long-handled clippers with blades like a parrot's beak, as well as stainless-steel garden forks and trowels, looked like an operating table. Jacko sat beside this terrifying display, with his Ruggie wrapped around Rosebud. On seeing Laura he did not so much run as bounce across the lawn in little jumps as if he were made of rubber and someone had cheerfully tossed him in her direction. First he hugged her and then pretended to growl and bite her. When he looked up and laughed at her, Laura felt her throat go tight inside, and her nose started prickling high up between her eyes, so that she had to shut them in order to avoid public tears. It was an attack of love and she knew how to cope with it . . . simply shut it away inside herself until it dissolved into her blood again. Sometimes it seemed to her that Jacko was not her brother but in some way her own baby, a baby she would have one day, both born and unborn at the same time.

'We've had another good day,' said Mrs Fangboner. 'He's a pleasure to have around, I'll say that for him. He can be a real little devil, but nothing nasty or bad-tempered. Your mum will be in tomorrow will she, with the . . .' She said this sentence every Thursday and never finished it, for she liked to pretend she looked after Jacko out of kindness, though she was glad to earn money without going out from behind her hedge.

'It must be tough on you two,' she said now, 'with your mum working late on Thursday. Mind you, I'm in favour of having a late-night Thursday. A lot of people who work late Friday in the centre of town come out here and it brings a bit of business into the area. But you must get hungry waiting for the shops to close.' She knew any implied criticism of Kate bothered Laura and had learned to offer criticism in the form of unwanted sympathy.

'I take Jacko home and give him his supper, and Mum comes home later with fish and chips,' Laura said. 'It's good fun, really.'

She was still staring at Jacko, quite entranced by him although he was so familiar. His hair was as curly as hers but softer and fairer, and light seemed to shine out of it as if he were a lamp, each pale, curling hair a little filament glowing in the sunlight.

'You'll be a mass of spots if you eat too much greasy stuff,' Mrs Fangboner warned. 'You watch it, Laura! You're just the age.' Laura nodded as Jacko brought his basket and took her hand.

'We eat salad the rest of the week,' she said. 'See you next Thursday!' and then set off to walk with her brother to the Gardendale Shopping Complex.

Kingsford Drive plunged like a dagger straight into the collection of shops and offices that made up the Complex. It still looked new and uneasy, as if it had only just arrived and might actually be folded up by the developers and taken away tomorrow so that they could start another subdivision, advertising the building sites as, 'close to a new Shopping Complex with all facilities.' Sitting on the very surface of the city's skin it had not had time yet to sink down and become a true feature.

For Laura and Jacko the library was the first stop and, once there, Laura forgot to be cautious because she thought the library was bound to be safe. She simply concentrated on getting a new book for herself and three for Jacko. He always wanted to take a book he already had at home because he thought it would be the same book he liked but made different in some wonderful way. Laura checked the box of old books the library had cancelled and was selling for twenty cents each. Sometimes they found a treasure (Jacko's favourite tiger book was one such) but there was nothing today and Laura was grateful because it was not the week Kate got paid and consequently it was a week of poverty at home. Laura's books were stamped at the big desk, but Jacko went to the children's desk and stood on the special red box so that he could watch his books being issued and put safely into his basket.

'Stamp please!' he shouted, and Mrs Thompson put a Mickey Mouse stamp on the back of his hand.

'Two hands, please!' he begged for he knew there was a Donald Duck stamp hidden at the librarian's elbow. However, another family had come up, making a little queue behind them.

'I'll stamp you twice next week,' suggested Mrs Thompson in reply.

'Two next time,' Jacko said to Laura, reluctantly giving up his place at the desk and walking beside her out of the library, his hands held in front of him like begging paws.

'This hand is sad with no stamp,' he announced holding up his left hand. 'It's lonely for a stamp, this hand.'

'Next time,' Laura said, guiding him anxiously across the road, though it was actually very quiet. They were now on the corner of the original Gardendale shopping centre which had been called Soper's Corner in the old days. They stood under the verandah of Soper's fish shop. Next to them was the old

Roxy Theatre, now transformed into the Gardendale Video Centre, twittering with electronic voices and there, tacked on to the end, as if the builders had had an extra yard or two of space to use up, was the smallest shop in the world, little more than a big cupboard with a tiny, angled window and little counter, all very, very thin. Once it had been used for selling newspapers, racing information, cigarettes and lottery tickets, but it had been closed for the last year. Jacko liked it and always looked in its empty window.

'My shop!' he would say, and indeed it was easy to imagine it as a shop run by a child for other children.

Today it was transformed, its window blossoming out into a cottage garden of tiny, pretty things: clothes-peg dolls, and doll's house furniture, matchbox toys, clear marbles with colour twisted in their hearts, pictures as big as postage stamps in frames carved from matchsticks, seven owls made of walnut shells, a peep-show shaped like an egg, and a box shaped like a book full of minute buttons and glass beads hardly bigger than grains of coloured sugar.

'In we go!' suggested Jacko with great enthusiasm and, of course, in they went.

OPEN THURSDAY NIGHTS, announced the notice in the window, LITTLE WHITE ELEPHANTS BOUGHT AND SOLD, and it was easy to believe that they would find a tray of elephants, small as grasshoppers, white as milk, milling around in the box on the counter, curling their trunks and trumpeting to each other in tiny, defiant voices.

Yet, once in this enchanting shop, all Laura wanted was to get out again for it was full of the stale, sweet smell, laced with peppermint, that had assailed her in the morning – the smell of something very wrong and unable to conceal its wrongness. The moment for which the morning had tried to prepare Laura was upon her. Now . . . now . . . she would begin to come apart. Now the first crack would begin between her eyes though no one would know it was there but Laura herself.

'Come on!' she cried to Jacko. 'There's no one here.' But at that moment, as if her voice had broken a seal of silence, a man suddenly rose from behind the counter where he had presumably been putting things away very, very quietly. He was grinning, his teeth apparently too big for his thin, rubbery lips to cover them. Indeed his whole face was somehow shrunken back around his smile so that he looked like a grinning puppet. He was almost completely bald, with what hair he had clipped very close, and there were dark blotches on his cheeks and neck, almost, but not quite, like bruises.

'Oh . . .' he cried when he saw Jacko, 'a baby!' He put a very heavy, bleating emphasis on the first half of the word. 'A baaaab-y!' he exclaimed again in a high-pitched voice, breathing out as he bleated, so that the air became sodden with stale peppermint, breathing in at the very end so that the word was finally sucked away to nothing.

'He's three,' said Laura. 'He's not a baby any more.'

'Oh, that's a baby to me,' exclaimed the man with a gusty giggle. 'If it comes to that, you're *all* babies to me. I'm extremely old, thousands of years old. Don't I look it?' he asked, and Laura thought he did.

'Naughty girl!' he cried, chidingly, and actually put out his hand and touched her hair, as if he were curious about its texture. 'You shouldn't look as if you agreed with me. But what a pet of a child your little friend – your brother is it? – appears to be. He looks so full of life, doesn't he? A rare commodity at *my* age – *tempus fugit* and all that – but he looks as if he had enough for *two*. He looks as if he sees colours the rest of us *don't*, or hears jokes we *can't*.'

Laura liked to hear Jacko praised, but the man leaned forward as he spoke and his dreadful smell struck her like a blow – a smell that brought to mind mildew, wet mattresses, unopened rooms, stale sweat, dreary books full of damp pages and pathetic misinformation, the very smell – she thought she had it now – of rotting time. It had to be the man's smell, for though they were surrounded with scraps of the past there was nothing else that could have smelt like that.

'He doesn't seem to think much of *me,* does he?' the man asked, coming round from behind the counter, his voice tittering on as he moved. 'He doesn't seem to care for me one teeny, tiny bit . . . Oh, it's not fair, because I think he's absolutely scrumptious.'

'What's his name?' For all his horrid smell he was immaculately dressed in a pale pink shirt and a very smart plum-coloured suit.

'Jacko!' Laura said, and thought to herself, Why am I telling him this? I don't have to tell him everything he asks.

The man's hand was extended towards Jacko and below his neat cuff she could see another discoloured blotch as if he were starting to go bad. 'We're just going,' she said. 'We don't have any money.'

'My name's Carmody Braque,' the man went on, as if she hadn't spoken. 'A name not unknown in the world of antiques and rare objects, and my shop is to be called *Brique à Braque.* Oh, I know what you're going to say,' he cried, though Laura had not been going to say anything, 'it's a wee bit obvious, isn't it? But how could I resist? And this isn't a serious shop you know – just a place to display a lot of little nonsenses.'

'We've got to go,' Laura said, wondering why it was so hard to walk away from someone who was talking to you, even when you didn't want to hear what they were saying. 'We just wanted to look around.'

'And so you did and so you shall,' cried Carmody Braque with fearsome generosity, 'and I'll make it up to the little brother, poor, wee lambie. Do I see a stamp on the right paw? How about another on the left? Hold it out, you little tiger, tiger burning bright, and you shall enter the forests of the night.'

Jacko had been pressing himself against Laura with rare shyness, but he was lured by the idea of the stamp and half extended his hand.

'Hold it out properly! Offer it to me or I won't be able to stamp it clearly,' Mr Braque commanded. Jacko thrust his hand forward. Laura found herself putting out her own hand to stop him but Mr Braque pounced with great agility, like an elderly mantis on an innocent fly. Incredibly he had a stamp in his hand which he had snatched from his counter, or even out of the air and he pressed it on to the back of Jacko's hand triumphantly, as if he had been working towards that moment for a long time.

'Look! Pretty picture!' giggled Mr Braque, but Jacko screamed as if he had been burnt and Mr Braque leaped back, still giggling.

'Dear oh dear!' he cried. 'It isn't my day, is it? I do hope I don't have this effect on all my customers.' Laura picked Jacko up, bewildered by his cry.

'Most children *like* a stamp,' Mr Braque said through his smile, and – as Laura looked into his eyes, across Jacko's shaking shoulder – she felt something very old looking back at her, something triumphant but also unappeasable. Those eyes, round as a bird's but clouded and slightly inflamed, looked away from hers immediately. 'Perhaps we'd better say bye-bye for the moment, hmmmmm?' he went on, gesturing to the door, and a moment later, Laura, still holding Jacko, was standing on the footpath amazed at her ineffectual self, feeling as if her mind had been glued up with the stale peppermint smell. Her clothes seemed to reek of it. She and Jacko had been lured in by pretty things, stupefied, and then quite ruthlessly thrust out again, having served some unguessable purpose.

Laura was glad to be out of the little shop, but wished she had escaped because of some splendid act of her own.

'Take it off!' Jacko was saying, wiping at his hand. 'Take it off! This hand doesn't like it.'

Standing in the centre of the Gardendale Shopping Complex Laura frisked her own pockets and the sleeves of her cardigan for concealed handkerchiefs. Standing in the everyday streets of Gardendale she began to scrub at the back of Jacko's hand. There, clearly outlined, even shaded in, was the very face of Carmody Braque himself, smiling back at her from Jacko's hand. The long teeth and the round eyes, the rubbery, stretched lips, were plainly seen. Not only that, the stamp showed no signs of coming off. It seemed to be *under* his skin, not on top of it, smiling, smiling, knowing it could not be touched by a mere handkerchief and the application of human spit. Laura had never seen such a detailed stamp before. It was almost like a real face in three dimensions, peering out through a window of human skin.

'I don't like it, Lolly,' Jacko said, sniffing and leaning against her.

'He can damn well rub it off himself,' Laura declared, swearing slightly because she was suddenly really frightened, but when she looked back at the door of the tiny shop it was closed. Mr Carmody Braque had sneaked out while they were not looking and had hung a notice from the door handle, 'Back in ten minutes'.

'What a weirdo!' Laura said. 'It needs soap, Jacko – soap and hot water,' and Jacko cheered up, though he was less than his smiling self as they went along the footpath and down the arcaded Mall. Laura herself was silent, for deep in her heart she feared it would take more than soap and hot water to remove the smile of Carmody Braque from under the skin of her little brother's hand.

3

A Guest for Supper

After Laura's father had left them Kate had taken a job as assistant in a bookshop and when the new Gardendale branch opened she had been promoted to shop manager, though she was not paid any extra for the privilege of being called by a grander title.

'We'll just give it a whirl, dear, and see how you go,' her boss, Mr Bradley, had said, and they were still whirling and seeing how it went a year later.

'Not to worry,' Kate declared. 'Wait until I've passed my bookseller's course. He'll have to give me a rise in pay then or I'll speak out in no uncertain terms!'

Kate did her course on one side of the table at home while Laura frowned over her homework on the other. Kate had a calculator to work out mysterious discounts and Laura was sometimes allowed to borrow it, although she was good at maths and could make figures behave themselves and give up their hidden secrets. It was cheerful to have someone to work with, and to have time alone with Kate when Jacko was washed and read to and tucked up in bed. Sometimes, late at night, Kate looked tired and rather old. But she was still pretty in her own special way, her fair hair shining and her long lips curved in a smile so that Laura found it hard to believe her father could have wanted to live with someone else – a younger woman, quite nice, but not nearly as nice as Kate.

'You're too kind to me,' Kate said when Laura mentioned this. 'It's best the way it is. We liked too many different things and I thought I'd change him to my way of thinking and he thought he'd change me to his. Well, we worked on one another for years and years and we both stuck half way. I miss him, but a lot of the time when we were together I just wished he'd go away.' These were true things, Laura knew, but they were only part of the truth which was something less orderly than Kate made it sound. Some parts of the full, disorderly truth were lodged in Kate and Laura like splinters of corroding steel. Their feelings had grown around the sharp, wounding edges which didn't hurt any more but were still there, fossils of pain laid down in the mixed-up strata of memory.

'He was a better housekeeper than I was,' Kate once recalled, smiling across the table at Laura. 'That was mean of him. He used to polish your shoes each night – you always had polished shoes in those days – and he'd help with cleaning without being asked, but then he had a miserable, long-suffering way of pushing the vacuum cleaner around our sitting room that really got to me after a while. It's funny to think that fifteen years of marriage – for that's what it was, you know – could come to grief because your father vacuumed the carpet as if he were St Peter being crucified upside down. Not just that, of course, but things like that. However, I must say he always loved you, Lolly. Write him a letter, or go and stay with him in the school holidays. I'd miss you, but I wouldn't mind.'

'You sound all reasonable, like a children's book on divorce,' Laura complained. She had been given such books to read and despised them, because they tried to be kind and sensible and Laura thought it was like being kind and sensible to a sacrificed Aztec whose living heart was being held up for all to see.

In the bookshop, wearing her round glasses (her intellectual glasses, as she called them) Kate managed to look quite dashing, even though her clothes were not very new. She took people by surprise because a lot of them did not expect her to be a keen and clever reader, as if reading were only something people went in for when they were particularly plain. Kate enjoyed talking about books to anyone who asked and spent quite a lot of time listening to other people describing books that they had enjoyed. Every evening Laura would ask about the day's takings, and they were compared with the same day last week or last month. Increased sales were always celebrated, but if they had fallen off in any way Kate would worry and start wondering if she shouldn't change the display, or run a little advertisement in the local paper.

The shop was between a window full of handbags and suitcases for people who wanted to travel elegantly and a shop full of dresses 'for the fuller figure' which showed large, tactful dresses all in wine-red and grey this week. Laura and Jacko ignored them and burst into the bookshop, Jacko already holding his hand out and shouting anxiously to Kate. There was only one customer, a tall man who made up for being a little bald in front by wearing his hair rather long at the back. He was reading a book, but gloomily, and not at all as if he intended to buy it.

'Look, Mum!' Laura cried imperiously, holding Jacko's hand out to her mother as if it were a vital clue in a mystery. 'The little shop next to the Video Parlour has opened for business again. There's a really horrible man in it and he frightened Jacko.' As she spoke she knew her words were reducing the experience to a childish complaint, not revealing its true quality.

'This hand wants to be washed,' Jacko begged. 'It doesn't like it.' Jacko and Laura talked together, their words winding in and out of each other in a ragged part-song of explanation and complaint.

'Dear me!' said Kate in a nervous, but fairly motherly, voice. 'That is clever, isn't it? What will they come up with next? However, I can see why it scares you, Jacko. Sweetie, I can't do anything about it now, but I'll get on to it with the scrubbing brush a little bit later – or rather Lolly will – and we'll soon have you pink and plain again.'

At work Kate was always nervous about being motherly, as if it had suddenly become a little illegal to be openly fond of her children. Even now, when there was only one customer, probably not wanting to buy, Kate knew she belonged to the shop until 8.30 pm and was not free to wash evil stamps off Jacko's hand.

'Have you got bus money?' she asked.

'Could we have just one game of Space Invaders?' Laura asked back, answering Kate's question by rattling the bus money in her pocket. She had once got into trouble for spending the bus money on Space Invaders and then walking home. 'It might cheer Jacko up.'

'You know I don't like you going in there,' Kate said, 'and certainly not with Jacko. For one thing it always looks foggy with cigarette smoke, probably worse. No – you go home, and I'll follow as soon as I can. How was Mrs Fangboner tonight?'

'Fanging around!' Laura said. 'Nice to Jacko and threatening me with spots from F. & C.'

'She's good-hearted really,' Kate said, looking around in case some friend of Mrs Fangboner had come into the shop.

'Why doesn't she show it more, then?' Laura asked. 'It's nothing to be ashamed of. Doesn't she realize that? She should embroider 'Be good-hearted!' on her tea towels, and then take the advanced course in it, and like me, too.'

'Don't let's push our luck!' Kate said, grinning, and Laura grinned back, comforted by seeing that Kate was really there, even if she was being more of a bookshop manager than a mother at that moment.

'All right! We're off and away!' she said. 'Don't forget the F. & C.'

'When have I ever forgotten the F. & C.?' Kate replied. 'It's worth a few spots not to have any dishes to wash.'

The fish and chips were always bought at Soper's fish shop, and sometimes they were lovely and sometimes disappointing, but the uncertainty of which it was going to be was almost adventurous, and the possible loveliness something to be looked forward to. As they waited for the bus Laura could smell the fish and chips cooking and patted Jacko, who was leaning against her leg like a tired dog. Laura was glad it was summer and that they would be getting out of the bus in broad daylight, for though the bus stopped almost exactly behind the telephone box that stood outside their gate, the few moments that separated them from their door often felt dangerous, and tonight such danger might also be depressing.

'I couldn't do anything about it,' she said to Jacko, who was peering at the stamp on his hand again, rubbing it anxiously. She wanted people to think she was talking to him, but actually it was with herself that she was holding a discussion.

'I did have the warning,' she admitted aloud, 'but it did me no good. I just stood there and let it happen. I knew it was set down to happen as soon as I went in at the school gate this morning.'

Laura usually enjoyed the bus ride up Kingsford Drive. It was slower and easier than the anxious morning rush. Often she felt a little of herself running out into houses and telegraph poles along the way, as if she were a blob of bright paint put down on wet paper, spreading out and dyeing the world with faint traces of her own colour, even as she took colour back from the world. This is what it feels like to be *this* shape, this size! Greenness feels like this! Every telegraph pole stood centred on a single leg gathering wires up, looping them over little stunted arms, and Laura felt her way into being a telegraph pole, or a roof rising to a ridge and butting against itself. The Baptist church squared its concrete shoulders, its doorway touching its own toes, carrying a great weight of square, white blocks on its bent back.

'Don't rub it! You'll make it sore,' she said to Jacko. 'Soap and water will get it off,' but he went on pushing at the back of his hand as if he would like to rub the very flesh from the bones. 'Pretend it's a mosquito bite and leave it alone.'

The dreadful stamp seemed deeper than ever as if it were slowly sinking down into him, visible, but subsiding beyond recall – like a coin dropped into deep water, reflecting light while vanishing for ever. Jacko sighed deeply and rolled his head against Laura's shoulder, and she felt a restless heat creep through her, almost like a little blush of horror, for she thought she detected the faintest touch of stale peppermint, as if Carmody Braque's breath was somehow coming out through Jacko.

'There's Brown,' she said with relief, pointing as much to distract herself as Jacko. Brown was a thoughtful dog, a familiar, rust-coloured acquaintance, wandering along, frowning and disappointed by the contents of the summer gutter – icecream wrappers and soft-drink cans. Jacko looked at Brown for a moment and then he turned his head away.

'He wasn't nice,' he said. 'That man wasn't nice, was he, Lolly?'

'Don't think about him!' Laura said, though she herself could not stop thinking about Carmody Braque.

They arrived home reasonably cheerful. Laura scrambled an egg for Jacko and went to extra trouble, dividing his orange into segments for him and cutting his sandwich into four little triangles like those sold in the teashop three places away from Kate's work.

After the scrambled egg and sandwich Jacko went willingly to bed – quite to Laura's surprise for it was often difficult to persuade him to go. Usually he wanted to stay awake until Kate came home and played a lot of energetic games, running and hiding under the bed and having to be pulled out by one leg, his pyjamas wrinkling and going grey with the sort of dust that likes a good bed to hide under. Space under beds was always dusty, filling itself greedily with coffee mugs, plates, and books. But tonight Jacko went quietly to bed and listened to his tiger book and a story read from one of the new library books, watching Laura trustfully, his stamped hand hidden under the pillow. Laura had, of course, tried to wash it clean again but the stamp was part of him now, more than a tattoo – a sort of parasite picture tunnelling its way deeper and deeper, feeding itself as it went.

'Ugh! What a thought!' Laura said. 'Grow up! Be mature!'

At half-past eight she heard footsteps on the path.

That was quick, she thought with relief and surprise, for Kate never closed the shop five minutes early even when the Mall was quite empty in case Mr Bradley should call in and find her gone. But it was not Kate. It was Sally, rather impatient at having to leave her television programme, with a message from Kate for Laura saying that Kate would be home a little late. Once the message was delivered, Sally added an invitation to Laura to come and watch television, pointing out that if Jacko woke up and cried they would probably hear him from next door, but Laura was not even tempted by this, for she was worried, and also rather hurt by Kate's delay. Perhaps something had gone wrong with the car, she thought.

Kate was about three-quarters of an hour late that night and when she did come home she did not come alone. The long-haired man, the single customer who had been in the shop – reading and not buying – was with her.

'We've got a guest,' Kate said unnecessarily. Laura stared at her for she looked mischievous and much more lively and lighthearted than she usually was after a Thursday night. She didn't kick off her shoes and collapse into a chair, resting her elbows on the table while she ate her F. & C. She unfolded Soper's fish and chips from their shawls of newspaper with the flourish of a waiter uncovering the speciality of the house.

'Isn't that classy!' she cried. 'Laura, I think it's going to be delicious tonight.'

The man's name was Chris Holly.

'Short for Christmas?' Laura asked, but apparently his full name was Christopher. He had an American accent which sounded strange in their New Zealand living room.

'This is just fine,' he said. 'It shows you can't afford to take any day for granted. I was feeling very remote, far away from almost everything, and then I heard that name. I could scarcely believe it.'

'What name?' Laura asked Kate.

'Fangboner!' Kate said. 'Chris asked me if he had overheard correctly and I had to admit that we did have a baby-sitter called Mrs Fangboner.'

'She just has to be Dracula's aunt,' Chris said, 'or even his sister.'

'I think Dracula was an only child,' Laura said. 'He doesn't sound to me like a man who had brothers and sisters. I think he drank blood because he thought everything in the world was his to begin with.'

'How could you leave your baby with a baby-sitter called "Fangboner"?' Chris asked.

'Desperation at the time,' Kate replied, 'but actually she's very kind.'

'She tortures her garden,' said Laura in a sinister voice. 'That uses all her energy. And somewhere there's a husband Fangboner who's had the name even longer. We never ever see him though. She might have his skeleton hanging up with one of those plastic covers that keeps the dust off velvet coats.'

'The mystery of Mr Fangboner!' Chris said. 'Anyway, Laura, we got talking about books, and on the strength of all that I took your mother out to have a drink with me and since I couldn't talk her into having dinner with me, I cunningly talked myself into having dinner with her. I professed an abiding love for fish and chips and I have to admit these are very good fish and chips.'

'It's not always as good as this, though,' Kate said. 'It's a lucky night.'

'Lucky for me, anyway,' Chris Holly said. 'I hope you don't mind a dinner guest, Laura?'

'No!' said Laura, but she minded dreadfully. Just after her father had left them Kate had gone out with several men, but part of the happiness of the last year was that she had stopped doing this and had seemed content to spend her time with Laura and Jacko.

The thought that an F. & C. night (a night of successful F. & C. into the bargain) had to be shared with a stranger who was trying – Laura recognized the signs – to be particularly nice to her, not because he was interested in her, but because he was interested in Kate, filled her with anxious discontent. Chris's was an understandable niceness, but was still something she was compelled to suspect.

'How's Jacko?' Kate asked suddenly. 'I knew there was something I had forgotten to ask.'

'He's asleep,' Laura said. 'Mum, there's something wrong with him. I don't think he's well.'

'We don't get sick,' Kate said firmly. 'None of us can afford to be anything but healthy. Jacko's tough.'

She gave Laura a glance that was faintly defiant but which seemed at the same time to be asking a favour, although quite what the favour might be Laura had no idea. She sat listening to her mother and Chris play the book-lover's game of finding which books of all the books in the world they had both read and enjoyed. They agreed about many of them – an ominous sign, and when they did not agree they argued like old friends, criticizing one another's taste with complete ease and confidence. Laura thought Mrs Fangboner had a lot to answer for. After a while she got up and tucked her own library book under her arm and said she was going to bed.

'Give me a kiss!' Kate commanded.

'It might be setting a risky example,' Laura said, making a joke of a serious thought.

'That's cheeky,' Kate said, without particular resentment, however.

'And shrewd,' Chris agreed.

'I'll give you two tomorrow,' Laura said, trying to be friendly though private, feeling they were laughing together at her, both happily retreating into an adult world where she could not quite follow them yet, even though she was the sort of girl a boy like Barry Hamilton could like from a distance. So she smiled politely and tried to mean it, going to bed because, after all, they did not really need her.

4

The Smile on Jacko's Face

Laura was talked out of sleep the next morning by her mother nagging back the shallow tide of retreating sleep, anxious because Jacko had had a bad night – a night of terrible dreams. Yet Kate was unexpectedly bouncy as if the day might hold something to be looked forward to. Sorting and cataloguing the various jumbled alarms of the previous day Laura washed herself awake and found an unexpectedly organized breakfast waiting for her – apple-juice, stewed apple and cornflakes, toast, and a cup of tea. She was at first taken aback, and then resigned, recognizing, by she knew not what clues, that Kate had managed her morning so well because of an energy of optimism that had nothing to do with her children.

'You like him, don't you?' Laura asked accusingly.

'Yes, I do,' Kate answered at once without asking who they were discussing, and added, half pleadingly, 'Don't you think he's nice?'

'He's all right,' said Laura grudgingly. All right, but unnecessary, she wanted to say – she *did* say – but managed to keep the words in her mind.

'He's going bald,' was the only criticism she allowed herself.

'Yes, but he's got a nice laugh,' Kate said. 'A nice laugh is deadly. He looks really mischievous about solemn things, not just big, solemn things like politics which anyone can make fun of, but little ones like – telephone bills.'

They had had a telephone once, but Kate had been unable to pay the bill and it had been cut off and had hung on their wall like a petrified insect hibernating through a winter of cold debt until at last post-office men had come and taken it away.

'Besides,' Kate said, 'he likes me, and, as far as I'm concerned, that shows he's a man of taste and judgement. All that stuff about Mrs Fangboner . . . it was a sort of line really. He just wanted an excuse to talk to me. Still, it was a cunning thing to pick on because it led to sharing jokes and that's a short-cut to getting to know someone. If your jokes match up, it's like being Alice in *Through the Looking-Glass.* Off you go through the third square by the railway and find yourself in the fourth square in no time.'

'He could have bought a book,' Laura said. 'That's a very attractive thing for a customer to do,' and she carried her breakfast through to Kate's room where Jacko, recovering from nightmares, was still in Kate's bed. Immediately, she saw he was duller, quieter and greyer than she could ever remember him before and as she approached he immediately held his hands out, backs up.

'Hey, how did you get the stamp off?' Laura cried, but Kate, dressing herself, was already beginning the patter by which she encouraged herself and Laura into a quick and occasionally competent morning, not realizing yet that this morning was twisting into a new and anxious form.

'Come on – eat up, Lolly! Jacko darling, you're going to have to shift your precious bones. It's not Saturday yet. We've got to be off and away. What stamp?' she concluded, as if she were moving in a different time from Laura and the original question had only just reached her ears.

'He had a stamp on his hand that wouldn't come off,' Laura said, and Kate suddenly remembered back to yesterday, striking her forehead with the palm of her hand.

'That's probably what's caused all these nightmares,' she cried. 'He was worried about his hand . . . I thought he must have a mosquito bite on it. Poor Jacko. Never mind! It's over and done with. The old dream's gone. Bright new morning! Look – the bad stamp's rubbed off over night.'

'No way!' Laura declared, staring at Jacko's mute hands, the right one haunted by the faint, purple ghost of Mickey Mouse, and the left hand slightly inflamed perhaps, but innocent of any stamp of any kind. 'Listen! Let me tell you what happened.'

'All right, if you must! But be quick!' Kate said.

However, it was not easy to tell after all. As Laura tried, the story, lively and indignant in her head, twisted itself in her mouth, limping out of her lips, sick and ashamed.

'I know it sounds mad!' she cried despairingly, thumping the quilt with frustration. 'I know you can't believe me.'

Kate rescued the almost empty cup and stared at her in surprise.

'I'm sure you're partly right,' she said. 'Laura, I really am sure you're right about what actually happened, but I can't help questioning your interpretation. Come *on,* Lolly! Warnings one morning, wicked signs the next . . . it's not like you to come over all superstitious. I thought the stamp looked quite horrid. I thought it looked like some advertising gimmick that had misfired. But if it hasn't rubbed off, then where is it?'

'I don't know,' Laura replied gloomily. 'Dissolved, I expect. Dissolved into Jacko's blood.'

'What a thing to say in front of a boy who's had nightmares,' Kate exclaimed reproachfully. 'Don't let's get carried away. Or rather do let's . . . We're seven minutes late already, and empires have risen and fallen on being seven minutes late.'

Later, Laura watched her mother and Jacko drive away. With a sigh she turned into the school gate, looking forward to Nicky's cheerful, gossipy company, sure at least that no matter what the day had to offer it couldn't be as threatening as yesterday. No jaws closed over her, there was no prospect of anything but ordinary school with ordinary, and therefore welcome, boredom. Disturbing ideas pursued her and nothing was reliable and straightforward any more. Sorry Carlisle stood by the flagpole talking to a girl, a sixth former called Carol Bright, someone he was quite entitled to talk to, but Laura thought she detected on his mild face the light of an interest that was more than casual. She stared very hard at him, trying to confirm this, and thought, not for the first time, that he was almost good-looking, and wondered how anyone with eyes full of reflections and dark staircases could enjoy the thought of Carol – except, of course, that she had wonderful, smooth, long, black hair which she wore in many different ways. Today it was in a ponytail – the tail of a circus pony, a curving fall of dark silk tied with school ribbon, inviting hands to stroke its shining descent. Laura, who had two ways of wearing her hair, long and woolly and short and woolly, now found she could actually be jealous of Carol Bright, and realized that, although she had never spoken to him, except as a fourth former speaks to a prefect and seventh former, in some ways she believed Sorensen Carlisle belonged to her because she knew what he really was and nobody else did. Almost as if in confirmation, he lifted his eyes directly to hers as she went by, and gave her a look of amusement, caution and something else . . . a look so complex she could not unravel, in the second of its duration, all its elements, but thought perhaps Kate would have called it ironic.

It was not usual for Laura to collect Jacko on a Friday since it was not a late night, for Mrs Fangboner did not mind having him until twenty-to-six, but Kate had suggested she might make an exception on this particular day when he was off-colour. So after talking to a mixed group of boys and girls, her usual acquaintances, and playing a game of tennis with Nicky who lived close to the school, Laura turned up on the Fangboner doorstep and was greeted with unusual enthusiasm by Mrs Fangboner, for Jacko had had an unhappy day and she was glad to be relieved of him.

'. . . like a different boy,' she said, sounding bewildered. 'Poor boy, I think he's going down with something. What on earth will your mum do if he's sick? She'll have to take time off and her boss won't like that, will he? I mean, it's not like a big shop where there's plenty of staff to take over.'

Jacko sat on a Fangboner stool, Rosebud smiling pink as ever out of his Ruggie, staring at Laura as if he could barely remember who she was. Then he got up and stalked over to her, stiff legged as a wind-up toy, dropped Rosebud and put his arms up, asking to be held. He wanted to be a baby again. Laura's eyes prickled with love, but it was of limited use, for he was too heavy to carry easily, and the walk to the shopping complex, usually gay and cheerful, was interminable today, for she had to make him walk at least part of the way and he grizzled in a dreary voice and continually dropped Rosebud who had to be picked up again and again. Laura struggled with her school pack on her back, history, maths and science, dragging at her shoulders, Jacko in her right arm, and his basket in her left. At last, in a moment of helpless frustration with the sheer difficulty of moving things around in the world, she gave him a small, sharp slap. He did not cry but simply bent his head against her.

'Poor Jacko!' he said in a sad, hoarse voice. 'Poor Jacko!'

She meant to hurry him past the tiny, wicked shop with its miniscule objects in its cottage garden window, in case his nightmares revived, but Mr Braque himself was out on the pavement painting the words 'Brique à Braque' on the window, and doing it rather well, too. Laura crossed over to the other side of the road but was very much aware of Mr Braque. Even as she struggled not to glance at him, he was projected into her mind, an invader of inner space and, turn her head away as she would, she could still see him. Her eye had trapped his image, her brain would not release it, and she felt she was looking into his ancient eyes once more, crocodile eyes, tied to a crocodile mind, and seeing something that could wear a human body and make it move, as an entertainer might wear and control a puppet-glove. With a sudden flare of – of what? – she wondered, for it was gone before she could define it, the hidden computer wired into her everyday mind (the very one which had informed her that her father was going to leave her, had warned her of Sorry Carlisle and only yesterday of Mr Braque) struggled to inform her yet again. 'Spirit!' it said. 'Incubus! Demon!' She knew, without looking, that he had turned and stared at her across the street, knew that his skin was less shrunken, his smile a little less deathly. Something was changing him, and she hardly dared to guess just what it might be.

It was late in the afternoon, but the bookshop was busy and Kate was selling a book to someone – a detective story.

'It's quite intriguing, though I liked his first one better,' she was saying, but the book was already sold and being slipped into a special paperbag printed with the bookshop's name so there was no risk in giving an honest opinion. Kate's eyes fell on Laura coming in at the door and her face lit up. Laura's heart warmed at the pleasure in her smile, but as it turned out Kate was pleased to see Laura for purposes of her own, with which Laura found it hard to sympathize.

'Lolly!' she exclaimed her blue eyes shining with pleasure. 'Lolly, would you mind if I went out tonight?'

'You've had your hair done!' Laura cried, outraged. 'I thought we were broke this week.'

'I've booked it up against next week,' Kate replied. She looked less like a mother in real life, and more like a mother on television, keeping herself nice for husband and family, thrilled to death with her new soap powder. 'I've fixed it up with Sally's mother to keep an eye on you.'

Kate was not to know how Laura had looked forward to arriving at the bookshop and giving part of the responsibility for Jacko over to someone else, and how dismayed she was to find Kate's concentration focused elsewhere.

'I suppose it's that American,' she growled.

'It is Chris Holly – yes,' Kate said. 'He's asked me to go out with him.' She spoke humbly as if Laura were bullying her. 'Don't be sour at me, Laura. I haven't been out for ages and I'd love to go to a nice concert and just get lost in lovely music.'

'But look at Jacko!' Laura pushed him forward, disconcerted to detect a certain triumph in her voice, pleased to use Jacko's despair as a move in a complicated private game where the rules were barely understood. Now Kate did look at Jacko.

'Oh dear!' she said. 'What can be wrong?'

She looked at her watch, a birthday present from Laura's father, still going, though the marriage had stopped ticking three years earlier. 'I can't talk now. Take him to the tea shop down the Mall and buy him an apple-juice. Get him a cake, too, if there are any left at this time in the afternoon. They dust them and pack them away at four o'clock.'

'You're flinging money about,' Laura grumbled bitterly. 'It's funny the way it stretches when it has to take in a bit of classical music, isn't it?'

She was not intending to be sympathetic, but Kate smiled warmly as if they were sharing a joke, hearing the words and ignoring the tone.

'Bless you, Laura, isn't it just!' she said. 'It's not long to closing time, thank goodness.'

Jacko really enjoyed his apple-juice, so Laura bought him some more with her own money and ate his cake herself thinking how awkwardly time was arranged so that there was either not enough of it or else great clots of useless minutes and seconds which it was impossible to use properly, and which had to be wasted.

Kate called for them where they sat in the tea-room, the only customers left among a forest of chair legs, for Jill, the waitress, put the chairs upside down on the tables as she swept up before going home. In the car, Kate dithered wildly. She wanted to go to the concert – she wanted to take Jacko to the doctor, she wanted to stay at home and look after him, but then she had promised Chris Holly she would go out with him, even though they had already had lunch together. Discussing this, backwards and forwards, Laura and Kate wound up visiting the Gardendale Health Centre and were actually able to see a doctor – not their usual doctor but another man who began by being impatient with them because they had come in at the last moment just as he was thinking seriously about dinner.

However, he became increasingly thoughtful as he examined Jacko, first frowning and then saying in a very puzzled voice, 'Well, there's certainly something wrong with him but it's not anything I can put a name to. Has he had any bad falls? Has he been shocked or depressed lately?'

'He's been fine,' Kate said, 'but yesterday someone played a trick on him that upset him. He had a bad night – a lot of bad dreams. Is it anything urgent? I might have to leave him for a little tonight – but his sister will be with him.'

'I don't think it's anything to be seriously worried about,' the doctor said. 'A good night's sleep might make a big difference. His reactions are very slow – you haven't given him any medication, have you?'

'None!' said Kate. 'I didn't think he needed anything this morning.'

The doctor looked thoughtful but not worried.

'If he isn't any better by tomorrow, bring him in again. Who's your regular doctor? I won't prescribe anything for him just now and we'll see how he gets on. I'll leave a note for Doctor Bligh attached to Jonathan's card.'

Laura forgot for long stretches at a time that Jacko's real name was Jonathan and only remembered it when places like the Health Centre remembered it for her, being too serious for playful names.

'Do you have to go out with this American?' asked Laura as they sat over a rushed and awkward supper of canned soup and toast.

'He's Canadian,' Kate said defensively as if being American was somehow a little disreputable.

'Well, it amounts to the same thing, doesn't it?' Laura replied. 'Canadians are Americans with no Disneyland.'

'It's not at all the same thing,' Kate replied calmly, 'and anyway I'm interested in Chris as a person, not as a nationality. He's not on the phone either, so I can't ring him.'

'You actually want to go out with him!' Laura said accusingly.

'Actually I do,' Kate said, and succeeded in smiling, though Laura's voice was not friendly. 'Oh, Lolly, don't be cross with me. It's over a year since I went out with anyone even vaguely romantic and I enjoyed having my hair done at 'Hair Today'. Peggy came and watched the shop for me, and it only took a few minutes with the heated rollers.'

'Suppose Mr Bradley had come in?' Laura said sternly.

'Well, he didn't,' said Kate.

'You wouldn't do that for Jacko and me,' Laura said in a cruel voice. 'All right! Go then! I expect you'll have such a good time you'll find it easy to forget about Jacko.'

Kate looked over the family table with a clear, cold expression.

'Laura, you're not to speak to me like that,' she said. 'You've got too much good sense to imagine I'd have arranged to go out if I had known that Jacko was going to be sick, but the doctor did say it wasn't anything to be seriously worried about, and you're going to be home, and Sally's mother is right next door. I'll leave you the number of the Town Hall – it's in the phone book anyway, but it's a council number – and, if Chris has booked the seats, I'll leave the seat numbers, too. If there's an emergency I can be back here in twenty minutes. You're not to worry – and you're not to be mad at me for taking one evening off.'

She sounded firm and, on the whole, Laura had to admit, reasonable. She felt confused at her own resentment and somehow mean-spirited, so she half apologized with a look, and later, when Kate was dressed in her best dress, and stockings without mends, told her as warmly as she could how nice she looked. In spite of good intentions she was astonished to hear how grudging her voice sounded, as if it were acting on hidden ideas of its own.

Nevertheless, Laura was even more astonished a little later to hear Kate say to Chris, when he came rather earlier than he needed to, that she could not go out after all because Jacko was ill and she would only worry about him and not enjoy herself properly. It would be a waste of a ticket, she said, because she would probably spoil things for Chris too. Kate had been thinking about Laura's protest and had changed her mind yet again. Chris, who had come in smiling and ebullient, was now uncertain whether to be sporting and hide his disappointment or honest and revengeful and display it openly.

'That's quite a blow!' he said in a gentle voice, but what he did not say was, 'That's quite all right, Kate. I know Jacko has to come first.'

'He's so much worse than I thought he'd be,' cried Kate apologetically. 'I was looking at him just a moment ago and he looks – well, I think he looks dreadful. Have you collected the tickets and all that, or did you leave it to chance?'

'For once in my life, I didn't leave it to chance.' Chris smiled, rather as if he were sneering at himself for his own good organization. 'You can take that as a sign of my enthusiasm. Never mind! If I hurry I'll be able to get them back to the desk before the concert begins and get my money back – or if I think for a moment or two I might come up with someone who'd be willing to drop everything at a moment's notice and come with me.'

'I'm so sorry,' Kate said. 'I'd offer to pay you for them, only I almost mortgaged the house to get my hair set. I'm really broke. Laura will bear me out – I've gone this way and that, ever since I realized how sick he was. I meant to come, right up to the last moment. See – I've got my best dress on.'

'And very charming it looks,' Chris said, which was a flattering thing to say except that he said it rather grimly.

'You are early . . .' Kate began. 'I can offer you doubtful compensation. Would you like some really terrible sherry?'

'I don't think I have time,' Chris replied, without looking at his watch. Then he shrugged and said with an unwilling smile, 'Maybe just one really terrible sherry.'

'You could come back and have coffee later – that is if you can't think of anyone who might go with you,' Kate suggested. 'Let me do something to make up for it all.'

'Oh, I'm bound to think of someone,' Chris answered. 'I have a wide circle of acquaintances and they can't all be busy, even on a Friday night – or have sick relatives for that matter.'

'You go, Mum,' Laura said, now changing sides herself. 'I'll look after Jacko and there's Sally's mother next door – and you can leave the theatre number. You said you would. We'll be OK.'

'No!' said Kate obstinately. 'I mustn't even think about it. Besides, by now I've probably spoilt it for Chris, anyway. He knows I'm half-hearted.'

'Well, you won't want me hanging around in a home stricken with sickness,' Chris said, sounding bored in an embarrassed way. 'I might catch up with you when the boy's over whatever it is that's wrong with him.'

Kate nodded. 'I'll change my dress,' she said. 'If I keep it on I'm sure to spill terrible sherry on it and I think it might burn a hole in it or make it change colour or something,' and she went into her room, leaving Laura and Chris Holly together, self-conscious and unwilling companions.

'Keep out of it!' Laura told herself, watching Chris sit, holding his terrible sherry, and making their room look disgraceful – dark with sickness and broken promises. He put the glass down and stood up with the look of a man who must be on his way. He had *goodbye and good luck!* written all over him.

Good riddance! Laura thought, and then said against all fierce intentions, 'She can't help it, you know.'

'How's that?' said Chris turning towards her, startled as if he had forgotten she was sharing the room with him.

'She's stuck with us,' Laura pointed out. 'She can't do anything about it. We're not books that you can put down, even in an exciting place, and then pick up again just when you want to. Jacko isn't being sick on purpose, you know.' Chris didn't say anything. 'Even I wouldn't do that,' Laura added, 'and I'm the one that feels spooky about Kate going out with a stray man.'

Having started, she meant to be rude to him, for she thought it could not harm Kate any more and, at that moment, hatred burned up brightly in her, for there was a feeling about his friendship with Kate, sudden and incoherent as it might be, that seemed to say, 'The happy year of Kate and Laura and Jacko on their own together is over and will never come again.'

However, instead of growing angry at being called a stray man, Chris looked at her thoughtfully and sat down again.

'Do I sound as if I was blaming you?' he asked. 'Or blaming Kate?'

'You do, actually. Well, you sound as if you're punishing her a bit for something that's not her fault,' Laura mumbled.

Where he might, justifiably have become aggrieved, Chris now began to look at her with increased interest, as if at last she had attracted his attention because she was herself, Laura, and not Kate's superfluous daughter.

'That's pretty unsympathetic of me if it's true,' he said at last, and Laura was forced to be gentler because he was being gentle with her.

'It's true all right,' she said, 'and it's awful for Mum. First I make her feel bad because she's going out and then you make her feel worse because she isn't.'

Her anger was draining out of her, and her voice became apologetic in spite of her efforts to keep it cool and expressionless.

'She really wanted to go. I thought she was a bit too pleased about it . . .' Laura stopped. Her aggressive beginnings were all exhausted.

What had started out as reproof was starting to sound like a confession, and Laura thought that in another moment she would find herself apologizing to him.

'Of course I don't blame her,' Chris said at last. 'The fact is, I was looking forward very much to going out with your mother – right? And suddenly – a sick kid – that could mean almost anything. It did cross my mind she might be standing me up, for example. I don't always feel so very confident of my own fascination. You'd be surprised – well I hope you'd be surprised – at the number of people who have found me perfectly resistible . . .' He paused, and Laura did not say anything for she was working this out. 'Kate was saying that your father left you all a few years ago and I was telling her that my wife did the same to me. Naturally, I think she did the wrong thing.' He smiled rather mockingly at Laura, inviting her to be amused at his judgement. 'But since then, all hesitations seem as if they could be simply that I don't measure up – right?' Laura felt uneasily that he had tricked her into an understanding she did not want to give. 'Kate's quite correct about one thing,' he added warmly, sounding as if he were continuing the conversation but trickily changing the subject, 'this is terrible sherry!'

'It was very cheap,' Laura said. 'We're great on bargains.'

'Sherry like this can never, ever be a bargain,' said Chris.

Laura felt obliged to explain further.

'It's not that we're poor.' She looked around her doubtfully. 'Not really poor. We own this house, and a lot of people don't have houses of their own. But we're usually short. The bookshop doesn't pay Mum a lot, and my father often puts off paying maintenance. Mum's lawyer has to chase after him every so often. Jacko and I cost a lot to run. We can't afford a lot of civilization.' Unwillingly she was treating Chris as though he were a member of the family.

At this moment Kate came back into the room wearing an old skirt and blouse.

'You're not only standing me up, you're trying to poison me,' Chris Holly said to her, and something in his voice eased Kate's expression and she smiled with undefined relief. 'How's the boy?'

'Still asleep, thank goodness,' Kate replied. 'Don't drink that stuff if you don't want to. It wasn't one of my brightest moves. It's a symbol really. It stands for the good sherry we'll have someday when we're rich.'

'I'd better get these tickets back to the Town Hall,' Chris said, standing up again, but even then he waited a little looking from Kate to Laura as if he were turning something over in his mind.

'Kate, I might take you up on that offer of coffee if it's still open,' he said.

'Oh it is!' cried Kate with such undisguised pleasure that Laura blushed for her. 'But let me confess – it's only instant coffee. The sherry's symbolic and the coffee's instant.'

'Nothing I can't cope with. I did my degree in philosophy, remember,' Chris said. 'It's a more practical study than anyone gives it credit for. Symbolic sherry – that's nothing to a philosopher,' and he left them.

'You shouldn't seem so keen on him,' Laura said, finding she disapproved of Kate all over again.

'Why not? It's flattering to him, isn't it?' Kate replied, beginning to tidy away the soup bowls, mute testament to a hurried and disorganized meal.

'He'll think you're out to get him,' said Laura darkly, and Kate laughed, looking back from the kitchen door.

'He's a grown man – he can look after himself,' she said. 'In fact I thought back there he was going to.' She was beginning to sound rather mischievous again.

'He's all right if you don't mind a bit of baldness,' Laura muttered, alarmed all over again at the ease with which Chris was insinuating himself into their lives, even though she had helped him to do so herself.

'Well, I don't mind it,' Kate said flatly. 'I'm bored with thick hair.' (Laura's father, Stephen, had particularly thick, dense hair like Laura's own.) 'And I'm bored at the thought of playing games – pretending not to be interested, trying to make out I don't really care if he goes or stays . . . If he's childish enough to need that, then I'd get bored with him too, sooner or later. I do like him and I want him to know.'

'What's this about philosophy?' asked Laura apprehensively. 'He's not a philosopher, is he?' She couldn't help seeing that if Kate had to have a man friend there would be wonderful advantages in a rich one, and felt instinctively that philosophers needed philosophy because they didn't have money.

'He's the next best thing to a philosopher . . .' said Kate. 'He's a librarian at the Central Library . . . in charge of the New Zealand Room.'

'A Canadian in charge of the New Zealand Room!' Laura exclaimed. 'What's wrong with a good, honest Kiwi joker?'

'It may be International Swap Over Year in library circles,' Kate suggested. 'Or they may be promoting Commonwealth understanding.'

'There's too much understanding in the world as it is,' Laura declared. 'I don't know why people think it's so great. A lot of the things you find yourself understanding are nasty.'

Chris came back an hour later saying the tickets had been successfully returned and, when Jacko was better, he and Kate might try to go to another concert together. He came with gifts . . . a bottle of lemonade, and a bottle of non-symbolic sherry which he suggested they try out to take away the memory of the symbolic sherry drunk earlier. Laura had a little bit in a glass topped up with lemonade.

'It makes it symbolic all over again, but in a different way,' Chris said. 'Kate tells me you need a clear head for your homework.'

In the room next door Jacko remained quiet.

Laura tried to concentrate on her homework while Kate showed Chris her bookseller's course.

'I freely admit it's not high-class entertainment,' she said, 'but I haven't got a piano at present, so I can't sing to you.'

They both laughed, though Laura did not think it was particularly funny. In Kate's bedroom Jacko suddenly gave a curious magpie cry.

'I'll go,' said Laura. 'I need a bit of a stretch away from history.' She pushed open the door of Kate's room and went in. She did not need to turn the light on, for a shaft of light, coming over her shoulder from the living room behind her, fell right across the pillows and she could see Jacko quite clearly.

The whole room seemed to gasp with a dirty sweetness, and she breathed it in before she could stop herself. The scent of used peppermint came unmistakably along with it.

Jacko slowly turned his head to look at her. His Ruggie lay on the pillow beside him, but he showed no interest in it. He was smiling dreadfully, his teeth unnaturally large, his face in retreat around the smile, but his eyes – at least his eyes were still his own, though brimming with a still flood of tears. A clammy hand pressed Laura down on to her knees beside Jacko's bed. It was the hand of terror, nothing less. A moment later her heart began to bang so hard it rang alarms through all her bones and made the world vibrate itself into rapid extinction, except for the feel of the bare floorboards under her knees. She concentrated on this feeling until, little by little, the world came back to her and she felt her own clothes sticking to her as if it were a hot day, felt too, the texture of Jacko's blanket which she had clutched between her thumb and forefinger as if she were taking a pinch of wool from it. Only a second or two had passed, but time, worked on by the excited energy of her fear, had altered yet again for her. There were probably small triangular formulas for it which she would have to do in fifth-form physics next year – time divided by fear multiplied by imagination and so on.

Jacko still wept and smiled, but the smile was fading now.

'All right, Lolly?' called Kate from the next room.

'I don't think he's too good,' Laura replied slowly. 'But there's nothing new.'

It was nothing new, but it was still something known only by her and inaccessible to other people. She could not sing in tune but she could resonate with mystery, and some part of her brain could understand and interpret the resonance.

'I don't like it,' Jacko said in a tiny, thin voice. 'Fox eat up gingerbread boy.'

'It was a bad dream,' Laura said, pouring him a drink of water from the jug Kate had put on his table. He was quite recognizable again.

'Laura will get that bad fox, Jacko,' she promised him. 'It just might take a little time, but Laura will get him.' A moment later he closed his eyes and went to sleep.

Laura returned to the sitting room. Kate glanced up anxiously, but Laura smiled and nodded reassuringly. She thought once more that Kate and Chris talked together like people who had known each other for years, instead of having met only the day before, but as she thought this Laura also realized that 'the day before' had stopped making a lot of sense to her. Time had indeed gone strange and the day before felt as if it stretched back as far as the limits of her memory. Mr Braque had stamped Jacko the day before . . . Sorry Carlisle had arrived at school the day before . . . her father had left them for Julia the day before. Jacko had been born the day before and so had she . . . There had only been one day in the entire history of the world, and that was the day before, so maybe Kate and Chris had known each other for ever.

'Mum, I've finished my homework,' Laura said, lying slightly. 'Can I go and see Sally for a few minutes – watch some telly, perhaps? You don't look as if you'd miss me.' She couldn't entirely banish sarcasm from her voice, so smiled to show she meant no harm by it.

'That's fine,' Kate replied, noting Laura's tone and smile and giving her a dry look. 'Don't be long though, will you?'

'No,' said Laura. 'I haven't seen Sally since Monday night, that's all. If I meet any molesters in the street I'll shout and Chris can come running and save me.' She was teasing him in an experimental way because he was a librarian and not some 'macho' gang member like those in the Gardendale Video Centre.

'Gladly!' said Chris. 'I'll have you know that I'm a black belt.'

'At Judo?' Laura asked sceptically.

'At philosophy,' said Chris. 'I am a great fan of Bishop Berkley. I'll confront any molesters with the theory that they are ideas in the mind of God and, as molesters are probably all atheists, they'll stop believing in themselves and cease to exist.'

'If you make it a really good argument I might cease to exist too,' Laura said.

'Oh, I don't expect you would allow me to convince you,' Chris replied, and Laura laughed a little reluctantly as she left the house.

It was a warm night, and she did not take her coat, although she was not going to Sally's at all. She had lied about her homework and lied about visiting Sally. She was going several blocks through the dangerous night to the very heart of the Gardendale subdivision and was, of course, intending to talk to Sorry Carlisle, seventh form prefect and secret witch.

5

Janua Caeli

Once upon a time the Carlisle family had lived on a farm on the edge of the city and had owned the whole Gardendale Valley, though they called it by another name. But the city crept out and out, an industrious amoeba, extending itself, engulfing all it encountered. The value of the land changed, it was re-zoned and, when the old farmer died, his brothers, city men themselves, subdivided and sold the fields where horses and sheep had grazed, turned away the cows and the bull, and sent in the bulldozer. For a little while the terrain became spectral as roads and street lighting went in ahead of any houses.

It shone at night, threaded with streets where nobody lived and pavements where nobody walked. However, in due course the sections were sold and the hectic homes of the Gardendale subdivision spread everywhere, each on its own little patch, a bright rash over the subdued land. A trim desolation had succeeded the farm. Now an instant coziness succeeded the desolation.

However, at the heart of the subdivision, set among the new houses with their small gardens, their bareness, and the constant autumnal fluttering of red nursery labels on young trees, there stood a wood of silver birches and poplars showing above a tall hedge that had marked, in previous days, the division between the Carlisle farmhouse lawn and the orchard and vegetable garden. Behind this hedge, among these trees, lived Sorensen Carlisle, the latter-day, stammering son of the old family, with his mother and grandmother. Every day, in order to go to school, he emerged from behind this woody hedge, flowering with a fairytale tapestry of Tom Thumb roses in the early summer, and travelled the two miles to school on a small motorbike.

The house had a name and a gate, both of which belonged to the vanished farm. It was called Janua Caeli and the letters were cut deep into the stones of one of the big gateposts. Locally, however, it was mostly known as 'the old Carlisle house'.

A scudding nor'wester beat clouds over the face of the moon, not yet full, but when it could it shone on the new gardens with an intermittent and threatening light, making them look stunted and strange by night, while, around the edges of curtains and blinds, light trembled with the constant pulse of television sets. Sometimes the curtains were still apart, and Laura could look into people's lives, see their lips move without words, watch them laugh at jokes she could not hear. It was like looking into a series of family peep shows, but Laura knew she was a stranger in the dark, spying on private moments, and hurried on.

Someone came walking down the street towards her, and Laura, hearing the ring of steps, turned in at a gateway and hid behind a family car until the shadowy man had gone by. The subdivision was filled with young families, but for all that it was dangerous at night. Two months previously an elderly woman had been robbed and murdered, tied up with wire in front of her own television set, and only ten days later a plain, lumpy girl from the seventh form, Jacynth Close, had been beaten and raped in the trees that bordered the Gardendale Reserve. People at school made uneasy jokes about how desperate the rapist must have been, but Laura was horrified at the injustice of the world, for it seemed as if the one advantage of Jacynth's plainness should have been to save her from this brutality. It made Laura realize that she herself could be chosen. All that was necessary was that her path should intersect with that of an appropriate savage at an appropriate time, and darkness was the most appropriate time of all. She was not altogether easy with the new, and in some ways blatantly female, body that had recently opened out of her earlier childish one, but was obliged to accept its advantages and drawbacks, as well as all the obligations of caution that came with it. So she went very carefully, skirting the overlapping circles of light, not sure whether to let herself be clearly seen and to see others or to stick to the shadows and run the risk that the savage might be lying concealed there, waiting for her.

Janua Caeli said the gates of the old Carlisle home in a single iron voice. They were locked, but not with a padlock and chain. Shaking them furtively to find the pattern of their resistance, Laura determined that they were bolted and spoke the name of the house like a magic spell as she wrestled with the bolt.

'Janua Caeli,' she said as the bolt yielded, and pinched her hand painfully. She slipped through, bolted the gates behind her and went on up a dark, shingled drive, sucking her fingers to help them recover from their sufferings.

The smell of untamed trees immediately surrounded her and with the smell came the conviction that wild beasts might spring out of the shadows at her . . . that she might have to run for her life at any moment. Still, she did not mind this feeling, for it had an edge of poetry to it that had not been part of the chilly anxiety of the street outside the gate. Better to be eaten by a tiger with golden eyes than beaten and raped by the savages of the Gardendale subdivision. Yet, after all, the world was ferocious one way or another, Laura thought, and could be just as savage behind the curtained windows of a family home.

For a moment she lost the path and, as she stood still trying to make it out, something soft and electric with life touched her leg, making her gasp with alarm. A moment later she realized it was the tiger's little cousin, a cat so indistinguishable from the shadows it could only be a black one. She saw then that the drive had actually swung to the left and she followed the faint clues of light which became stronger as she came out of the trees and into a courtyard that appeared to be full of giant chessmen and barnyard roosters. She was accompanied now by two shadows, a faint, grey moon shadow and a much blacker one flowing away behind her, cast by a welcoming light over the door. As she approached this door the moon shadow ignored it, but the lamp shadow shifted and shrank around her like a nervous dog.

The population of shapes in the courtyard was something Laura had read about but never seen before – a topiary company, trees, some of them in tubs, clipped into shapes they would not have chosen, left to their own devices. Laura walked between them nervously. It was easy to believe that one of the giant roosters might be real, might even now be twisting its head to look down at her passing under its beak, but she arrived at the door safely and noted with pleasure that it was made of heavy planks, very thick, old and secure, well able to keep unfriendly forces at bay. For a moment she thought that a face looked at her out of the depths of the wood, but it was only a door knocker, an iron gargoyle obligingly holding a ring in its mouth. Laura knocked boldly, for she had not pursued this dark, half-enchanted journey to be hesitant at the end.

Sorry's mother, Miryam Carlisle, opened the door. She could not have been much older than Kate, but her hair was quite white. She was very tall, perhaps as much as six feet in height, and though Laura could not see her face clearly she found she could fill it in from memory – very cool and calm and always about to change to another less ordered expression, but never quite doing so.

'Mrs Carlisle,' Laura said, 'I'm sorry to come so late but I wondered if I could have a word with Sorry – with Sorensen, that is.'

'Laura Chant!' exclaimed Miryam Carlisle, astonishing Laura who had certainly not expected to be recognized. 'Do come in. We've been hoping you would come and see us some day.'

Laura stepped into a hallway that smelt of flowers, light falling softly through a big arch opposite the entrance and revealing wonders: a carved chest, a slender table inlaid with scrolls of ivory and pearl, a huge vase of mixed flowers, the purple and pink spires of foxgloves standing out against the white wall, and a shallow bowl on a second glass-topped table filled with pot pourri and embossed with blue and green hummingbirds. All these objects spoke of people with a different sort of time in their lives from that available to Kate and Laura. No wild searching in the morning for missing shoes, no racing down the path, or pushing a car into life so that school and work could be reached at the appropriate time. These people had time to make pot pourri and arrange flowers. They might be better organized than Kate – Laura was fair enough to acknowledge this – but she realized, too, that this hall spoke of the advantages that money could confer, and one of these was time. It might be fair to love Sorry for his riches because one loved the chance they offered to become harmonious and beautiful.

A figure appeared in the lighted arch – old Mrs Carlisle, quite as tall as Miryam if she were to straighten herself, but pillowy in shape, head pushed forward like an elegant tortoise. She watched Miryam and Laura in silence as they stopped outside one of the doors leading out of the hall.

'This is Sorensen's study,' Miryam explained, knocking on the door, and Laura tried to imagine having a door that people actually knocked at – a door behind which she too, could be silent and mysterious.

'What is it?' asked a voice behind the door – Sorry Carlisle's voice, no doubt about that, not deeper, but darker than it was at school.

'It's Laura Chant,' said Miryam, opening the door for her, and Laura noted with astonishment the familiarity with which her name was used. She was known here, singled out from the rest of the population of Gardendale, though she had never visited the house before. Out of sudden and unanticipated embarrassment she looked at the room beyond Sorry who was half-rising from his desk to meet her. She saw, first of all, real bookcases filled with books, few, if any of which had been acquired out of the 'Cancelled' box at his local public library. She would have expected books, however. Sorry also had an old leather settee, battered but still good, brightened with patchwork cushions, and real pictures on the wall, the marks of the painter's brush giving its texture to the painted surface. Among the pictures was a large poster of a naked woman and beside it, standing in its own wooden frame, a complete human skeleton, yellowish white, shining and smiling. Directly above this was a painted mask, funny – and frightening because it *was* funny even though it was so still. Laura felt a sigh trying to force its way out of her lips at the prospect of owning such beauty and of living with it day after day. But then she saw that one complete shelf in the bookcase was filled with women's romances, such as she and Kate despised, and this made her feel strong, as if they proved Sorry to be stuck at some inadequate level of understanding which she herself had grown beyond. The cat pushed slickly past her legs and jumped up on to Sorry's knee where it disappeared, for he was wearing black and his greater blackness swallowed the cat's lesser one. Laura saw, even before she looked at him properly, that this was a different version of Sorry Carlisle from the one she had known at school. His black dressing-gown, or caftan, was part of the change; his hands, redefining the cat by stroking it, were another. For they were covered in rings, some of them old and beautiful, gifts perhaps from his grandmother who also wore many rings. However, when she looked into his face, as she was bound to do, at last, her hair stood quite simply on end, for in this room he was somehow expanded, less simple, less mild, less *good* – overflowing with blackness. At the same time he stared at her incredulously as if she had had a precisely similar effect on him, appearing in his doorway, a visitation hoped for and feared, a test he was forced to take before he was ready to do so. To be taken aback and frightened is one thing; to find that in some way you are frightening someone else is another. If it had not been for the picture of Jacko she carried in her mind, she would have turned and run out of the house.

At the same time Laura saw, with relieved satisfaction, that Sorry had a few pimples at his hairline and the thought that this witch might have pimples like anyone else gave her confidence. The cat on his knees began to knead and purr, looking up at her with luminous eyes.

'Come on in,' he said. 'What's eating you, Chant?'

'Tigers!' Laura thought of saying as she sidled nervously into the room. Miryam Carlisle continued to stand in the doorway watching her. Sorry, for his part, recovered from his strange astonishment and began to smile a smile both inquisitive and sinister.

'What's brought you into my parlour?' he asked ominously. 'It's late to be visiting a man in his rooms, Chant.'

'I'm wearing my school uniform,' Laura said. 'Does that make it better or worse?' She had never worked out why he had always chosen to call her by her surname, but she had not minded. Sorry laughed a little as if he were surprised at her answer.

'I don't know the etiquette on that one,' he admitted. 'I don't think it's dealt with in any books I've read. Sit down.'

Laura did so, feeling shabby among the patchwork cushions, and Sorry watched her as if she were a model, displaying herself on his sole behalf.

'Your school uniform's too short, for that matter,' he added. 'It should come down to your knees when you're sitting down. It's in the handbook.'

Laura looked at him cautiously. She did not want to misunderstand this remark.

'I've let down the hem as far as it will go,' she explained.

'You need another,' Sorry said. 'There's the rest of this term and then two months the other side of Christmas before you can change into winter gear. And you'll probably grow over the holidays.'

'Sorensen, you're not at school now,' said his mother.

'I know that,' Sorensen replied. 'And she knows it. I was being subtle, letting her know I was looking at her legs. She's got very sexy legs but I'm not allowed to tell her about them at school.'

'There's a difference between being oblique and being obscure,' said his mother, while Laura tried to hide her consternation.

'You must forgive Sorensen,' Miryam went on, turning to Laura, quite as if she were an honoured and adult guest who mustn't be offended. 'He can be very inept at times.'

'I'm not being inept, Chant,' Sorry said. 'My mother knows that. She's just worried because I'm not doing an impression of polite conversation – weather or health – "And how are you, Laura Chant, are you keeping well, and your dear mother, is she well too?" . . . all that stuff.' He spoke in a rapid, light voice that picked subjects up and abandoned them before his listeners had caught up with them, and there was a slight breathlessness haunting his words at times, the remains of his original stammer. 'My mother finds "sexy" a very aggressive word, but I think it's accurate and I'm more likely to know about such things than she is.' Laura was being used as part of an argument between two little-known people. 'Whatever else I may miss out on,' Sorry added, smiling at his mother.

'Sorensen!' she said in a soft voice, soft but quelling, a velvet cushion used to smother a prince in a tower.

'Do go and do something else, Mother,' he said, looking away. 'Please do. It's very inhibiting to talk to a visitor with you listening in. I won't hurt her. I won't even frighten her.'

'I haven't noticed much evidence of inhibition so far,' his mother said dryly. 'But I shall certainly go. It's nice to see you, Laura, but don't let him alarm you.'

And they both looked at her with their matching eyes showing unmistakable appraisal, as if they were ancient priests assessing the quality of a sacrifice.

'I won't,' Laura said, but certainly feeling she was getting out of her depth, not because she had gone out too far, but because a totally unexpected tide had come rushing over her. Perhaps coming to see Sorry in his own house had been going too far after all. Mrs Carlisle closed the door and went away.

'What do you want?' Sorry asked immediately the door closed, giving her a very close and private stare that suggested he knew a great deal about her, much more than the shape of her legs. The glances exchanged at school for a year and a half had given them a certain power over each other, which was why Laura was here at all, but she found this particular gaze so close it was suffocating.

Now she also found she could not ask him about Jacko as simply and directly as she had planned to do, and looked around the room at the books, at the skeleton, at the naked woman whose revelations seemed to her to cross some unspecified boundary and somehow made her shy. This woman had been photographed as if she were on her own in a private reverie over her own private skin, but of course she had agreed to be photographed, the photographer at least had been present, and the picture was intended to be looked at by men. There was a small snapshot pinned to one corner of it, but Laura could not make out what it showed and was almost frightened to look closely, at least while Sorry was watching her.

'D-don't you like it?' Sorry asked her, watching her eyes. 'The poster, I mean.'

'It isn't meant to be liked by me,' she answered, and then added, 'it's too personal, really . . . like standing in the dark and looking in at someone's window.'

'But that's quite an interesting thing to do,' he said. 'And harmless, as long as people don't know you're there.'

Laura struggled with a difficult idea.

'It still seems too private though, as if looking at her somehow lets you look at other people too . . . who mightn't want to be looked at,' she ended hurriedly. Sorry studied his poster and then studied Laura.

'That's art, isn't it?' he said after a moment of silence and speaking as if he did not expect her to understand him. 'Like dissecting a possum in biology – private occasions having their skins pinned out and their guts identified and labelled. You read, don't you? Unless you carry books around for the look of the thing! Do you think there are any private moments in art? Better still, tell me what you really want to talk about.'

'Whose bones?' Laura asked, moving on to the skeleton whose privacy was, after all, violated even more than that of the woman in the poster.

'It belonged to my great-grandfather who was a doctor,' said Sorry. 'I've inherited it. It's called 'Uncle Naylor', but I've not managed to find out if it's just a name or if he really was a relation. I expect you know that, except for my chromosomes, I'm a recent arrival in the Carlisle family. Do you take science at school?'

'I know what chromosomes are,' Laura said primly. 'More or less.'

'Chant, you can't have come to see me simply to talk about my skeleton and my poster,' Sorry suggested.

'No!' Laura agreed, looking at the bookcase. 'Why do you read all those romances?'

'For romance!' Sorry answered promptly. 'Research and romance. There's not a lot of romance in being a prefect, you know.' He pointed his fingers at her, making a gun out of his hand. 'Stand and deliver, Chant. What are you doing here?'

Laura stood up. 'I thought you might help me,' she said. 'I need help, I think. And you're a witch, aren't you?'

Sorry's face went quite blank as if every expression had been cleaned from it with a cloth, but she had the impression that he had become very angry and couldn't think why. Now it had become impossible to ask a favour of him, and impossible not to. She looked around the room again, at the indisputable seventh form homework, the skeleton, the poster, the photograph. Out of anxiety and confusion she made a half move to look at the photograph more closely, for it seemed as if it might offer another diversion, but Sorry took hold of her wrist and shook it slightly.

'What do you want?' he asked and added, 'I might provide a love philtre, but I don't do contraceptives.'

Laura felt herself colour, as much with anger as embarrassment. 'You know it's nothing like that!'

'How do I know? You won't tell me. Except you've come to consult a witch.'

'I need help for my brother,' Laura said at last, and Sorry looked taken aback and then openly angry.

'Your brother!' he said. 'You've come all the way here to . . .' He broke off. 'How did you get here?'

'I walked, of course,' Laura answered.

'You were asking for it, weren't you?' he asked. 'Think of what happened to Jacynth Close.'

'I did think, but how else could I get here?' she said. 'Things like that don't happen often.'

'I expect once is enough if you happen to be the one,' Sorry said. 'You came here about your brother . . .'

'He's terribly sick,' Laura said.

'To hell with that!' Sorry exclaimed. 'Take him to a doctor. I'll punish your enemy, cure warts, release the winds . . .' He raised his hand and a breeze actually rippled the pages of his seventh form chemistry, very eerie in the small room. 'If you wanted to make a neighbour's goat have fits . . . I'd be the right person then, wouldn't I?'

Laura knew she had hurt his feelings but could not see why.

'He's terribly sick,' she said. 'Sicker than anyone knows. A doctor won't help.'

Sorry was still holding her wrist. He stood up. 'You should be careful, knowing what you know,' he said. 'I might drive a hard bargain. I might ask to drink a pint of your blood or goodness knows what. Get a doctor. They're subsidized by the government. I'll see you to the gate.'

'A doctor would be no good,' said Laura, but she walked out of his room passively enough when he held the door open for her, though she felt her own anger building up in her in a gratifying way.

'Sorensen?' called a voice. 'Does Laura drink coffee?'

'Not here she doesn't! She's on her way,' said Sorry. 'For eighteen months we've given one another these looks across the school playground and I thought she'd come because . . . well, never mind why I thought she'd come, and she thought I was a bloody witch doctor who could cure measles free.'

'Sorensen, please don't swear like that,' said the older Mrs Carlisle, old Winter, who, coming forward, looked exactly like Laura's idea of a witch, for she was getting ready for bed and wearing a dressing-gown instead of the tweed skirt and twin-set she often wore, and her white hair, usually pulled severely back, hung over her shoulders in two plaits.

'I'll tell you what,' Sorry said, looking at her, speaking as if he had just had a brilliant idea, 'why don't we put on the opening scene from Macbeth for Chant? You, me and Miryam.

"When shall we three meet again

In thunder, lightning . . ."'

'We don't do Macbeth until next year,' Laura interrupted him.

Winter ignored them. 'Just how far do you have to go?' she asked Laura.

'I can easily walk,' Laura said stiffly. 'It's not far.'

'She lives in Kingsford Drive,' Sorry said crossly. 'I'll run you home on the Vespa, Chant. Of course that might turn out to be more risky. You never know your luck.'

He was starting to look more at ease, more inquisitive again, but Laura's anger was reaching its peak. Their tempers were not synchronized.

'Did you think I came because I liked you?' she asked indignantly, remembering, however, that she had felt jealous of another girl talking to him earlier that day.

'Why not?' asked Sorry. 'Let's be honest . . .'

'Don't let's be honest!' his grandmother interrupted him. 'Go and get your motorbike, Sorensen. I don't think Laura should walk home alone through these streets.'

'I came by them,' she replied. 'At least I live a real life in a real house, Sorry Carlisle, not shut away behind a high hedge in a sort of museum – a museum of spare time.'

It was impossible to be rude to Sorry, without being rude to his mother and grandmother, too.

'Look – stuff real life!' Sorry said. 'I've tried it out and believe me it's nothing but rubbish.'

'And double-stuff your broomstick!' Laura retorted in a low, fierce voice. 'I hope you get splinters.'

'Terrific!' said Sorry, walking out through one of the doors. But in the doorway he stopped and half turned as if he might be going to say something else. However, if this was so, he changed his mind and walked away, shutting the door after him.

'At least come into the kitchen, Laura,' said Winter Carlisle. 'He will have to change his clothes and then he'll bring his bike round to the kitchen door.'

Laura let herself be led into what was surely a farmhouse kitchen, though the farm had ceased to exist. In spite of the warm night she had begun to shiver, but she did not wish to show it. Also she found something sinister about the unremitting kindness these women showed her, for she had come as a stranger and quarrelled with a member of the family in their own hall. Besides she knew herself to be scruffy and tired and forlorn. They gave her lemonade – the second glass she had had that night, but this was not fizzy, shop lemonade; it was a home-made kind, made with real lemons. Indeed a slice of lemon floated in it like an opaque island. It was in her hands almost before she knew where she was, and a plate with tomato sliced over home-made bread was put in the other. They both watched her from under their peaceful eyelids and she felt the pressure of an unspoken expectation, and an anxiety which their calm faces did not reveal.

What's going on? she thought, wondering if she might not enlist these new witches – for looking at them she saw they could not be otherwise – on Jacko's behalf. Sorry's nature, when she first saw him, had been almost flamboyant in its declaration, but his mother and grandmother were softer and more secret. The faces of the witches looked out through their own faces as if through masks of grey lace.

'What did you want Sorry to do for you, Laura?' asked old Winter.

'My little brother is so ill,' Laura began, but they were not really interested in Jacko, only in Sorry himself and for some reason in Laura, too. Miryam interrupted her, something Laura thought this polite woman would not normally have done, except that she was anxious to say something before Sorry came back.

'Please be patient with him,' she said. 'I know he can be very difficult at times, but for reasons I can't go into now I have to tell you that Sorensen's difficulties are partly my fault.'

'But he's not wicked,' said the older woman, more to herself than Laura, 'not yet! A wicked witch can be a very terrible thing,' she added, to Laura's further confusion. Laura took a mouthful of bread and tomato, not so much from hunger as from nervous politeness, and felt their anxiety ease a little though she had no idea why.

'He wasn't really so very difficult,' Laura said. 'It was more as if we started talking about two different things, but he's different from the way he is at school.'

'Ah, yes, I imagine he is,' said Miryam, 'but he has to go to school, you know. He's talked a lot about you. It seems you recognized that he has this ambiguous nature and perhaps, by now, you can see that it's an inherited thing.'

'I thought he was a witch,' Laura said. 'That's the word that came in to my mind.'

'It's very much a feminine magic – or so we think,' Miryam said. 'And Sorensen sometimes resents it. He doesn't like being called a witch, although of course that is really what he is. Sometimes he feels that he's not completely a man or a witch but some hybrid, and he struggles too hard to be entirely one thing or the other. But he can't give up either nature. We do try to reconcile him, but so far, at least, our efforts have met with very mixed success. However, the real difficulty lies elsewhere.' And once again Laura felt their glances fall on her, outwardly calm, inwardly concerned, as if they were depending on her for something, but could not tell her what.

'He thought I came to see him because I liked him,' she said. 'Not that I don't,' she added hastily, 'but – you know – because I specially liked him.'

'Well, perhaps you do,' suggested Miryam smiling at her. 'Or perhaps some day . . .'

'I wouldn't come to see him at night because I liked him,' Laura said, horrified that they should think she might have. She stared down at the bread in her hand. There was only a crust left, and she was holding it between finger and thumb, as girls in old-fashioned pictures sometimes held roses. She couldn't remember eating it, though the taste of the salted tomato was fresh in her mouth. Already, out of nothing, she had moved into a vague alignment with these women, become a conspirator without knowing the nature of the conspiracy. She took a deep breath and turned to ask them about Jacko again, but in came Sorry himself in an expensive motorcycle jacket and blue jeans and wearing a motorcycle helmet which transformed him into a moon walker.

'I've got a spare helmet,' he said. 'Come on, Cinderella, let Prince Charming put it on for you. My darling, you must have the smallest head in the world.'

Laura couldn't help laughing. The Vespa was waiting at the kitchen door. Sorry climbed on to it with the nimbleness of much practice.

'You'll come back again, Laura,' said old Mrs Carlisle with satisfaction. 'After all, you've eaten our bread and salt, and that's a sign.'

'Did you?' said Sorry sharply. 'Chant, you haven't got the sense you were born with. Mind you, everyone warns you to watch out for someone like me, but who's going to teach you to watch out for two nice, middle-class women with money and private-school accents? OK, hop on the bike behind me. Hang on to me if you like, but don't pull me backwards too much, will you?'

'Take her straight home,' said Winter as if this was in doubt. But the journey only took a few minutes and, since she felt very tired and the moon was now permanently hidden by a warm bed of nor'west cloud, she was glad of the lift and thought once again that life was very easy for Sorry Carlisle in the same ways in which it was very difficult for her.

At her own gate she hesitated, struggling with the unfamiliar fastening on the helmet until he began, rather impatiently, to take it off for her.

'By the way, Chant,' he asked as he did so, 'just what is wrong with the little brother?'

'He's bewitched,' said Laura, 'but *you* don't care.'

'Not so very much,' Sorry agreed. 'Besides, most likely it's just chicken-pox or something.'

'It's a sort of vampire,' Laura explained, and he laughed.

'This isn't a village in the Carpathians. You've been watching the Sunday night horror movie.'

'We don't have television,' Laura replied shortly. 'Besides it's not exactly a vampire. More a spirit, an incubus, a demon.'

'What a load of rubbish!' said Sorry derisively. 'Which one is it?'

'I don't know,' said Laura, 'and that's a funny thing, because I knew what you were straight off, didn't I?'

She turned her back on him and marched up the little concrete path, its square edges lined by alyssum and a few poppies. The door looked very light and flimsy after the Carlisles' front door, which seemed to be built to withstand battering rams. Still she had lived a very happy life behind that door and was comforted to see it again.

'Hang on a minute, Chant!' Sorry called behind him, but she opened the plywood door, went through it and shut him and his blue Vespa out in the dark where he seemed rightfully to belong. He was something different from what she had thought him and she wanted to think carefully about him before she saw him again.

Inside the house, Kate and Chris Holly stared at her in a self-consciously innocent way.

'How's Jacko?' Laura asked.

'Very quiet,' said Kate, remarkably cheerful. 'He might sleep it off. You never know.'

Laura, however, thought that she did know. She looked at them carefully. She had been away a great deal longer than she had implied she would be when she left, but they did not seem to have noticed. There was so much traffic up and down Kingsford Drive, even at this time of night, that Sorry's motorbike might easily have gone unnoticed, or perhaps they had been thinking of something else . . . She had a strong feeling that they had not missed her.

6

Different Directions

'Laura! Laura!' Kate screamed suddenly, and then, 'Laura!' again and, immediately terrified, Laura found herself on her feet, dizzy with the last traces of sleep and an early Saturday waking. Rushing into Kate's room she found something frightening in progress, something that she could only watch aghast, for Kate had called her out of the need for an instant companion, not because she really thought there was anything Laura could do. The room reeked of Carmody Braque and Jacko lay on his sheet drumming with his heels, his eyes open but turned up so that only the whites showed, his body arching before their eyes into a stiff bow, collapsing and arching again. A single drop of blood suddenly trickled from his left nostril and ran down the side of his face, as if something in him was being wrung out, reluctantly releasing its juice.

'Oh God! Oh God!' Kate cried, panting with horror. 'Laura, he's dying!'

However, Jacko wasn't dying yet. He collapsed and grew limp at last, opened his mouth once or twice so widely they could see past his teeth, deep down into his throat, then fell into a quick, snoring sleep. Kate fluttered around him, longing to pick him up and hug him, terrified that she might harm him by moving him.

'Ring the doctor,' she cried. 'I must ring the doctor. Don't leave him, Laura.'

'Run to Sally's,' Laura shouted.

'They're out!' Kate replied. 'Saturday morning – early swimming lessons. Where's the phone money?'

There was a frantic search for phone money, but though there usually seemed to be too many useless little coins in the world, when you really needed them they behaved like nervous beetles and crawled into cracks or under things and refused to come out. At last, after going through her coat pockets, sobbing and complaining, Kate found sufficient coins to make two phone calls if necessary and ran out, leaving the door open. Laura sat by Jacko, whose sleep grew quieter and easier as she watched over him, and then Kate was back, soft-faced with relief, for she had been lucky and, after one encounter with an answering service, had got on to the very doctor she had seen yesterday who was also the doctor on duty for the weekend. Perhaps her distress had carried conviction, for he had said he would come at once, something doctors could not be relied upon to do, and Kate, relieved of her first anxiety, was free to bend over Jacko once more and stare at him with desperate tenderness and sadness.

'He looks so old,' she said, and her expression and her voice ached with such pain that Laura could scarcely bear to watch her. 'I've heard of a dreadful disease where children turn into old men and women, but I don't think it comes on suddenly like this . . . Oh, Laura! Suppose it *is* that that's wrong with him. What could make him shrink like this? It must be something terrible.'

'I don't know,' cried Laura, affected as much by Kate's hysterical cry as by Jacko's spasm, and then she added, 'Well, I do know, but you won't believe me.'

Kate stood up in her old, blue dressing-gown that had once been so pretty. Laura could remember five long years ago, seeing her father notice Kate in the blue dressing-gown and embrace her and stroke her fair hair while Laura watched, impressed with the feeling of a grown-up mystery, and thrilled because she thought this might at last be the happy ending of their arguments and that from now on things would never go wrong again. Kate's eyes had been sleepy and smiling then. Now they turned on her, wide, distracted and beginning to be angry.

'You're blaming all this on the junk man and his stamp?' she asked disbelievingly.

'Something is draining out of Jacko and into him,' Laura said stubbornly. 'It's his life force that's being stolen.'

'Great Heavens above!' exploded Kate. 'Don't frighten me any more with your Space Invaders rubbish! Don't make me think that you're going crazy, too.' She stopped and took a deep breath, rubbing her cheek as if someone had struck her.

'I know you can't believe it,' Laura said resignedly, 'but it's true. Sometimes the room smells of peppermint and that was Carmody Braque's smell, horrible peppermint, and sometimes Jacko smiles with his smile. I have to say what I know. He's bewitched.'

'It's not a game,' Kate said. 'I'd believe you if I could – I'd believe anything that would help me to understand what's happening. But your ideas are symbolic, like the terrible sherry . . . whatever is true in them has disguised itself as a fairy tale.'

The doctor came and looked at Jacko without enlightenment.

'I think we just might put him into hospital for observation, Mrs Chant,' he said at last. 'Can you afford a private hospital?' Kate looked doubtfully around.

'Not really . . .' she began and then said, 'Oh, his father can! I know he will, in a case like this. And if not – we can always sell the house. It's just a question of what's best for Jacko.'

'It might be hard to fit him in at the state hospital,' the doctor said with a sigh. 'I'll ring, if I may, and . . .'

'We're not on the phone,' Kate explained and the doctor said he would go to the clinic and make arrangements from there.

Kate was to ring him in an hour or two and he would tell her what he had organized. Just as he was leaving, Jacko had another spasm, twisting and arching a little less alarmingly than the first time, but it was easy to see the doctor grow very concerned.

'The trouble is, Mrs Chant, I haven't the ghost of an idea what could be the matter with him. It could be some sort of epilepsy, but there are some other symptoms that just don't fit into that category at all. He's best in hospital. There's one doctor – Dr Hayden – he's very good. I'll see if I can't speak to him.'

Jacko, in bed at home, already seemed to belong partly to the world of medical mystery, no longer a son or brother, but a puzzling case that would have to be solved. The doctor drove away and Kate looked unhappily at Laura.

'Well, that's that!' she said. 'What shops are open on a Saturday morning? He'll need new pyjamas at least. Isn't it mad to think of such a thing, but everything he's got is either too small or in the wash. I don't want him looking neglected.'

'New Brighton's open on a Saturday,' Laura said. 'Have you got any money?'

'I'll write a cheque if I have to,' Kate said. 'Let me see – quarter-of-an-hour to get there, quarter-of-an-hour, say, twenty minutes to buy something for him, and quarter-of-an-hour to come home. It's the best part of an hour. I'd better not go. I wish you were old enough to drive.'

'I'll stay by him. I won't move,' cried Laura. 'I'll look after him just as well as you would. But don't be long, will you?'

'After all it doesn't matter so very much,' Kate said. 'They'll only put him in hospital pyjamas probably.'

In their family most of their money went on outside clothes not private ones. Jacko was not neglected but his pyjamas were, and Kate finally decided she must go. She went to the door, then rushed back and hugged Laura.

'Darling!' she said in a muffled voice. 'Darling Laura! You're *both* so precious to me. Look after Jacko and look after yourself.'

'You look after yourself,' Laura said. 'You're the one that's going out into the world, not me.'

She watched through the window as Kate began pushing her car, leaping into it as it began to roll. A moment later she heard the sputtering rattle of the engine reluctantly consenting to fire. Laura was alone in the house. This house which had been a happy house now felt threatening, for its present desperation flowed back into the past and ruined not only the present day but the memory of all that had gone before it, which suddenly seemed to be only a mocking cat-and-mouse game the world had played with them. Jacko was lying very still, scarcely seeming to breathe at all. His fair hair was dull, his lips the colour of the clay used for pottery during arts and crafts at school. He had the slightly withered look of an apple unexpectedly discovered at the bottom of the fruit bowl. His skin was lined by tiny furrows as if it were becoming minutely loose on him, crinkling over shrinking flesh. Never had she seen a human being look so removed from the world, hidden behind closed lids, tightly sewn with invisible threads, and certainly looking as if they might never open again.

'Jacko!' she whispered. 'It's me, Jacko! It's Lolly.' But his eyes and lips remained sternly shut. She took his hand, and nearly dropped it, for it was cold with a still, deep cold, as if no blood or any other function of life moved in it. She held it and kissed the palm hoping he might respond to this small affection, but he remained inert and silent.

Laura went back into the big room and looked out of the window, though there was no chance that Kate would be coming back yet. A light rain had begun to fall. Outside, the world had matched itself up with her own grey, weeping mood. Outside there were two splashes of colour – the red telephone box at the corner of the picture, framed by the window, and the blue Vespa parked beside it. Coming up the path was a moon-walker in a white motorcycle helmet. Laura waited, like someone in a haunted house, for the knock to fall on the door. After a moment it came. Laura opened the door. Sorry stood with his helmet, like a spare head, under his arm.

'Good morning, Chant,' he said in rapid but pacific tones. 'I've come to make peace.' Under his jacket he wore a high-necked black jersey which made his pale hair look a definite yellow. He was quite brown with summer and his light-coloured eyes were startling against his dark skin, but more ordinary this morning – less highly charged and threatening.

'What do you want?' she asked, thinking she sounded childish, rather than cool and slightly cutting as she would have liked to be. However, he seemed to be looking a little beyond her into their house, almost as if he were testing it for clues to other presences.

'Isn't your mother at home?' he said. 'You have got a mother, haven't you? You don't run this place alone.'

'She's out!' said Laura shortly.

'Good enough! I'll be normal then, not charming,' said Sorry. 'I've a good line for charming mothers, but I'd rather not. Come on, Chant! Take a risk! Invite me in!'

Laura stood aside to let him in but he still hesitated on the doormat.

'Ask me in!' he told her, smiling. 'I have to be asked, but then – after that – I'm hard to get rid of.'

'Oh, all right! Come on in!' said Laura rather impatiently and he stepped cautiously through the door.

'We call on each other at odd hours, don't we, but mine's a more respectable hour for a visit than yours. Do you always wear pyjamas like that?'

Laura remembered how she had stared at him in his black robe the night before, and how she had looked critically around his room while the cat purred on his knee. Her own pyjamas were scarcely more respectable than Jacko's, but at least they had all their buttons.

'It isn't my best pair,' she said trying to joke a little. 'I keep the black satin ones for special occasions.'

'This *is* a special occasion,' Sorry said, opening his eyes in apparent astonishment, 'but don't rush off to change or anything. Tell me again, what's this about the little brother?'

'He's in here,' Laura said. 'But a doctor has been. He's going to hospital. It won't do any good though. Only I know what happened and Mum won't believe me. She can't. No one can.'

'I promise I can believe six impossible things before breakfast,' Sorry said. 'That's why I gave breakfast a miss this morning before coming to test your hypothesis. Do you do science down in the fourth form? You didn't tell me last night.'

'It's compulsory,' Laura said. 'I'm not too sure about a hypothesis if that's what you're asking, but I know *Through the Looking-Glass*.'

'A hypothesis is a suggestion of what might or might not be true,' Sorry explained. 'You can disprove it, but you might never completely prove it. I think that's how it goes – more proof the world's lopsided. Let's see the boy before your mother comes home and tears a strip off you for entertaining older seventh form men in your pyjamas.'

'You really do think you're terrific, don't you?' Laura said with a faint grin.

'Someone has to,' Sorry replied, following her into Jacko's room. 'Those harridans at home have been . . . Heavens above, Chant!' he suddenly exclaimed. 'What's that smell?' Laura could almost have hugged him because he could smell the peppermint too, but she held her breath and waited while he looked at Jacko.

'Well, well!' he said after a moment. 'You clever girl! You were right and I was wrong.' Laura released a gushing sigh of relief. Sorry sat down on a chair by Jacko's bed – a chair draped in Kate's underwear.

'Go on! Tell me all!' he said, as he lifted first one of Jacko's eyelids and then the other, not so much to look at his eyes as to notice the way they closed. Laura told her story as tersely as she could.

'Demon! Spirit! Incubus!' said Sorry. 'It sounds to me as if whatever faculty you have that makes you – you know – able to guess at some of the extreme people drifting around in the world – it sounds as if that faculty was stuck for the right word. Does this Carmody Braque have any – did he have a word branded on his forehead, say, or any mark that might have been a word crossed out?'

'No, nothing like that,' Laura said definitely. 'He was quite bald – his hair was thin and clipped very short. I'd have certainly seen it.' Sorry appeared to abandon a briefly-held hypothesis of his own. He stared at Jacko – picked up his hand and sighed, shaking his head.

'Have you ever heard of the lemures?' he asked at last.

'Monkeys?' Laura said.

'Primates!' said Sorry absentmindedly. 'No – not those. The lemures were the wicked spirits of the dead . . . the lavae or lemures. I don't think your Carmody Braque is actually an incubus. I think he's a wicked spirit that has managed to win a body for itself once more and has probably gone on by absorbing the lives of others – their energy – to keep himself alive. You were almost right when you said he was a vampire, but it's not mere blood he's after. It's the essence of life itself.' He looked at Jacko as if he were some sort of a rare flower whose stem had been bent by a storm. 'The fact is . . .' he said after a moment, and then grew silent. 'You're a big, brave girl, Chant, aren't you . . . the fact is I think your little brother has had it.'

'You mean you think he might be going to die?' Laura cried, hearing her voice high and hard in the dim room.

'He's sealing up,' Sorry said in his light, remote way. 'Even if I had come last night there's nothing I can think of that I could have done about it.' Laura began to feel very cold – as cold perhaps as Jacko lying in his blankets but not warmed by them.

'You really think he's going to die?' she repeated.

'He's sealing up.' Sorry also repeated himself in a reasonable voice as if stating a fact she must accept. He looked quite lighthearted, interested in the problem but not affected by it.

'Sealing will help for a while, I suppose. It's a form of hibernation – aestivation really . . .'

'I don't want a lecture,' Laura said, staring at him incredulously, for he sounded like a teacher at school.

'You really think he's going to die?'

'You asked me that a moment ago. I'm sorry,' Sorry said and shrugged. 'I shouldn't think he'd stand out for very long against this sort of possession. Well, it's not so much a possession as a consumption.'

'Come into the tidy room,' Laura said after a moment. 'You could have a glass of symbolic sherry.'

'At nine-fifteen in the morning?' Sorry asked, 'and on an empty stomach?' He followed her out and sat down opposite her at the table. Laura lifted her eyes to his and looked at him steadily, and his grey eyes went blank and then shifted away from hers, turning silver in the oblique light from the window.

'You upset, Chant?' he said in a careful voice.

'He's my brother, and I love him, and you say he's going to die,' Laura said. 'He was a terrific little boy and you talk about him dying as if you just didn't give a stuff about it!'

'I used to have some brothers,' Sorry said. 'I don't know what I'd think if one of them was about to die, but I'm sure of this – none of them would worry about me. My feelings worked really well for years but I know they're not too good now. I suppose I did my own sealing off – a different sort from Jacko's – some time ago. But I'll do what I can for him, which is to ask Winter. She knows everything – Winter. So take a deep breath, Chant. You're no worse off and you might be better off . . . and at least you're not quite on your own with it any more.'

This was true. Laura did take a deep breath and realized as she did so that Sorry was not watching her face, but the rise and fall of the breath under her old pyjama jacket. He sighed himself, met her eyes, and gave her a smile both deprecating and conciliatory.

'You did invite me in,' he pointed out, 'even though you knew I was a mixed blessing.'

'I didn't invite you to watch me breathe,' Laura pointed out.

'You didn't make any conditions, either.' Sorry looked away from her again. 'An invitation means a lot to a witch. And the lemure could only put his mark on your brother's hand because it was held out to him. Sometimes these little rituals carry a whole lot of significance. Now you'll have to get him to take his mark off, and I think the only way to do that might be to put a mark of power on him and command him through that.'

'Could I do it?' Laura asked disbelievingly. Sorry shook his head.

'I shouldn't think so,' he said. 'I think it would have to be a witch who did it – or someone similar. But the difficulty is he wouldn't let a witch get anywhere near him, let alone hold out his hand for any reason whatsoever. However, let's see what Winter comes up with.'

'Well, I'm going to get dressed,' Laura said. 'Why don't you look at some books?'

'I'll make a cup of coffee if you like?' suggested Sorry. 'Don't try and tell me where things are. I'll guess.'

'You'll guess wrong,' Laura said. 'Mum puts them in funny places.'

'But I have an instinct for coffee,' Sorry said. '*You'd* swear it was witchcraft!'

'It's only instant,' Laura told him, like a true hostess.

'I prefer instant,' Sorry cried triumphantly. 'I seem cosmopolitan now, but I'm suburban at heart.'

'I'm not even sure what cosmopolitan is,' Laura replied. 'Suppose you make the coffee and stop talking about yourself.'

'You're a bloody ruthless hostess,' Sorry shouted after her, 'You're supposed to make a guest feel relaxed.' However, he sounded good-humoured.

'Well, watch out for the kettle,' Laura said. 'Don't worry if it hisses. It's got a slow leak. Fill it quite full, and when it whistles it's boiling.'

She dressed rather more carefully than usual, borrowing a white shirt of her mother's to wear with blue jeans. The kettle screamed savagely and was silenced. As she was brushing her hair she heard Kate's voice and came in to find Kate, with Chris Holly at her elbow, staring with surprise at a stranger standing in the kitchen door offering her a cup of her own coffee. Sorry was friendly and polite and seemed completely at ease. He had found and set a tray and in the centre of it in one of the ex-peanut butter jars, was a bouquet of pink rose buds as perfect as if they had just come from a florist's window. Kate exclaimed over them, but Laura knew they were not natural flowers. They were the second outside proof she had had of Sorry's double nature.

'I'll be spending most of the day at the hospital,' Kate said wearily. 'Chris, what can be wrong with him?'

'Hospital's the place where they'll find out,' said Chris.

Laura looked at him suspiciously, wondering what he was doing there, but it seemed that he had offered to come round and bring Kate a particular book and, knowing she would be out in the afternoon, she had called in at his flat to explain this to him. Chris had immediately offered to drive her to the hospital in his own car which was larger and had a heater that worked so that Jacko might be more comfortable. Laura thought he looked rather bewildered to find himself there and thought, too, with prickles of dismay that Kate had really gone to him because he was important enough to her for her to be anxious about letting him down. With most people she would have remembered afterwards.

'Laura, I don't know how long I'll be . . .' Kate began.

'Mrs Chant, my mother suggested that Laura might like to come and stay with us for the day – and for the evening too, if necessary,' Sorry said. Laura knew he was inventing on the spur of the moment. Kate hesitated.

'That's very kind . . .' she said in a doubtful voice.

'We've plenty of room,' Sorry went on, 'nothing wonderful, but we'd love to have her.' He had cunningly made his invitation difficult to refuse by suggesting humble hospitality.

'Oh, look, I know it's an imposition,' said Kate, 'but the family next door – we usually work in with them – are away. I can't be sure when they'll be home. It would be a great weight off my mind if . . . are you sure your parents – that is, your mother – won't mind?'

'Winter counts as a father, Lord knows!' Sorry answered. 'They'd be angry if I didn't bring her back with me in these circumstances.' He sounded grave and responsible, but then he said to Laura, 'Pack your toothbrush and your black satin pyjamas, Chant,' in a noticeably different tone. Kate, however, did not notice, though Chris Holly did and gave first Sorry, and then Laura herself a quick, curious glance.

Two phone calls later, Chris carried Jacko out to his large car and settled him down with Kate, and then with kisses and hugs exchanged between Kate and Laura, and to the sound of instructions about locking up, turning the electricity off, and promises to ring, they drove away to a private hospital which was expecting Jacko as a patient. It had a special rooming-in service, Kate said, so she could stay with Jacko for as long as she liked, all night if necessary. Chris and Kate and Jacko looked so like a family that Laura couldn't help feeling a desolate resentment that Chris should have gone and that she should have been left. Of course, she could not drive the car, but Kate's ready acceptance of his offers of help continued to disturb her.

'Now you're in my power!' Sorry said pleasantly. 'Think of that and tremble.'

'Big deal!' Laura replied. 'I'm used to it from school.'

'Well, then,' said Sorry, 'I'll have to come up with something novel, won't I? I'll check through my romances when I get back. *For the Love of Philippa* might have some good ideas in it. Or *Stolen Moments*.'

'Why would you want to make me tremble?' Laura cried out in irritation. 'What a male chauvinist sort of idea.'

'I am old-fashioned,' Sorry agreed. 'I didn't bring a helmet for you. I'll just crawl along but we'd better watch out for cops. Shall we take a risk and sneak a look at this antique shop?'

Laura was glad to be diverted. Later, with a few possessions in a shopping bag, she rode on the Vespa, holding on to Sorry, but following in her mind, with her truest attention, the progress through the city to the unknown hospital of Jacko and Kate. Even without witchcraft, the world grew slightly unbelievable, as if part of her were a reading eye and most of her was a character moving through a story – a character, moreover, who had begun to suspect that she might not be entirely real, might be nothing but a puppet, or words on a printed page.

7

The Carlisle Witches

'Of course Sorensen was right to bring you,' said the younger Mrs Carlisle. 'It must have been very distressing for you, and for your poor mother. I do hope Sorensen behaved appropriately.'

'He was very polite, mostly,' said Laura, 'but very strange, too. He behaved as if something had gone wrong with a car, not a brother. But then he took me to the Gardendale Shopping Complex and we looked at the little shop. It was all shut up. Sorry said every chink was closed, that it was even sealed up along the bottom of the door. He said that I would have to make Mr Braque take the mark off my brother, but that he didn't know how I would do it because Braque was an old and careful demon.'

'Well, we'll have to think about that,' said old Mrs Carlisle. 'We are not without our powers, you know . . . We are the daughters of the moon. But we'll talk it over later on.'

They were in a big, light room with a polished floor and woven rugs, the white walls so covered in pictures that they seemed to be full of windows into different worlds. One at her side showed the heart of a silver fire. Beside it was a scene in fresh, clear colours. Among little hills and trees and sparkling fountains, smiling monsters played cards or gathered flowers. In the background a great face, which was partly a building, watched the scene with melancholy detachment, and in the very front of the picture a man covered in short feathers turned an owl's face to stare out of the frame, but whether he was wearing a mask or whether he was some sort of man-bird Laura could not tell. It was one of many remarkable things in the room she would have liked to look at more closely, but the presence of her hostesses made her too shy to stare as much as she wanted to.

'I hope Sorensen has been kind to you,' his mother said. 'We cannot depend upon him not to make mistakes, but I should explain to you that it is not entirely his fault. I am to blame. I sometimes make the same sort of mistake myself.' She wore a plain, pink dress with a dull finish, like the outside of a rose petal, which looked remarkably beautiful close to her white hair and cool, blue eyes. It made Laura immediately homesick for Kate who could not have worn a dress of such a colour for five minutes without smudging the front of it.

'It would be easier to explain to you if only you had known the farm in the old days,' said old Mrs Carlisle. 'It's probably a mistake to become too fond of land. But, you know, we loved our farm. Once the whole valley out there was ours, and it was like owning a whole world – a world with a forest, a river, a plain . . . We made a dam of stones and we swam naked there. It sometimes makes me sad to think that I'll never be so close to water again – there are no private places left. There's always magic, of course, but in the past it was simple and direct.' She sighed.

'We could see the city if we climbed the hill a little way,' Miryam said. 'It was like, well, it was like the army of a neighbouring country amusing itself in its own way, always manoeuvering on the horizon. My mother is right you know – it is probably wiser not to love land too much. It never really belongs to you. No matter how you cherish it, it comes and goes. In the end it owns you.'

'The army came closer you see,' Winter said. 'My husband was an oddity in his family, one of us really – a moon man – not a strong magician and not a witch. He was more like you, yourself, a sensitive. Now, his brothers have none of his touch. They're business men, big in the city. Still, we should have been warned, Miryam and I.'

'The army came closer,' Miryam chimed in, taking over, rather than interrupting. 'Suddenly we no longer needed to climb the hill to see it. When we went out of our gate on what was then a country road we could see it coming towards us. That was already years ago . . .'

'Twenty years ago perhaps,' Winter put in.

'I was very young and opinionated in those days,' Miryam said, smiling back at a past self. 'I thought the world began and ended at the farm gate and was quite prepared to mistrust everything beyond it. On rainy nights the city's lights began to take over the entire sky. My mother and I thought that we would try anything to save our valley and we decided . . .' She glanced at her mother.

'We decided to raise what we call a cone of power over the farm,' Winter said calmly. 'We would still be visible, but somehow not observable. The city would know we were there but would pass us by. However, such a condition is hard to create and even harder to maintain. We needed a third witch.'

Miryam leaned forward almost pleadingly.

'We work best as a trio, you see,' she explained, 'as the three female aspects.'

'I was the old woman,' Winter said.

'And I was to be the mother and my daughter the maiden.' Miryam sat back again. 'I thought that if I had a child it would certainly be a daughter. We have had daughters for fifty years – never a son in all that time. All the time I expected my baby, I spoke to it as if it were a daughter – promising her the valley – but as you know, I had a son.'

'Sorry!' said Laura. 'I mean Sorensen.'

'It's an old family name,' Winter said. 'Even though we didn't expect him to be one of the family, we still gave him a name that tied him in with us. I suspected, when I realized Miryam could not exchange dreams with her unborn child. She had a difficult time having him. We were told he would be her only child and – to be frank – when he was born neither of us wanted him.'

'Wouldn't he have done to be the maiden?' Laura asked with a faint grin. 'He is a sort of witch, isn't he?'

An expression of bafflement crossed Winter's face. A little storm of anger passed through her at the perversity of past events.

'We didn't realize what he was until a long time after,' she said. 'Perhaps the signs develop later in men or perhaps . . . anyhow we didn't realize. However, it was not just one mistake, but a combination of two. We underestimated Sorensen, and we overestimated ourselves.'

Now they were suddenly both silent. Laura, filled with her own anxieties, bewildered by their eager confidences, knew they had come to the heart of their story, and having come there they now hesitated and looked at each other.

'I'll tell . . .' said Miryam with a sigh. 'In the end it was my decision.'

'My dear . . .' Winter turned to her and spoke gently. 'In the beginning it was mine.'

'Laura,' Miryam said, 'I am not a motherly woman and, when I thought of my son, I felt quite trapped. The thought of watching him grow up, so close and yet so much a necessary stranger (as I thought then) unable to help me protect my home from the army – from the city, that is – marching towards us, swallowing market gardens as it came . . . well, I could not bear it. I decided to have Sorensen adopted. Yet I'd no sooner decided this than I realized that I didn't want to lose sight of him, either. I don't want to try and conceal just how self-centred I was . . . I didn't want to look after him, but I still wanted to have news of him, even some control over what happened to him. I know it was self-centred . . . Well, as it turned out perhaps it was lucky that I was well enough off to have the best of both worlds.'

'We found a foster home for the baby,' Winter said. 'It was almost like a story-book home . . . a wonderful, motherly mother, all the cake tins filled with home baking, kind father, such a dependable man, and four brothers . . . the sort of family that goes to church on Sunday morning, and then off for a picnic in the family car on Sunday afternoon. They liked children – didn't want to have any more of their own – and had decided to foster a child.'

'I did make certain conditions,' Miryam said, 'and to this day I'm not sure if I did wisely or if I was stupid. If things turned out well it was certainly for different reasons than I thought at first. You see art and learning have always seemed to me to be some of the most powerful consolations the world has to offer us . . .' She broke off and said smiling, 'You're too young to know what I'm talking about. What I mean is I did tell Sorensen's family what school I wanted him to go to and ask them to encourage him to read and listen to music . . . I also promised I'd never get in touch with him directly . . .'

'You could have done things quite differently and it still would have made no difference,' Winter said. 'He was a witch at heart, and all other differences are nothing to that one.'

'We followed his progress from a distance,' Miryam continued. 'Everything always seemed to be going well. Every day for a while I wondered if I had been fair – but there was no way I could ever have been fair – and after a while I forgot to be concerned. The city came. My father died, my uncles forced us to sell the farm (though we kept the house and its closest gardens) and then one morning, three years ago, I walked into the courtyard and found Sorensen sitting there. He looked so like my father that I knew him at once, though he was in a dreadful condition, filthy, dirty, exhausted, injured, quite unable to speak. He couldn't even tell me his name. And then for the first time I realized that this shattered boy – he was fifteen then – was all I had planned in the first place: a true child of power.' She shook her head, less at Laura than at Winter, sharing a memory that could not be described.

'How did he know where to come?' asked Laura. 'If you'd never written to him or anything.'

'It seems that, without any of us realizing it, he was still tied to us,' Miryam said, 'and when he needed a place to run to, he ran to Janua Caeli as a spider might retreat along an invisible strand of its web. When he needed to find people of his own kind he had the power to find them. In the circumstances we had to be glad, but we were rather frightened too, to think there was no way we could hide from him.'

'We struggled to save him,' Winter continued, 'oh, not his life – he was in no danger of dying – but,' – she looked at Miryam doubtfully – 'his humanity, I suppose. We realized the danger we were in. You see, Laura – you can probably imagine – a witch without humanity is a black witch nine times out of ten. We took him to doctors, we patched him together. He imitates normal life very well now, when he has to, but no wonder he talked about your little brother as if he were a broken car. Sorensen is very much a broken-down car himself, and none of us can tell how badly broken. He doesn't appear to feel very deeply, though he can seem quite clever.'

'Smart!' said Laura. 'Smart, and sort of tricky!'

She could not help being distracted by this story, though her deepest thoughts were always of Jacko. 'What went wrong with his other family?'

'Too many things to tell you now,' Miryam said. 'I've tried to let you see the judgements we made. But now I suppose we're paying the price because we've grown very fond of Sorensen and, having made such mistakes in the past, we don't feel very confident. We can't tell much of what he really thinks or feels – perhaps he doesn't know himself. We work by guesses a lot of the time.' She looked at Laura very directly but her voice grew quite shy. 'We felt very pleased when he began to talk about you because it seemed to us . . . we both thought . . . We both thought that simply by recognizing him you had set some machinery free, that he had begun to move towards . . .' She hesitated and seemed to wait for Laura to finish the sentence, but Laura was silent.

'But of course,' Winter seemed to be starting a different topic, 'it might have its dangers from your point of view. We can't promise he's safe company.'

Laura looked at them uncertainly. Inside her clothes was the body that still surprised her, not yet completely herself, its powers of attraction, great or small, largely unknown. It was because she was a girl that they thought Sorry might be dangerous to her. However, she knew she must not give in to fear.

'I'm all right!' she said indignantly. 'Or I will be when Jacko gets well again.'

Old Winter stirred, and then said briskly, 'I'll talk to you about that after dinner. I'd better move my bones and get it served. It won't take long. Perhaps you can go and call Sorensen from his study and tell him dinner will be in about ten minutes. Remind him to wash his hands.'

Laura was learning the geography and landmarks of this house – the carved chest just outside the arched doorway of the big room, the table with its slender legs and its top inlaid with ivory leaves and the telephone set in the middle of it. Laura passed it, willing it to ring and for the caller to be Kate saying, 'I'm coming round to pick you up immediately,' but the phone was unobliging. She walked to the door of Sorry's study and knocked, but there was no reply. She knocked again and, after a moment, boldly turned the handle.

The door opened as silently as the door in a dream and she went, like beautiful Fatima, into Bluebeard's chamber. Of course, there were no previous wives hanging by their hair, stabbed to the heart, cut throats smiling with terrible knowledge, only seventh form homework spread across the floor and desk. Laura looked at the maths with the interest of someone seeing something written in a language they are beginning to learn themselves, and lifted her eyes to the backs of the row of romantic novels along the bottom of the book case. There, no doubt, she would find *For the Love of Philippa* and *Stolen*

Moments. Behind the door, Laura now saw many photographs of birds and a shelf holding Sorry's camera and square bottles labelled *Developer* and *Fixer.* Laura had seen most of them before at the Science Fair and turned to look at other pictures. In a heavy frame, as though through a window, a painted man watched her. His face was shadowed by enormous wings rising high above his shoulders, but his forehead sprouted leaves and, from among the leaves, either horns or branches. Beside him, the photographed woman, naked, and smooth as satin, reclined, smiling at Laura just as she smiled at Sorry, but the glance meant something different. To Laura it was the smile of a sister, not a siren. Pinned to the corner of the poster over the woman's head was the small photograph she had observed with curiosity nearly twenty-four hours earlier. The skeleton looked at her, smiling anxiously, but she refused to meet its gaze and walked instead to the foot of the couch, stepping in between islands of homework to study the photograph. She was staring at herself – made grainy with enlargement – as if a detail had been selected from the background of some other photograph and blown up beyond the capacity of the image to hold a clear outline. Yet there she was, caught in a moment of recent, but past, time, half turning, speaking to someone, perhaps Nicky, who was out of the picture, her knees showing guiltily under the school uniform. Laura, looking from her own picture to that of the naked goddess extending herself langorously to the left, sighed and shook her head.

Frowning, she turned to find Sorry standing in the doorway watching her narrowly, his cat coiling around his ankles. He did not look so very different from one of his own pictures, and, once again, just as she had when she saw him in this room for the first time, he looked more than himself, a wild man framed in the heavy architraves of the door, the telephone dimly visible in the hall beyond him.

'If you had read *Wendy's Wayward Heart,*' he said, 'you would recognize my expression. I'm trying to look rueful at being caught out in an act of sentimentality.'

Laura said nothing.

'How am I doing?' he asked.

'I don't think you look sentimental,' she said, nor did she think that pinning her photograph to the poster was a sentimental thing to have done. He immediately moved close to her so that he was standing almost over her, and though he was not much taller than she was, she was caught between the wall and the couch and could not step past him. He looked at the photograph over her head.

'It's not very clear is it?' he said. 'I was pretending to photograph the school library. You wouldn't stand still.'

'You could have asked me,' she replied. 'I don't mind being photographed.'

'I was too shy,' he said, and Laura could not tell if it was at himself or at the idea of shyness to which he directed his black smile. Laura did stand still. She remained as still as the heroine of a jungle movie who, waking to find a serpent coiled on her breast and unable to move in case it bites her, lies breathing slowly and watching light rippling over its wonderfully coloured scales. At that moment Sorry seemed brilliant, his own breathing uneven, his eyes almost luminous.

Something is going to happen, Laura thought. She was going to be kissed. On one side of a kiss was childhood, sunshine, innocence, toys and, on the other, people embracing, darkness, passion and the admittance of a person who, no matter how loved, must always have the quality of otherness, not only to her confidence, but somehow inside her sealing skin.

However, Sorry did not kiss her, but put his left hand on her breast without once taking his eyes from her face or ceasing to smile at her. Laura felt her own expression become incredulous. Nevertheless, his touch was real, and immediately changed Sorry, whose air of menace had given him only a moment earlier a sort of impervious glitter, for his face softened somehow, became a little unfocused as if he were more disturbed by it than she was.

'Don't!' she said, inspired. 'Remember, you've got to be invited.'

'W-well invite m-me then,' he demanded, beginning to stammer, but as his voice lost confidence his half-threatened embrace became more intrusive. At that moment the phone rang, and she felt Sorry, leaning against her, catch his breath in surprise and, perhaps, relief.

'Saved by the bell, Chant,' he remarked.

'I wouldn't have invited you,' she called after him as he went to answer the phone. 'You were saved as much as I was.'

'I was planning to be very nice to you. You might have enjoyed it,' he replied. He answered the phone and then turned, holding it out to her. 'It's your mother,' he said. 'Isn't that wonderful! She might have known you were in difficulties.'

'Not real difficulties,' Laura said, seizing the phone.

'It was touch and go,' Sorry said. 'And this is me going.'

He left her alone with Kate's voice coming from another world. Laura thought she could smell the hospital over the phone.

'How are you, Lolly?' Kate asked.

'Fine!' said Laura. 'They're being terribly kind to me. Everything's fine. How's Jacko?'

'No one knows yet,' Kate said after a pause. Her voice was careful, but Laura could hear desolation eating its way through her words. 'No one knows yet,' she repeated. 'Tell me truly – do you think the Carlisles mind having you?'

'I don't think so.' Laura had to speak truly. 'But I mind. I hate being away from you and Jacko.'

'I hate it too,' Kate said, 'but there's nothing you can do here except just sit around with Chris and me.'

'What's *he* doing there?' Laura's voice sharpened with jealousy. 'Why is he there and not me?' Kate was silent. 'Mum?' Laura cried.

'I don't know,' Kate answered at last. 'I just don't know. I didn't plan it that way. It's just happened out of the blue. I don't know why you're where you are either. Everything happened so fast . . . an offer was made . . . it was convenient at the time and I just grabbed at it. I've wondered about that too, sitting here by Jacko's bed. Laura, I'm staying with Jacko tonight. I can't bear the thought of going home to an empty house.'

'I could come home, of course,' Laura cried. 'I'm not a prisoner. We could be together.'

'I wouldn't sleep,' said Kate. 'I might as well be here.'

'I'd sit up with you,' Laura promised, but Kate had made up her mind. She had made up her mind about something else, too.

'Laura, I think I'd better get in touch with your father,' she said. 'I think Jacko's so ill that he'd better be told.'

To her dismay, Laura felt herself going rigid with a pain so old that it seemed unfair she should still suffer from it. She thought she was over mourning her vanished father and was furious to find she still suffered, and while she stood, momentarily struggling with this remembered anguish, Sorry came into the hall again, pointing through the arch, perhaps suggesting dinner was ready.

'It might cheer him up to know there's a chance he won't have to pay so much maintenance in the future,' Laura said at last, in a hard voice.

'Don't be like that, Lolly!' Kate pleaded. 'It's too serious a time to give in to thoughts like that. Part of what we like in Jacko is your father. The same with you. I mean, he's got a share in you. And he was so very fond of you. He never really got to know Jacko.'

'All right!' Laura said. 'Do what you think best.'

'It has to be what I think best,' said her mother. 'I'll ring you first thing in the morning and tell you if there has been any change. And Laura – I know I'm more incoherent than usual, but I do love you and I am thinking of you. Don't forget!'

'Me too!' Laura cried. 'Give my love to Jacko.'

'Things no good out in the world?' Sorry asked as she put the receiver down.

'Not very!' Laura said. 'I hope it's all right if I do stay tonight. I've forgotten to pack a clean shirt but maybe I could get one tomorrow morning.'

'You can see that Winter and Miryam are delighted to have you,' Sorry answered courteously. 'And I've proved my enthusiasm, haven't I? The perfect host, I'd say.'

'You're different out of your room,' Laura commented, hoping she sounded more casual than she felt.

'Well, maybe!' Sorry replied restlessly. 'I'm very powerful and sexy in there, but the further away I go from my room the meeker I become. At school I hardly exist. Are you hungry?'

Rather to her surprise, Laura found she was starving. They came into a room where a big window looked out on a vine-covered verandah, though now, as evening deepened outside, the vines looked like ghostly serpents, less real than the reflection of the table and the four people around it.

It was a proper dinner, with thin, clear soup, a salad, and a chicken casserole, and even pudding. Laura felt quite weak with delight at the sight of food, though it seemed heartless to be eating while Jacko was so sick and Kate so worried.

'I have been giving your brother's situation some thought,' said Winter Carlisle. 'Sorensen – help Laura to her chair.'

'I'm all right!' Laura said in astonishment. 'I can sit down myself.' Such courtly manners were part of an alarming foreign ritual. There were girls in her class at school who had boyfriends they slept with, but not one of them behaved particularly nicely to the girls. Any boy who was publicly good-mannered, unless forced to be, was doomed to scorn, for everyone, in Laura's class at least, knew it was boys against girls in the world, and good manners were either a surrender or part of a trick, a manipulation, and deserved nothing but contempt.

'Be that as it may, Sorensen can be civil in order to make me feel comfortable,' his grandmother said. 'We are a fond family rather than a loving one, so consideration is doubly important. We can't afford to abandon it as loving families may choose to do out of confidence in themselves. Now, Laura – perhaps in a confrontation I might be a match for your Mr Braque, but I can't make him take his mark off your brother unless I get a certain power over him. Sorensen is right in thinking we should put a mark on Mr Braque in order to get that power, and that it will be a very difficult thing to do.

'It's not very different from casting the runes,' Winter continued. 'In the past, many magicians cast the runes. In Australia, the tribal magician points the bone and his victim withers and dies. The mark used by Carmody Braque is the same sort of thing. It is a mark of possession and has become a door into your brother, through which Mr Braque can come and go at will. He could give, but he chooses to take. He knows his own power and he would recognize ours. He wouldn't put out his hand to Miryam or me or even Sorensen.'

'My mother says Jacko is terribly ill,' Laura said.

She did not have to say, 'Isn't there anything, anything, that can be done to help us?'

'There would be no danger,' said Winter casually, 'if you were a witch yourself.'

Miryam smiled at Laura. Sorry lifted his silver eyes to look thoughtfully at his grandmother.

'You want to work a changeover?' he asked.

'Why not?' Winter asked back.

'It c-could kill her,' suggested Sorry.

'Oh, no – surely not!' Winter replied quickly. 'She's half way there, isn't she? You must admit it. You feel it yourself.' She turned back to Laura. 'As you know, you're what we call a sensitive, my dear. You stand on the threshold of our condition, and we can invite you in – Sorry, Miryam and I. We could help you to make a witch of yourself. Common nature, which trembles a little before you now, would let you in. And then we think that, if you found a way to mark Mr Braque, you would – what was that phrase, Sorensen?'

'Rupture his integrity,' Sorry concluded.

'I don't think he's got any integrity,' Laura exclaimed. 'I think he's just horrible all through.'

'His wholeness!' Sorry said. 'The way his system holds together in one piece! We think he might begin to fall to bits if you put a mark on him. He's very old by the sound of it and it gets harder and harder to maintain an unnatural body.'

'If I was a witch he'd recognize me too, wouldn't he?' Laura asked. 'Carmody Braque, I mean.' There, in the centre of the table, was a perfectly ordinary milk jug. The dishes at her elbow were dirty in an ordinary way. They helped her to be matter-of-fact about this extraordinary suggestion. Sorry stared at his grandmother as meditatively as if she had simply proposed Laura approach Mr Braque dressed in her best clothes, but Winter had actually suggested she become a witch.

'He might do so,' Winter said, 'but you see he knows you. He's met you. He already knows you are not a witch. Now, if you wore dark glasses so that he could not look into your eyes (for they can be very treacherous windows, eyes can) and some one of us, Sorry perhaps, went with you and was recognized as a witch, we think it very probable that you yourself would not be suspected. Your own changed state would be masked. You would then have to talk him into accepting something from you, or trick him into wanting to take it . . . anything to make him put out his hand. And once you have marked him it is important then that he should recognize you and know exactly what you are and what you intend.'

'Would I be able to change back from being a witch?' Laura asked.

'No!' said Sorry. 'You can only make one changeover in your life.'

Laura frowned to herself.

'It's hard to imagine,' she said. 'You seem different, but you don't act differently from any other family. What do witches do?'

'We're like scientists,' said Sorry. 'We compel nature – move it around according to our wishes – but scientists use rules that they've worked out through thought, and ours comes through imagination, I suppose.'

'. . . and exchange,' Miryam agreed. 'The scientist reasons and then, by experimental or industrial processes, applies his reasoning. The price that's paid for altering nature is often paid outside the scientist himself, but witches, when they institute a change, bleed something of themselves out into the world. It builds up again, but it takes time – seconds, hours, days . . . changing the weather can take a long time to recover from and even then it's no use trying to make it rain if there isn't a rain cloud in sight. Or we can dip into the future a little, but only blindly. Sometimes it's useful, sometimes . . .' As she spoke Sorry lifted up his hand, the air twisted above it and a moment later a kingfisher was sitting on his finger clicking its beak but otherwise seeming quite unperturbed. 'Not that any of this solves Chant's problem,' he said, staring at it in astonishment. 'Suppose she doesn't want to change over?'

'She doesn't have to make up her mind immediately,' Miryam said in her calm way, 'though you should decide within twenty-four hours, Laura.'

'The hospital might work out a cure,' Laura suggested, and encountered a look from Sorry that was distinctly harassed – the bare beginning of an apology for the suggestion his grandmother had made. Something about it had troubled him in a way he did not want to admit. Finding himself noticed by her he turned his head away to look at the kingfisher, which vanished a moment later as mysteriously as it had come.

'Was it from the future?' she asked, and he nodded.

'But not very far in the future,' he told her. 'Not much over a day. It'll fit in somewhere.'

'Don't give yourself a headache,' said Winter warningly. 'He's showing off,' she added to Laura. 'A materialization like that, even though it is only a little thing, is quite hard to achieve and very wearing.'

'It was really beautiful,' Laura said. 'Like getting a little present from tomorrow.'

'Sorensen has a real affinity with birds,' Miryam said, and for the first time Laura heard a note in her voice that suggested she might be proud of him in her own cool way. But Sorry looked into space as if he half expected it to punish him for taking liberties, and said very little for the rest of the evening.

Laura's bedroom was upstairs, looking out over the courtyard with its leafy population of birds and chessmen in the form of topiaries. From her window she could see the wood, the last remnant of Winter's farm, and through its leaves and branches the occasional light of the Gardendale subdivision, quite as pretty as Christmas lights, set among the poplars and birches. Though she knew this was a beautiful and mysterious house of numberless rooms, she was briefly homesick for the noise of traffic, the dangerous streets, even for the Supermarket from Outer Space, all part of the happy year now breaking up around her, becoming something to be remembered, not a time she was actually inhabiting. She pushed the bolt on her door, wondering if she was, perhaps, frightened of Sorry, and deciding that really what she wanted was to feel contained, shut off with her own thoughts, away from all the seductions and persuasions of the Carlisle witches.

'Chant!' said Sony's voice urgently in her ear, and she woke, startled, to find she had been sleeping. The darkness was thick and soft as if she had been wrapped in fur.

'What do you want?' she cried, really frightened now, first by the darkness and the unfamiliar room that lurked beyond it and then by Sorry's voice somewhere close to her face.

'Shhh! Don't be scared!' he said. 'I haven't come to . . . I don't mean any harm. Listen, don't let Winter con you into anything, will you? She's a tough proposition, old Winter, and she always thinks of her own advantage first. Don't let her work a changeover on you unless you are quite sure it's the only way to save your brother – and even then – make sure it's what you really want to do. Don't give in without making her tell you whether or not there's an alternative. She will tell you honestly if you ask her, but make sure you ask her.'

'Is it so terrible – being a witch?' Laura asked, sitting up in bed. She put out her hand in the dark and after a moment touched Sorry's face.

'No – it's not terrible, but it separates you off,' he said. 'You mightn't want to be stranded over here with Miryam and Winter and me.'

Listening to his voice in the dark, Laura found herself remembering the exact feel of his hand in the touch at once intimate and remote earlier that evening, and to her astonishment wanted to feel it again so that she could think carefully about it. She touched his face in the dark like a blind girl trying to find out what expression he was wearing.

'How did you get in?' she asked. 'I bolted the door.' She felt him smile.

'Very sensible,' he said, 'but it's a poor witch that can't go through a door.'

'Aren't you pushing it a bit far?' Laura asked sternly. 'I think what you've been doing to me counts as sexual harassment.'

'You've been reading *Woman's Weekly,*' Sorry replied. 'Never mind – as harassment goes I expect it's the best sort there is.'

'It's not fair!' Laura hissed.

'Fair!' Sorry answered. 'You know what you can do with "fair"! Besides, one way and another, I didn't think you'd mind. I thought we could take a short cut perhaps. You don't want to go through all that "getting to know you" bit, do you?'

'I don't know,' Laura said. 'I don't know anything about that. I've never been out with a boy. Have you – with a girl, I mean?'

'Do you want a reference?' Sorry asked.

Laura's hand still touched his face.

'Have you ever been to bed with a girl?' she asked, and he was silent. 'Have you?' she persisted.

'Not here,' he said at last.

'Did you like it?' she asked. 'Was it like it is in the last five lines of a Barbara Cartland?'

'It was nice in bits,' Sorry said. 'As a matter of fact I got into a hell of a lot of trouble over it. But then I might have been the villain, not the hero. If only I knew for sure.'

'What's it like being a witch?' Laura asked.

'Nice in bits,' he said again. 'Sometimes the two things seem to go together. Listen – I'll show you – I'm very good you know. Think of some place – some place you remember as wonderful.' Before Laura could stop it a certain memory came into her mind.

'Not that!' she was about to say, but Sorry said, 'Got it!' as if she had passed him something in the dark, and the room began to lighten towards the window.

'Nature is like a holograph in some ways,' he said. 'Any part contains the whole picture.'

Just for a moment Laura was looking into something like a peephole no bigger than a small coin, the next moment a most peculiar sensation overcame her, as if she had suddenly been asked to contain a memory of every place in the world. Whatever she named she saw, what she saw she struggled to name, not one ocean but all oceans, deserts of ice, coloured only with sunrise, sunset and the shifting lights of the aurora, sand sifting to the very boundary of sight. Somewhere in the flesh of the earth the dreadful earthquake shuddered, the tide walked to and fro on the leash of the moon, rainbows formed, winds swept the sky like giant brooms piling up clouds before them, clouds which writhed into different shapes, melted into rain or darkened, bruised themselves against an unseen antagonist and went on their way, laced with forking rivers of lightning, complete with white electric tributaries. Out of this infinite vision an infinity of details could be drawn, but Sorry had settled on one, and from the endless series a particular beach was chosen and began to form around Laura – a beach of iron-dark sand and shells like frail stars, and a wonderful wide sea that stretched, neither green nor blue, but inked by the approach of night into violet and black, wrinkling with its own salty puzzles, right out to a distant, pure horizon.

Laura had once, many years before, visited this beach with Kate and her father. Now she smelt the strange smell of salt, mingled with the organic scents of rotting seaweed, and of sand, alive with more lives than she could begin to number.

'That's restful,' Sorry commented. 'Sweet dreams, Chant. See you tomorrow.'

He was gone, and Laura, both disturbed and comforted, watched the waves break on the curving sand and went to sleep again at last.

•

In the morning she woke early to the song of many, many birds and went down through the old house, still and empty at that hour of the morning, its rooms inhabited only by the abstract brownish-gold of early sunlight. Then a noise drew her out of the back door and she found Sorry himself, squatting half-naked before his motorbike doing some unexplained maintenance.

'I made some coffee a moment ago,' he said as casually as if he were used to having her around. 'There should be enough for you, too. It's still hot, if you hurry.'

Laura found the coffee and came out to sit on the step and watch him.

'Doesn't your bike go?' she asked after a moment. 'I need to get home and put on a clean shirt.'

'Have one of mine,' Sorry said. 'No, I suppose it would be a bit too big. OK. She's jake! Give me ten minutes and I'll be able to take you home and check the bike at the same time.'

Laura sat on the step, leaning back against the door, and felt for the first time completely comfortable in Sorry's company. Later, she climbed on to the back of the bike with the skill of increasing experience, and they roared off down the drive, opened the gate, closed it again, and came out of the enchanted world of Janua Caeli into the Gardendale subdivision. There it lay, innocent, and sleeping its Sunday morning sleep, streets almost totally empty, houses washed over with early, tawny light, but beginning to turn pink along the ridges of the roofs and the rims of the narrow chimneys.

Laura saw with amazement Chris Holly's car outside their gate.

'Sorry,' she said climbing off and standing beside him, 'that's Chris Holly's car.'

'Is it indeed?' said Sorry in a disinterested voice.

'Kate went off in it,' Laura frowned uncertainly. 'She must be back – something's wrong.'

'Something's still wrong with this bike,' Sorry said. 'I'll tell you what – jump back on it and we'll have a little burn up round by the estuary and pick up your shirt on the way back. Anyhow, it's very early. Your mother might appreciate not being woken.'

'You don't understand . . .' Laura cried scornfully. 'All I want is news of Jacko . . .'

'No, you're the one that doesn't understand . . .' Sorry exclaimed almost desperately and at that moment, almost as if given a cue in a play, Chris Holly opened the door and walked down the path to collect the milk. At the gate he glanced around rather self-consciously. He was wearing Kate's good raincoat which was very long, and his feet were bare.

Almost at once he saw Laura and Sorry staring at him.

'Damn!' muttered Sorry mostly to himself. 'Don't take it to heart, Chant. Stay cool.'

Laura was more than cool. She climbed back on to the Vespa and said very coldly, 'Let's go somewhere else.'

'It's none of my business,' said Sorry, 'but I don't think you should take it seriously. It's nothing really.'

'Laura . . .' exclaimed Chris Holly uncertainly, looking appalled.

'Go at once!' Laura commanded and thumped Sorry on the back. He nodded, and they shattered the early morning silence tearing off down Kingsford Drive.

8

Changing for Ever

'It's not so dreadful!' Sorry said, sounding rather bored. 'Your mother thought she might feel more cheerful if she spent the night with Chris. Well, why not? I'm in favour of anything that makes people feel better about bad times.'

'Jacko's so sick,' Laura said, but Jacko's sickness was only part of the reason for her pain.

'It won't make him any worse,' Sorry said, 'and it might make her feel better.'

'You don't understand about things like this,' Laura cried. 'You haven't got a heart.'

'Lucky me!' Sorry replied. 'But it doesn't mean that what I'm saying isn't true.'

It was going to be a very hot day. They were walking along one of the tracks around the estuary where the city's river, after turning through ranks of houses and small factories, met the sea and fell under the influence of the moon. The hills were on their left, the water on the right, though as the tide was out there was more mud than water. Ahead of them were two lakes, settling ponds for a sewerage system speckled with ducks, black swans and geese, and reflecting the jagged rim of the hills as exquisitely as less ambiguous water.

'You'll forget it,' said Sorry, trying again. 'Forget it now.'

'I won't!' Laura said, with sullen determination. 'I'll never forget it.'

'Well no, perhaps not totally forget it.' Sorry grew increasingly perplexed and irritated. 'You'll just stop thinking about it. Other things will happen and you'll start thinking about them instead, so you might as well stop thinking about it now.' He took off his jacket as he spoke, so that the sun fell on his back and shoulders. They came round a bend in the path and looked into a bay where the film of water, no thicker than a sheet of paper over the mud, nevertheless reflected the morning light with an intense silver whiteness, but as they walked towards the shining expanse, a gust of warm wind blew across the bright surface and it vanished, turning suddenly grey. They disturbed a heron sitting on a partially submerged log, and it rose and flew past them sinking its head on its breast as its flight settled down, trailing its long legs behind it. Laura wished she could fly off alongside it, and then dissolve into the honey-coloured air like sugar under the warm stirring of the wind, and never have to feel anything again.

'No chance!' said Sorry beside her, reading her thought by some uncanny skill of his own. 'We've just got to grin and bear it. Look at the mud. It's very calm, isn't it? Let's calm ourselves by looking at mud for a while.' However he was staring after the heron as he spoke as if part of his attention were flying with it.

'It's easy for you to bear it,' Laura said sharply.

'Thank goodness!' Sorry agreed. 'I don't mind if you think I'm insensitive. It's my triumph that I am. It's a victory. Holy cow! Why suffer?'

'I didn't choose to suffer,' Laura answered resentfully.

'You can choose not to though,' he assured her.

They sat down among the cocksfoot and clover and stared out over the mud, pocked by crab holes and woven across with tracks left by the crabs in their steady, sideways commerce, scavenging and threatening assiduously. Sorry put his arm around her shoulders, but it was not comforting and not even very distracting for he had grown remote. It was rather like being embraced by a tree.

'I know what I'm talking about,' he said. 'Look – I only met my mother three years ago. She sent me off when I was a month old – did she tell you? She feels obliged to confess from time to time.'

'She did mention about that,' Laura admitted. 'She seemed guilty about it.'

'Don't think I blame her,' Sorry added. 'I think she did the right thing. It wasn't her fault that it didn't work out.'

'What went wrong?' Laura asked, willing to be distracted a little.

'I went wrong,' said Sorry. 'I could go through the looking-glass and the others couldn't. It was as if everything around me had an extra piece tacked on to it that I could see and work with and no one else knew about. I could make trees blossom, cabbages grow . . . I could make the rainclouds roll away . . . I couldn't make it rain then (that's a lot harder) but still, I could find anything lost and I could read any book. Actually, that wasn't witchcraft but it might just as well have been. At first I made them uneasy and then they seemed to get used to it. The oldest brothers left home and I went cheerfully on. But then my father lost his job – redundancy they said, but I think he'd upset somebody there in some way. He got another job, but not such a good one, and besides he was beginning to get a bit older and that worried him . . . he had to blame someone and he chose to blame me.'

'How could he?' Laura said, bewildered.

'There was no difficulty at all,' Sorry assured her. 'It's not a skill, blaming other people. It's an instinct. He got very frightening over it.'

'But you weren't adopted,' Laura said. 'They could have given you back, if you made them feel uncomfortable.'

'Oh, no,' said Sorry, and laughed. It was a light laugh, amused and not in the least angry, but for some reason it chilled Laura to the bone. 'There was one really important reason why they couldn't give me back, or get rid of me in any other way, and if I tell you what it was it makes them sound . . . it makes them sound mean and trivial, but they weren't. It wasn't a trivial reason, though we're brought up to think it ought to be. She paid for me. Miryam paid them quite a lot to look after me – more than it cost to keep me – something over for their trouble – and by the time things got really bad they had absolutely come to depend on getting paid. Their standard of living – the house and car for example, partly depended on getting that money every six months.'

'Like maintenance!' Laura said, understanding at once.

'I got sinister in every way to Tim – my foster father. Well I'd always been illegitimate (Miryam tells me she really doesn't know who my father is and tried to arrange it so she'd never know). Then I'd always been left-handed. And there was the – I suppose I have to say the supernatural element, though it seems to me that I'm more a part of nature than most people, not outside it or above it. I always feel I work with it, not against it. Well, whatever it is I learned to hide it pretty quickly once I could see how it was upsetting him, and then, blow me down, he moved on to my left-handed-ness. Poor Tim! He started to drink a lot about that time. He'd get terribly drunk about – oh, say once a month – then he'd spend the next three weeks repenting, and we all had to repent along with him. Part of my repentance was learning to become right-handed. He said it was for my own good. I've always stammered,' Sorry said. 'I think nature intended to balance out a tendency to talk too much by making it harder to talk at all. Well, my stammer just got worse and worse and at home I lived like a one-handed babbling idiot. Even when Tim wasn't there I was always practising for when he was. Then he lost his job again and was home a lot more. In the end I got so peculiar at school they sent a welfare officer around to see what was going on . . . and that just . . . it was the end.' Sorry laughed despairingly. 'Tim went absolutely bananas. He thought I'd complained, or so he said, but really I think he just wanted an excuse to have a real crack at someone. He said the country was run by sinners – hard to argue with that, one way and another – that the wrong people had the money. He mentioned Miryam by name and then quoted the Book of Revelations and f-finally,' Sorry said, 'he gave m-me the m-most terrific hiding he'd ever g-given me. I mean he was a really b-big man and he b-beat me up. When I was little he used to play a fighting game called "Bears" with me. This was a game of "Bears" for grown-ups, I suppose.'

Laura stared at him in alarm, for though his voice was perfectly cheerful, the emergence of his stammer was somehow unnerving. He smiled at her lightheartedly but as he did so the stigmata of an old punishment discoloured his face, even displacing his summer tan so that his cheeks swelled and his eyes blackened, and she could not be sure if he knew what was happening to him, there before her, or if he was quite unaware how memory was betraying his apparent unconcern.

'I c-c-c-could h-have k-k-k-' Sorry was abruptly unable to speak. He frowned, closed his eyes and then said in a strained but calm voice, 'I could have killed him, but I was too sc-scared, and besides that, in my head he still felt like my f-father. Look!' he cried with relief, 'there's the kingfisher.'

It was perched on a projection on the bank behind him, which rose at that point in great steps of clay and rotten rock, partly overgrown with bushes of white daisies, bracken and periwinkle, as well as late foxgloves. The kingfisher flew down to Sorry's outstretched hand, so that Laura could see, once more, its creamy breast the colour of primroses, and its blue-green back.

'Would it come to me if I were a witch?' she asked, and Sorry nodded absently. Perhaps he was brooding on the story he had told to demonstrate his light-heartedness and which had, instead, illustrated to Laura the harsh interaction of event and memory. 'What happened then?' she asked.

'Then?' said Sorry derisively. 'Oh, then the f-f-f-fat was in the f-f-fire.' But he was over his anxiety and merely making fun of his impediment. 'No way could I have gone to school the following day and told people, "Oh, yes, I do have a few bruises. I walked into a door." I would have done it. In a way I wanted to protect him, but he didn't want to take the risk. He pushed me down stairs into the basement, and locked me in a little cupboard down there. I could sit up in it but I couldn't do any thing really energetic like standing, and he said I had to stay there until I'd got rid of the devil in me. I wasn't even allowed to go to the lavatory, can you imagine, not that that was urgent. What with one thing and another I'd just been.' He laughed and fell silent.

'Your father doesn't sound to me as if he could have been really very kind in the first place,' said Laura.

'I think life got to be like war for him.' Sorry looked for a moment as if he were overwhelmed by any explanations he might try to give. 'I've thought a lot about it and I've talked about it, and I've read books written by people who've watched other people very closely, and what I've worked out is this – that Tim managed really well in a certain setting, but being out of work put one part of his mind into a state of constant despair – even panic, and who can live with that? I think being violent with me was one way he tried to make sense of it. I mean by having someone or something to blame.'

'It was an awful way – stupid too,' said Laura.

'Lord knows how much choice he had,' Sorry replied. 'Once he started it was hard to stop. He couldn't admit weakness.'

'Well, you must have got out,' Laura said at last.

'I must have, mustn't I?' Sorry said. 'I don't remember. I don't remember anything for ages after that. The next thing I remember is Miryam crying, but I was in hospital then. I was brought back to Janua Caeli later. Apparently, after about a day, Tim began to come to his senses a bit, opened the cupboard . . . and no Sorensen! I'd gone. I don't know how. I turned up in the courtyard among the clipped trees, quite out of my skull and then Miryam realized something she hadn't realized before – that I was all that she'd intended me to be in the first place, give or take the little matter of my sex.'

'Not so little!' Laura said.

'Well, thanks for your confidence,' Sorry replied. 'About average, I suppose!'

'I didn't mean that,' Laura cried furiously. 'You know I didn't mean that.'

'OK, OK,' he said. 'It was just a smart answer. I'm sorry. See? Events have conspired to make me name myself everytime I apologize.'

'Do you mind? Being called Sorry? It's just a nickname,' Laura said.

'I'm used to it,' Sorry replied. 'Miryam took me to a witch doctor over in Sydney – a real witch doctor – but a psychotherapist, too. I mean she was a witch like Winter, Miryam and me, as well as having university degrees and all that. She was terrific – she really used her capacity for something other than special effects. If I ever live to grow up, which sometimes seems doubtful, I'd like to be like her.'

'A psychotherapist?' Laura asked doubtfully.

'Heaven forbid,' Sorry replied. 'I'd like to work for – I don't know – the wild-life division, or be a ranger or something. I could use what I've got in some tactful, useful way, helping damaged bush regenerate, helping threatened bird populations. Anyhow Chant, there's a moral to all this and it's that you can get over anything . . . People have got over much worse things than this sort of rubbish.'

'But you haven't got over it,' Laura pointed out bluntly.

'Don't let's tell anyone that!' Sorry said quickly. 'Look at my school record. Helping in the library, photographing all sorts of unsuspecting birds, and climbing the heady ladder of success to be a prefect. I'm in the top-half of the class for most things and Katherine Price and I fight it out for top place in English. If that's not getting over things, what is it? I don't want to die, really. I'm interested in what happens next, so I've got to keep on. My advice is . . . just say good luck to your mother. Being miserable won't change a thing . . . not a thing.' He flung his arm into the air and the kingfisher took off like a brilliant dart. 'Away with it all!' said Sorry softly. 'So – all right – it's not fair. Another thing that isn't fair is that I'm sitting here in the sun with you, while poor old Tim is currently doing cane work or whatever, in occupational therapy in some nuthouse. I'm a tribute to the power of money and education. Miryam knew what to do and had the money to do it. She just dropped everything and carried me away. If ninety-percent of the world thinks I'm normal then I *am* normal . . . talking of which, there was something I was going to ask you.'

The flat greyness of the estuary made Laura's heart (furious a moment ago) begin to feel flat and grey, too. She tried to think beyond Sorry's tale back to Kate and Chris Holly.

'Just because things have been worse for you,' she said slowly, 'doesn't make any difference to me . . .' But, for all that, the place, the time and the story had had an effect. Her indignation had been altered, had almost gone, but it's place was taken by a bleak depression and she began to cry, not for any one reason, just for the breakdown of her life into pieces that no longer held to a safe pattern. What she had been warned of in the beginning had come to pass. A week ago she had been complete and continuous with a true face turned to the world, but now she had come entirely to bits.

'Don't cry!' said Sorry, without much sympathy. 'Don't cry! I'm starting to feel I've got all the disadvantages of being married to you and none of the advantages.'

Laura found it was possible to sniff furiously.

'What advantages?' she yelled at him. 'Come on! What advantages? You want to make out? All right then. It doesn't take long does it? And then you can just shut up about it. It'll be over and done with.'

Sorry stared at her in consternation.

'That's really terrible,' he said at last. 'Is it my fault?'

Laura looked down at her hands, locked together so tightly that for a moment she could not be sure herself just which fingers belonged to which hand. 'See, I admit I do have the odd thought about you, Chant, stalking around in the school playground – a sort of grey heron girl, angular and a bit knobbly, but graceful too, and you recognized me, so I've watched you – and you've grown up over the last year and just look as if you might . . . The really awful part is that you've only offered because you're miserable and even then . . .' He laughed to himself. 'Well, I'm not a hero,' he said. 'That's for sure – but I can *pretend* to be one. Let's go back and see how your brother's getting on.'

Perversely enough, Laura now found she was really longing for Kate once more, as if by offering herself so insultingly to Sorry she had in some way caught up with her mother or got her own back on her. She felt suddenly easier, smiled shakily and let Sorry pull her to her feet. She began to feel free of the gnawing anger that had been eating her.

'I'm a bit jealous of Chris Holly, I think,' Laura said, and became even lighter as she named her demon.

'I don't get jealous,' Sorry answered, 'but I can't congratulate myself on it really.'

'If I had a boyfriend wouldn't you be a bit jealous of him?' Laura asked.

'No!' said Sorry and then asked 'Who? Anyone in particular?'

'No – well – say Barry Hamilton,' Laura suggested.

'Barry Hamilton!' exclaimed Sorry. 'Barry? Surely not!'

'He's very good-looking – and he's got a car,' Laura pointed out.

'But he can barely spell his name,' Sorry exclaimed.

'He can. He's not stupid!' Laura cried. 'You're so busy praising yourself you probably wouldn't notice. *And* he's got a car,' she repeated.

'Holy cow!' said Sorry, startled. 'I've got a rival – and a bloody fifth former at that.'

He looked at her, and for a moment the enhanced – the magnified – quality he had shown in the study the night before shone out in his more commonplace face. Laura, with astonishment, alarm and unexpected pleasure, felt the glance like a little electric shock affecting not so much her heart as the pit of her stomach. She looked away from him.

'Hey,' said Sorry as they came up to the Vespa and looked in the long grass for their hidden helmets, 'I dare you to make me another offer, Chant.'

'You turned me down,' said Laura. 'You missed your chance.'

'Hang on tight, then,' Sorry commanded. 'I can't really roar away on a Vespa, but I'll do my best.'

Chris's car was still outside the house, and Laura went in, while Sorry, like an obedient dog, waited outside with the Vespa.

Kate sat at the table in the very place where, in happier days, she had done her bookseller's course, and Chris Holly sat beside her talking to her in a soft, urgent voice which broke off as the door opened and they both turned to look at Laura. Kate had been crying, though she looked calm now, and she was messy, even for Kate, for she had not brushed her hair, which hung around her in disordered curls, duller than it should have been, while yesterday's mascara was smudged under her eyes, recalling the bruises which Sorry's violent memories had projected into his present skin.

'I'm glad to see you back,' Kate said in a careful voice. 'I wasn't expecting you to turn up quite so early in the morning.'

'Anyone could have told that,' Laura said, pleased to hear herself sound easy rather than angry. 'It's all right! It gave me a surprise, but I've got over it. How's Jacko?'

'Dreadful!' Kate answered bleakly.

'I'll make you both a cup of coffee,' Chris said. 'It's one useful thing I can do. And then I'm going to go home, have a bath, tidy myself, meditate a little and come back to collect you.'

Kate turned her apparently battered face to Laura as soon as he was out in the kitchen.

'It wasn't that I didn't care about Jacko,' she said. 'It was because I care so much. I felt so dreadful I needed some sort of consolation and escape.'

'I wanted to comfort you,' Laura cried. 'I'd have kept you company – me, not a stranger.'

Kate looked around the room as if she might see some advice written up on the walls.

'It's the wrong time . . .' She sighed. 'It's the wrong time to say these things. But it's the only time, as it turns out. Everything happens all at once. First I met Chris, and then Jacko grew ill, and the two things have run into one another so that they've become part of the same thing. I've got to say things, even though I know it's the wrong time to say them. Laura, you are a consolation to me, but you can never be an escape, because I feel responsible for you. I have to try and protect you and look after you, and anyway one of the things about sex . . .' She stopped and began again. 'You make me more myself than I want to be, at times, you and Jacko between you. And there are times when people make love that they get a rest from being themselves. Just for a few moments they can become nothing and it's a great relief. That's what I mean by escape. I've been myself, unrelieved, for a long time now and I've loved it, loved being with you and Jacko, even loved work, although I grumbled so much. But I wanted escape. Chris didn't ask me last night – I asked him.'

'Suppose someone like Chris isn't around?' Laura asked. 'What do people do then?' She thought of herself watching the heron fly and longing to dissolve into nothing. Her voice sounded severe in her own ears, but Kate said mildly, 'They get by, and I would have got by.' Then she gave a grin which, weak as it was, was still her own grin. 'It was just my good luck that this time I didn't have to. Lolly, I've said enough. I'm not going to apologize because I don't feel ashamed enough for that. I'm sorry if you were upset, but not enough to wish I'd done anything different.'

This speech made Laura think she had forgotten something and a moment later Chris came in and said, 'Is that your boyfriend waiting out there at the gate, Laura? Do you want to ask him in? What's his name again – Sorrow?'

'Sorry!' Laura cried. 'No! I'll just yell to him from the door.'

From the door she shouted, 'I'll ring you later! OK?' and Sorry gave her a thumbs-up sign and rattled away down Kingsford Drive.

'He's kind of spooky,' Chris said to her when she came back. 'I don't know why I think so, but I do.'

'Don't start her on that,' Kate begged. 'It's only Sorensen Carlisle, the dark secret of the Carlisle family recently brought out into the open.'

'He certainly suggests more middle-class affluence than we usually see around these parts,' Chris said critically.

'Oh, they're a well-to-do family . . . spread all over the city.' Kate sounded careless. 'Every now and then one of them is mentioned in the New Year Honours for services to industry or something. There are two women and that boy living not very far from here. Goodness knows why they stay. I'm sure it's not really their scene.'

'He doesn't look as if he's got much to put up with,' Chris said disapprovingly. 'I thought the other day that the cost of his haircut alone would keep a family of refugees in food for a week.'

Laura felt moved to defend Sorry.

'At least he's not going bald,' she said, and was forced to like Chris, rather against her will, because he laughed and passed her her coffee as if he were giving her a prize.

'Chris has never forgiven himself for being a well-off middle-class boy instead of a refugee,' Kate said almost cheerfully. 'He feels obliged to be hard on others for his own good fortune.'

'Sorry wants to be a hill-and-beach doctor,' Laura said, 'and make sick forests better. Or help with rare birds.'

'So he's into conservation, is he?' Chris said. 'Well, it's better than nothing, I suppose,' and a few minutes later he went off in Kate's car, starting it perfectly because, while she was at the hospital, he had taken it to a weekend garage and had the battery recharged. 'Though you really need a new one,' he said. 'I'll pick you up in three-quarters of an hour.'

Left alone, Kate and Laura looked at each other cautiously, like people just getting to know one another after a long and transforming separation.

'Even if you just did it for consolation and all that,' Laura said after a moment, 'doesn't sex . . . I mean it only works with enthusiasm too, doesn't it?'

'I did feel enthusiastic,' Kate said, getting up, 'but I've dealt with enthusiasm before now. I can manage enthusiasm. It's sadness I find difficult. Laura – they think Jacko is going to die . . . I know they think it. They haven't managed to do anything much to help him. He's just got worse and worse and worse. I've rung twice this morning and they say there's been no change except that he's got a bit weaker. I can't help knowing what that means. I didn't really want another baby, you know. I only had Jacko because I thought your father might leave – he was already having an affair with Julia then and I knew that this time it was serious, so I had Jacko! Still it's a rotten reason for having a baby, just to tie someone to you, isn't it?'

'Jacko didn't care,' Laura pointed out. 'He has always behaved as if he thought life was lovely.'

'Yes, that's the wonderful thing,' Kate said. 'Given half a chance, babies are certain that the world wouldn't function without them. They know they're marvellous. Once I stopped caring about your father so much . . . I really loved my days with you and Jacko and now it looks as if . . . I really don't believe it's my fault – yet in a superstitious way I feel that it's a sort of punishment for past mistakes.'

'I don't believe that for a moment,' Laura cried. 'But I know more about Jacko's sickness than you do. It's just that you won't believe me. Can I come with you? Can I see Jacko?'

'May I,' corrected Kate. 'Yes – you probably may, though really you'd do better to remember him as he was, bright and cheerful and always ready for some sort of mischief. Still, of course you can come with me. There's a sort of sitting room, a little waiting room with TV where Chris spent a lot of yesterday, and I'm allowed in Jacko's room at any time. They offered to make up a bed so that I could stay with him, and I'll probably do that tonight. Now let's get going. Bags first bath.'

From the bathroom she called a moment later, 'You know, Laura – you should be pleased that I can go out and get involved with someone like Chris. The day's going to come when you want to be free of me, and it'll be much easier for you if I've . . . if you don't have to leave me always on my own.'

But Laura was staring into her mirror wondering just what sort of face Sorry had seen looking across the playground at her and just what she'd think of her own face if she hadn't grown up with it day after day.

She decided that she would put on her best clothes in case she saw Sorry later, for she thought it would do no harm for him to see her wearing her one nice dress, even if it was only a sundress that had been too small for Sally. She brushed her hair hard until it actually shone a little, though its lambswool surface did not really give light a fair chance. She put on her best sandals and asked if she could also put on some makeup.

'A little bit of lipstick to brighten yourself up, if you feel you must,' said Kate, but Laura couldn't resist using eye-liner and mascara and thought she looked like the heroine of some foreign film.

Later, at the hospital, staring at Jacko, all this seemed childish. He had become part of a hospital's machinery. Fluid dripped into his arm, a plastic tube was taped up his nose. Hospital sheets and blankets did not so much tuck him in as strap him down and he lay beneath them looking like a shrunken doll, but still unmistakably Jacko, still her brother. All the upside-down events of the last twenty-four hours, the intrusive new people like Chris Holly and the three Carlisle witches, grew faint, like memories from an earlier less important life. Laura longed to pick Jacko up and hold him, to remind him somehow, even in his coma, that he had a sister who loved him and would do anything to stop the shadows inching up over him. But all she could do was look at him and say his name to herself in a stubborn voice.

'Lolly,' said Kate. 'Dearest girl!' She started to say something but could not finish it. 'Cry if you want to,' she said at last. 'I do, on and off, all the time.'

Only a few hours earlier, Laura had hated Kate for spending a night looking for comfort with Chris Holly, but already her own reaction seemed like that of a child with limited understanding. Confronted by Jacko's great stillness, seeing a ghost of hope haunting the despair in Kate's pale face, all such judgements became insignificant. However, Laura did not cry. The feelings she longed to dissolve with tears were part of the power that might still save Jacko and must be hoarded and invested, not easily spent.

While Kate and Laura stared at Jacko, as if they were looking at some mysterious and tragic work of art, a doctor came in and began to check up on him, and at this moment Laura smelled the unforgettable smells of stale peppermint and decay. She felt her chest and throat heave violently, Kate looked at her anxiously, and she said quickly, 'It's all right. He's going to have one of those fits – that's all.'

As she spoke Jacko began to bend, but very weakly. She saw, as nobody else apparently did, Carmody Braque look out at her through Jacko's eyes, then grin and vanish.

'Don't you see?' she asked Kate despairingly. 'Don't you see . . . can't you smell him?'

'How did you know he was going to do that?' the doctor asked.

'I could smell he was going to,' she said. 'He begins to smell of peppermint.'

'My daughter thinks he's possessed,' Kate said lightly to the doctor.

'It's not a possession – it's a consumption,' Laura said,

repeating the diagnosis of Sorry Carlisle. 'He smells of peppermint cough-mixture and of going rotten.'

'That's strange,' the doctor said to Kate. 'I think he smells of peppermint at times myself. Sister says she can't smell it and Dr Roper says he doesn't notice anything either. Mrs Chant, I can't accept such a diagnosis, but there's not one thing we've done that's made him better, I must admit. His heart is under a lot of strain from something – some pathological condition no doubt – which I cannot recognize or prescribe any treatment for. The glucose and protein solution probably added to his capacity to last out, but that is all we've been able to do for him. When you've guessed at everything but the one thing, then maybe that one thing is the only possibility you're left with.'

'Could I go and telephone?' Laura asked. 'There's a telephone in that little waiting room, isn't there?'

She knew by the crackling voice on the end of the phone when she finally got through, that she was speaking to old Winter Carlisle.

'Winter . . .' she said in a way that was familiar and yet somehow the only way she could claim any power over this old woman who had offered her a strange bargain. 'It's Laura Chant. My brother is a lot worse.'

'Remember there is a possible solution,' said Winter's voice.

'I've got to ask you,' Laura said, 'and you'll tell me honestly – Sorry says you'll tell me honestly – is there no other way you can think of to save him except what you said last night?'

'I promise by the cup, the sword, the coin and the wand,' Winter Carlisle said, her crackling voice committing ancient symbols to modern wires which delivered them through Laura's listening ear into her reasoning mind. Like her brother she was, for a moment, part of a machine.

'Is it hard?' she asked.

'Very hard, but not too hard,' Mrs Carlisle replied. 'It changes you for ever, but you are changing for ever anyway.'

'Is it a bad change?' Laura asked.

'It can be, if people use it badly – but the same can be said of all human changes,' Mrs Carlisle replied.

'There's some reason that's nothing to do with Jacko that you want me to do this,' Laura said. 'There is, isn't there?'

'There is,' Winter agreed, 'but I wouldn't have suggested it if it hadn't run along with your own necessity.'

'Can we do it at once?' Laura asked her last question. 'Now!'

There was a silence and then the old voice said, 'I think we can – tonight – but you are not to eat anything all day. Tell me, Laura Chant, are you a virgin?'

'Yes,' Laura said. 'Does it matter?'

'It makes some differences,' Winter replied. 'It makes it easier to change if you aren't too tied to your present state. There are three of us to help you over, but you are the one that must remake yourself. Don't eat. Food will hold you back.'

'I'm not hungry anyway,' Laura said. 'Is Sorry there?'

'In his study doorway, watching me,' Winter replied. 'Do you want to speak to him?'

'No. I'll wait and see him tonight,' Laura said. 'Just give him a wave from me.'

She hung up, and was pleased to find she was not shaking or apparently nervous in any way. She turned to meet Chris Holly's curious gaze. He was sitting in one of the waiting room chairs reading a book by Graham Greene and looking at her.

'What are you up to?' he asked. 'It sounds like a black mass or something.'

'It's nothing like that,' Laura said, though she thought it might be a little like one. 'It's a private arrangement.'

At that moment a shadow loomed in the doorway and a voice spoke.

'Can this be my woolly baa-lamb?' it said. 'Oh, Laura – you've grown up.'

Laura turned and found herself looking at a man she knew. Just for a fraction of a second he seemed totally familiar, but she could not remember his name or how she knew him, and then realized he was her dark, powerful father, rather heavier than he'd been when she saw him last, wearing clothes she had never seen him wear before, while his second wife, pretty Julia, quite noticeably pregnant, watched him lovingly from a tactful distance.

9

The Changeover

Before she went back to the Carlisles' that night Laura was allowed to visit Jacko once more.

'Talk to him!' the doctor had said. 'Talk to him as much as you like.'

So Laura bent over him and whispered, 'Jacko – listen Jacko – it's me, Lolly! I'm going now, but I'll be back soon. Hold on a bit longer and I'll save you. Be a good boy, Jacko, and hold on.'

She stared at him as if she were going to print his face in her internal sight, so that even when she was far away she would still have him directly before her. She held her expression quite still, but Kate was not deceived.

'Laura, don't *suffer* so much!' Kate exclaimed wretchedly.

'You don't make sense,' Laura replied, 'suffering yourself and then telling me not to.'

'I'd bear it for you if I could,' Kate cried. 'In the end, I know I can put up with anything, but I want to protect you.'

'Is that why you didn't tell me that Dad was coming?' Laura asked. Kate was silent.

'I wasn't sure he *was* coming,' she said at last. 'I didn't want you to be disappointed.'

'Disappointed!' exclaimed Laura dangerously. 'What's he doing here at all? He scarcely knows Jacko. He didn't even remember his last birthday.'

'Lolly – shhh!' Kate said. 'He'd have to be a hard-hearted man not to be affected, knowing his little son was so very ill. And Stephen was always affectionate, given half a chance. It was just his bad luck I wasn't content with affection.'

'Well, I don't mind about *him'* Laura said. 'I'm not too crazy about Julia because she's going to have a baby and it seems creepy when Jacko's so sick. It's as if he was being replaced even before he's gone.'

'Is that why you won't stay with them!' Kate exclaimed.

'It's part of it,' Laura answered, for she could not tell Kate about the Carlisle witches and the changeover that loomed ahead of her, the thought of which lay like a black, impenetrable fog, blurring the whole evening.

Her father insisted on driving her back to Gardendale, and his car purred like an obedient beast through familiar streets made suddenly strange by being seen through the eyes of strangers.

'What a monstrosity!' exclaimed Julia as they went past the Gardendale Shopping Complex. 'God! It's a form of pollution. Do they play piped music in it?'

'Only in the Mall,' Laura said, thinking the piped music was not so very different from that playing over the car's stereo system. 'It's not too bad.'

'Sounds awful,' said Julia. 'Is that where Kate works? Poor

Kate.' The car moved on, and a few moments later drew up outside the Carlisles' gate.

'That's good timing,' said Stephen, for Sorry, warned of her approach by some instinct of his own, was opening the gate.

'I'll get out here,' Laura said hurriedly. 'Then you won't have to go all the way down the drive.'

She knew Julia and her father would be impressed by Janua Caeli, but she did not want them moving into the magic circle of its shadows and trees.

'Who's the boy?' asked Julia slyly.

'Sorensen Carlisle,' Laura answered stiffly, and Julia and her father both burst out laughing, as if they now understood something that they had not understood before, and were not only amused but relieved by it.

'He's not a boyfriend. He's a prefect,' Laura mumbled.

'I thought there must be some reason why you refused to stay with us,' Stephen said. 'I thought maybe it was me. Oh well, you're growing up, Baa-lamb.'

'Thank you for bringing me,' Laura said to him.

'Don't I get a kiss?' he asked so sadly that she surprised him, and herself too, with a kiss and a warm hug, and smelt his smell, wonderfully preserved in her memory, of tobacco and after-shave lotion.

Julia waved amiably, Laura waved back uncertainly, and then the big car drove off, leaving Laura to watch Sorry close the gate and to walk down the long, dark drive with him, feeling first in him, then in the air, and particularly in the old house ahead of them, a preparatory tension, a wild winding-up for some test that could only be guessed at.

'How's the little brother?' Sorry asked. 'And how are things with your mother?'

Laura told him everything she could remember, anxious at being alone with him in the darkness under the trees when he was in such a witchy mood, but he said very little until they came on to the lighted terrace before the front door.

'Let's get back inside – you'll feel safer out of the shadows,' he said.

'The worst shadows are in my head,' Laura said, and certainly they followed her into the kitchen.

'You're probably a bit faint with hunger,' Sorry remarked. 'But that's part of the idea. I can't offer you anything to eat, though actually I wouldn't mind a slice of cake myself. That's a pretty dress, Chant. Did I tell you?'

'It's old now,' Laura said, 'but I still like it. I won't be able to wear it much longer. It's getting too small.'

'Not so!' said Sorry. 'It's you that's changing, not the dress. You're getting too big for it.'

'I can't take credit,' Laura said seriously. 'It's just a thing that happens.'

'Chant –' he exclaimed suddenly. 'Cut and run! Go while you still can. Forget your brother, sprint away down the drive, open the gate and get out into real life again. Find some nice boy with a real heart, fall in love, have kids, grow old and die like a real human being, not an imaginary one.' But as they stared at each other across the table his mother appeared in the kitchen doorway.

'Don't mind him, Laura,' she said. 'Sometimes I think all women are imaginary creatures, as Sorry chooses to put it. He doesn't mean that we're simply imagined, you know, but that our power flows out of the imagination, and that's the faculty that makes magicians of all of us. Witches just act upon it with such conviction that their dreams turn into reality. Come with me.'

Sorry sighed as Laura moved over to Miryam, who laid a pale hand on her bare arm, gently but compellingly.

'Goodbye, Chant!' he said, as if she were going away for a long time. 'Sometimes I've thought I might change over too, by going the other way. Sometimes I thought I might use you as a bridge so that I could get back to . . .'

'You're forgetting, Sorensen,' said his mother. 'You've tried that and it didn't work for you. You've no real choice.'

'Then I'm saying goodbye to the idea of it,' Sorry replied. 'I'll see you on the other side, Chant – or a bit before that, really. I've got a part to play, too. I'll go and psyche myself up for it.'

'Sorensen has so many missing pieces,' Miryam murmured as she led Laura upstairs, speaking of Sorry as if he were a jigsaw puzzle. 'We don't despair that he may remake himself, but for now you are our only concern . . . you and your change-over. The first part is easy and even pleasant. We'll get rid of all the world that we can.'

Laura had a bath, lit by candles as thick as her wrist. In one corner on an iron tray stood a little brazier made in the shape of a black cat. The cat's eyes glowed red and the slow smoke rising from its open mouth smelt not so much sweet as herbal, a little like new-mown hay, but richer and somehow very confusing. In the soft, uncertain light, the bath sometimes seemed to be a pool of water set among slender trees with fiery leaves. The walls of the room came and went, mostly close and damp with steam, but at other times entirely vanishing, giving her unexpected views of plains of grass where wild horses grazed, or yellow sand and red volcanic rocks where lions prowled and yawned, or green jungles haunted by birds of paradise and jaguars. Once she saw a long curve of coastline where fires burned and painted men struggled in the sand,

and again from a great height she thought she looked dreamily down on a road like a blue-black weal struck across a green land, crawling with cars like coloured flies.

•

Miryam helped her out of the water, shaking a few drops from a nuggety little bottle of thick, green glass and rubbing them in her hair. The candles smoked and flared.

'Did the world creep around you? Did it come and go?' she asked in a tense voice.

'Everything kept changing,' Laura said, looking at the bathmat under her feet, and felt Miryam relax once more.

'For tonight, this room is a crossways of many lines of space and time,' Miryam murmured. 'They cross in all of us all the time, these lines, but only the witches and similar people can catch fish on them – strange fish sometimes. Outside, the moon is rising higher – a full moon. You couldn't have chosen a better night, really. I am the Preparer,' Miryam went on in a more formal voice, 'Sorensen is the Gatekeeper, and Winter will be the Concluder.'

She hung chains of silver around Laura's neck and then dropped over her wet head a white, silky shift laced across the breast so that the chains showed beneath it. Laura looked down and thought she was standing on grass and then that she was standing in sand. There were words written upside down in the sand and she turned her head trying to read them, TAM HTAB she read between her feet. The surrender of her will to the scent and the steam and the changing proportions of things made her feel a little light-headed. Miryam brought her a cup that appeared at first to be made of black glass, though its inner surface was shot with dark crimson and kingfisher blue, so she wondered if it was made of black opal or some other semi-precious stone. It was quite empty but Miryam filled it from a tall jug.

'What is it?' Laura asked, for the drink was hot and smelled of several familiar things all at once.

'It's mulled wine,' Miryam said. 'Heating it destroys the alcohol, you know. You won't get tipsy. Believe me, you'll need all your wits and all your will.' She put it on the little table beside them. 'Give me your hand!' Laura did as she was told, then tried to take it back again, but Miryam, as quickly and efficiently as a good nurse, pricked the top of her finger with a silver pin and held it over the cup so that a dark drop of blood fell and was lost in the dark wine.

'Ouch!' said Laura indignantly. 'Why didn't you tell me?'

'Better not to know, I think,' Miryam said smiling, watching Laura suck her finger. 'Do you suppose the Sleeping Beauty had a moment to suck her finger after she pricked it? And what dreams did she have because of it? She'd never pricked her finger before, so perhaps that was the first time she'd tasted her own blood. As for you, you must travel back into yourself Laura. Don't worry! It's only a little nature magic . . . a sprinkle of cinnamon, an orange stuck with cloves, the blood of grapes, the juice of a girl . . . it will just start you on your journey. So drink it slowly, and make yourself into a woman of the moon.'

Laura drank the wine, but it was Miryam's suggestions that filled her head, shooting her full of crimson and kingfisher blue. She thought her drop of blood was trying to find its way back to its proper place and that she must follow it. At the same time, as if hands had been softly but forcibly clapped together behind her eyes, she felt a gentle concussion in her head. Then something like an insistent wind parted the silken curtains of her thoughts and feelings, moved through them, and let them fall together once more and, though she could not name the intruding presence, it had a name and might even have been recognized if she had been expecting it.

'Are you sure it's only mulled wine and a drop of blood?' she asked anxiously.

'Were you touched?' asked Miryam looking up, still smiling but very alert. 'It's because you are a halfway girl. It's not the wine so much as something in you that recognizes the signs we are making out here, and signals back. Look at yourself. You could almost be one of us already.'

She turned Laura slowly so that she looked into the watery depths of the looking-glass where she saw herself, shadowed and delicate, her wrists and ankles as slender as if she had hollow bird bones and could rise up against gravity, her woolly hair a dark halo, glittering as if touched by gold dust, her eyes like black holes burnt into a smooth, olive face. She licked her lips and would not have been too surprised to see a serpent's tongue flicker between them, but it was her own tongue, surprising because it showed she was solid all the way through and not just a phantom created by Miryam and the night.

'Not that it will be easy for you,' Miryam continued. 'But for the moment – look – it's a wonderful, mysterious thing to be a girl.'

And, looking at her reflection, Laura thought this might be true.

'They don't teach us that in social education,' she said, with a slanting smile at her reflection which smiled back obediently.

'Witches came before the simplest societies,' Miryam answered, 'back in the time when people slept outside under the moon. And the moon crept into their sleeping thoughts and polarized their dreams. You're not a witch yet – only a halfway house, but at this moment the room will accommodate your wish.'

Across the space of the city, back through time into the morning, Laura's wish showed her Jacko. He swam in a soft, hazy gap connected with wires and tubes to the body of the hospital. But from this room, in this company, she could see, spreading through him like a blight, the progress of Carmody Braque's possession. It was as if a line of bruises was inching forward across Jacko, discolouring him as it went. She could see how soon and how completely he could be devoured by blackness. Laura looked at Jacko with incoherent love, even as she clenched her teeth at the thought of Carmody Braque.

'No!' said Miryam urgently and made a move that broke the connection. 'If he chose this moment to visit your brother, Carmody Braque might become aware of you, and of your plans. It is time for you to begin. We will marry you, if we can, to some sleeping aspect of yourself and you must wake it. Your journey is inward, but will seem outward. I'll give you these – we call them the coins.' The discs she placed in Laura's hand were of stone, not metal, worn smooth and thin, engraved with words that Laura could not read.

Miryam led Laura to the door.

'Is Sorry out there?' asked Laura as the door opened on darkness. She wanted to think there might be a friend waiting for her. 'Is he being Gatekeeper out in the dark?'

'Indeed he is,' Miryam replied and Laura could feel, rather than see, her peculiar smile. 'But he's not out there. He's inside your head. Didn't you feel him move there? Don't you feel him there now, waiting for you? You must be brave, Laura, and never turn back.'

'What if I can't do it? What if it doesn't work?' Laura asked.

'Never ask that!' Miryam told her, softly but very seriously.

'I'm not scared. Only curious!' Laura insisted.

'Well, Laura – let me put it like this,' Miryam said. 'Once you walk through the gate that Sorensen will show you, you *must* succeed. It's your life you are gambling with.'

'Good!' Laura said fiercely. 'I don't want any way back. It must work – that's all there is to it.'

'Winter is certain you will succeed,' Miryam told her.

'Will it hurt?' Laura asked. 'I want to be warned.'

'It will seem to hurt,' Miryam replied, not very comfortingly. 'Do what is shown to you to do. I can't warn you. A changeover is never the same twice over. Each person pictures their own.'

'It's very dark,' Laura said, taking a hesitant step. 'Where are we? I can't remember. Are there stairs?' There was no reply. 'I can't remember,' she repeated and put her hand back to the door, but the door had gone. She could feel nothing before or behind her. She realized at last that she was alone and in such darkness that she could not see an inch ahead of her. If she had been an Egyptian mummy waking into the bandaged dark of a triple coffin under tons of ancient stone she could not have been blinder or looked into a deeper blackness.

She stood there a long time, unable to tell if she were alone, or in company. Sometimes her isolation seemed so great she wondered if she had been projected into the heart of a black hole somewhere. Yet at other times the darkness, while losing nothing of its impenetrability, seethed with the spirits of people and events. She thought she smelt flowers, and then something peppery. Something apparently breathed next to her ear; a finger soft as thistledown, cold as ice touched her lips and immediately she tasted a birthday cake made for her by Kate when she was nine years old, remembered the sweet, smooth texture of a whole crystallized cherry that had slipped in unchopped, glowing like a jewel in the dark, moist slice that had been passed to her. A ghostly hand, perhaps Sorry's, touched her breast with scarcely any more weight than sunlight. She thought he might have become some sort of demon lover in her head and might dictate her own possession, so that she would feel it like a memory although it had never happened, but the sensations went by like dreams.

She was woolly Laura Chant, sitting in the dark preparing to pit herself against the lemure, the evil spirit, wicked Carmody Braque who had chosen her brother to sustain him in his unnatural existence. 'Lolly!' said Kate in her ear. 'Laura,' said Chris Holly. 'Baa-lamb!' said her father. 'Laura Chant,' said old Winter. 'Chant,' said Sorry in his prefect's superior voice, touched as always with self-derision. Jacko did not call her. He floated in his hospital womb, tied to life by wires and tubes, devoured from within by the ravenous lemure.

Laura could not be sure if she sat there for minutes or hours or days, for this blackness was the solvent of time, holding seconds in a disordered suspension. But then she saw a crack of bluish light. The darkness was splitting an inch before her eyes, or perhaps it was the actual pupil of her eye painlessly but inescapably dividing. Darkness had confused her. The light was quite a distance away from her. A door or gate was opening. 'Do what it is shown to you to do,' said Miryam's voice, and Laura moved to the door, stepped through it into a vague half-world where everything she saw wavered as if she were looking at it through tears. She moved along, and slowly the wavering grey-ness settled down and she began to recognize the place in which she found herself, under a strange, dark sky with clouds so heavy and low she felt she could have put up a hand and touched them. Every now and then the lightning wrote across them in an instantaneous scribble of power, but Laura did not bother to look more than once at this electrical graffiti.

She was in Kingsford Drive once more, walking towards the Gardendale Secondary School. Other pupils, all in school uniform, pelted by her – she recognized no one; they were gone before she could name them. The gate of the school was visible and around it the Gardendale subdivision lay revealed, entirely familiar but made eerie by the lurid light which the sky poured over them. First bell was gone . . . she would be late again. Laura began to run – the big trucks rumbled by beside her, the earth-moving machines clashing their jaws over her head. The crowd of uniforms passed in ahead of her. The prefect on gate duty was Sorry Carlisle, sitting there, not at, but on, a school desk, whistling to himself, studying his fingers, bright with rings, just as they had been when she first saw him sitting in his study. He wore his black dressing-gown with its girdle of rope and she could not tell, when he looked up, if he were hero or villain, for he was both threatening and savage, and yet consoling. Two distinct and contrary faces had tangled into one, both smiling with the same set of features as if he were offering to save her and ruin her simultaneously, and to initiate both with the identical hand, now held out to her. He was the boy who had touched her and warned her, and she had invited him in twice and thought that now he might have decided to eat her. However, she was to be brave and do what it was shown to her to do. She walked up to him, looked into his eyes and saw her reflection, tiny and flaring, with light on the silver surface.

'First bell's gone, Chant,' Sorry said, 'and you're not wearing a school uniform.'

'Neither are you,' Laura pointed out, returning his intent, private stare without faltering.

'Right on, Chant!' he said and then, 'Have you got any money? I'd do it for you free, but you know . . . even to cross the Styx you have to pay the ferryman.'

'You couldn't call Gardendale "the sticks",' Laura protested, showing her stone coins. 'It's right in the city.'

'But built of sticks,' Sorry said. 'Sticks and stones. Styx and stones!' he repeated with a different, darker emphasis, taking one of her coins. 'Now, I'm to give you the sword. You're inventing the terrain, but we're putting in a few of our own symbols.'

'What do I use it for?' she asked as he buckled the sword around her.

'Anything that won't let you pass,' he said. 'I'll put you on the path and you're not to leave it, and not to look back.' Laura thought he was looking down the front of her dress and put her hand over it.

'And give me a kiss,' he added.

'Do I have to?' she asked him, but in a different voice from the one she would have used yesterday morning.

'I cannot tell a lie,' Sorry said. 'I invented that bit. I thought it would be nice.' The black clouds behind his head flared as if a reddish light had fallen on them from some unseen source.

'Where are we?' she asked, looking around, suddenly uneasy, and feeling a faint jolt as if the ground had shivered under the Gardendale subdivision – as if her abrupt uneasiness was the uneasiness of the whole world.

'Never ask!' Sorry cried, suddenly furious. He took hold of her arms so tightly it hurt, but she realized that she had suddenly frightened him, for his upper lip and forehead shone with a faint, dewy bloom. Relaxing, he laughed a little shakily. 'That way philosophy lies!' he declared. 'And it's instinct alone in this country. It can't stand the pressure of doubt. You'll kill yourself if you ask questions, and me too, since I'm shut up here with you.'

'I'll kiss you because I want to,' said Laura, 'not because you do.'

'I'll settle for that,' Sorry replied. 'But be gentle with me.'

However, he was not gentle himself and neither was Laura. Thunder munched around the edge of the clouded sky. Sorry looked up and smiled.

'I love your sound-effects,' he said. There was a little gate she had never noticed before tucked in beside the big school entrance. A track of uneven yellow paving led away from it. Sorry unlocked the gate.

'Follow the yellow brick road and remember, don't look back. Just keep on going. If the road divides, look for a sign. Cut down whatever crosses your path. On your way, Chant, and thanks for the kiss – I think you've got natural talent.'

'It's not as if it were hard,' said Laura and left him behind.

She was in a forest that was all forests, the forest at the heart of fairy tales, the looking-glass forest where names disappeared, the forests of the night where Carmody Braque devoured tiger cubs, the wood around Janua Caeli inhabited by yet another tiger which might have a human face behind its mask, and Laura's own forest, the forest without trees, the subdivision, the city.

Between the straight trunks of the birches, the earth-moving machines lumbered like shadowy, disinterested beasts, a distant supermarket parking lot showed like a little desert of cars. Mrs Fangboner, hair newly set, came out from between the ferns and called, 'Laura – don't get into dangerous spots. Don't let yourself go.' But Laura was already going. The shop for fuller figures could be seen through broad, green leaves, its windows full, not of dresses, but fat zeros, pot-bellied legless sixes, and bosomy eights, and threes like pregnant, primitive goddesses. In the teashop the chairs were being stood on top of the tables and made a forest of their own, sprouting upwards in fountains of coloured leaves. Among them Jacko sat, hunched and very frail, looking at Laura with the face of a little old man, his can of apple-juice in front of him.

'Don't you worry, Jacko. I'll nail the bastard,' Laura promised and walked on.

The bookshop was alive with leaves, and each one written on. Novels took a whole tree, but poems were cheap. Kate was selling Chris a poem and giving him too much discount. Laura almost went over to tell her so, but the thunder growled at her . . . the tiger growled at her and lifted its striped face out of the grass beside the path. Its face was so heavily striped it was more black than golden.

With the coming of the tiger the forest shifted, becoming older and darker. Moss hung from the trees, and the only sound was the faint trickle and gush of distant water. Laura now began to feel an ache in her neck and shoulders, as if she were pushing against an intangible resistance, and vaguely thought it might be something like the past, or reality, for a stream of shadowy figures began to flow past her, all going in the opposite direction from the one she and the tiger, slipping distantly through the trees, were following . . . She saw dwarfs, lost princes, beautiful girls who had committed themselves to silence in order to save brothers turned into swans or ravens, young men who thrived on sunshine and dwindled with darkness, mutilated maidens who wept over their own silver arms, and then simpler people, three bears, the girl in the red hood, the lost children who found their way home, the lost children who didn't and were covered with leaves by the robins. Once the road divided, but the true path was always marked by her own drop of blood and she followed it faithfully. On her right the unicorn knelt to dip his horn in a pool of water, watched by the pale, radiant eyes of primroses; on the left, three hanged men dripped and fell to pieces among shining flowers, while beautiful butterflies fed from their corruption as readily as from the honeysuckle and wild roses. The trees cried out to her as she passed, some seductively, others in voices of pain, and Laura herself began to ache and throb down her back and in her chest. Briars crept over the road and she pushed through them, scratching herself so that she dripped blood once more. The path was distinct and she pushed on into a forest of monstrosities, a tree of snakes, a tree whose rosy apples, once clearly seen, were the hearts of Aztec sacrifices. A bush, whose branches ended in hands held aloft (as if Laura had pointed a gun at it) allowing her to see a tiny eye on the end of each finger tip, watched her go by. The brick road now began to trickle with water. Moss showed between its cracks and then a green ooze and then water itself bubbling up so that the bricks moved soggily underfoot and yielded their colour, staining the bubbles yellow. The briars thickened and Laura at last drew the sword and began to cut her way through them, but though this lessened her troubles in one way, it increased them in another. The sword slid easily through the woody stems, and the briar immediately reared up, then thrashed about in anguish, screaming with a voice Laura dimly recognized as her own, while, as if the stroke had fallen in her own head, she felt a shock of pain, followed by a spasm of rank sickness. Still she knew she must follow the road and hacked away, while the water ran more and more strongly. The only way she could follow the road was to feel for its stones with her blind feet, while she shivered and retched on her way through the screaming, writhing briars which now began to drip her own blood on her, streaking the water which came up to her waist.

How far is there to go? she wondered. How far have I come? And she turned her head and looked back, though as she did so a voice out of memory warned her, 'Never look back!'

Behind her the road branched infinitely. Kate and Stephen stood together in church being married; she saw herself born, her first day at school, saw Winter Carlisle, much younger and softer, feeding hens, saw Mrs Fangboner looking at her dahlias with a rare, solitary pleasure, saw Miryam, stricken, hold a baby who must be Sorry, and Sorry himself crouched under a rain of blows, though she could not see his assailant's face. She saw Chris, in another country, holding a letter he hesitated to post, saw herself looking in a mirror, saw all the possibilities, her own and other people's, that had brought her to this point. At the same time she experienced another jolt similar to that she had felt when she asked the question, 'Where are we?' and a big piece of the forest vanished. Beyond it she could see either smoke or steam rising from nowhere. A fine shuddering began to run through everything and, huge in the sky, in faint letters hundreds of miles high the words TAM HTAB appeared, becoming more and more distinct every moment. Laura knew what had happened and immediately ducked down under the water. At first it was like being in mist. She breathed easily.

'I'm drowning, I'm drowning,' she told herself, forcing reality back into her surroundings, and suddenly her lungs were filled with chilly water. She coughed and spluttered, but there was only more water and she began struggling to find the surface again with no clear view of which way to go. Yet the weight of water lessened. She held out her hand and it broke a surface somewhere, was seized even before her head came free by a hand cold with gold and silver. Sorry helped her to her feet in a furious cloud of clear water. He was as white as paper but the shadow of tiger stripes lay across his face. Like her, he was gasping and soaking wet.

'I thought you'd blown it there,' he said, 'but you brought triumph out of disaster. You took a short cut. Look!'

He pointed and she saw Miryam and Winter sitting high on the bank watching them.

'Give me the sword,' he said. 'Come on, quickly. And I'll give you the wand in its place. There's nothing much more I can do for you now.'

'I won't look back again,' Laura promised shaking, as he took the sword from its sheath at her side and gave her instead a long rod with a silver tip.

'It doesn't matter now,' he said. 'You're too far in. There's only one way out for you now.'

Laura came up and looked boldly at Winter.

'You took a risk too,' she said. 'What are you doing it for?'

'I hope to make something right that I did wrong a long time ago,' Winter said. 'We all have separate purposes hidden in your changeover. Look around you.'

They were high on a range of hills as bare as if they were covered with nothing more than a sinewy, brown skin, stretched over stones – no grass, no flowers, no butterflies, no trees, only tanned soil, red rock and grey slopes of shingle, the only sound that of water leaping and flowing down the naked hillside. Far below, a plain billowed with the irregular green surges of a forest that stretched away from them, vanishing into the mists and thunderstorms that had marked the beginning of her journey back through dreams and time to this place of powerful simplicity. At her feet the water leaped and fell into a wide pond lined with stone, and was directed down a channel of stone by a shutter that swung on a pivot. Another dry channel led away from the pond to a forest lying beside the first, but apparently dead. Though she was many miles away, Laura could see its skeletal trees make an intricate but rhythmic lace beside the green flanks of the forest she had traversed. Beyond the forest was the estuary and the long straight line of breakers rolling in from the sea. Laura looked behind her and saw the bare, silent land continue folding and falling away to another ocean she recognized in a mysterious inner way, for she had never seen it before.

'I've been here before though, haven't I!' she said, not asking a question but answering one that hadn't been spoken. 'I was here before I even began remembering. It's the beginning land.' No one said anything. 'It's bare, but isn't it beautiful?' she said. 'Have we all got this inside us?'

'It's partly the memory of space we're moving in now,' Winter said. 'And partly the memory of all living things. But the forests are all your own, and the bare forest down there stands for the forest that, by some accident, grows green in Miryam, Sorensen and me. You don't need me to tell you what to do. But only you can do it.' She touched the shutter as she spoke, and her hand flowed through it as if it was made of water.

'No,' said Laura and leaned against the shutter so that it swung half-way over and water began to flood out of the pond in two directions, turning in double spirals in the pool without seeming to be any less than it had been when she first saw it. She felt the shift painlessly in her head – in every last part of her.

'You must find your own way back now,' Winter said. 'I am the Concluder. You must pay to pass me. Give me the coin.' Laura hesitated. 'You do have it?' cried Winter, suddenly horrified.

'I think so,' said Laura, and creakingly opened her clenched left hand. The stone coin was there, clutched so desperately that the skin on her hard palm was swollen and bruised around it. She picked it up with her other hand and passed it to Winter, who received it gravely and then lifted a measuring gaze to her face.

'You'll make a very strong witch, Laura,' she said thoughtfully. 'But you can't return the way you came. Follow the water to its source,' Winter said. 'You can use the wand to begin with.' Laura looked at Sorry.

'I can't walk any further,' she said. 'I just can't walk any further.' Her skin was stitched and seamed with thin, red lines, scratches from briars and from the lines of her own blows severing the briars.

'Then crawl, Chant, crawl,' he told her, smiling and growing even paler. 'I'd even crawl beside you, Chant, but as things are I can't, I can't.'

'It'll never get into *Poetry Today,*' said Laura, naming a well-known school textbook, and began to crawl on knees largely made of cotton-wool and rubber, but unlike cotton-wool and rubber able to bleed. At first the rocks shrank back from the wand but as she went on, they closed in, tighter and tighter, so that she had to squeeze through cracks no bigger than that under a door which grudgingly gave way to the wand and let her slide through. At one moment she seemed to be climbing a wet, helical path leading upwards, but a sudden twitch of perspective made her see she was, in fact, climbing down. It grew so tight she began to despair, for though the wand, like a rod divining spaces in solid rock, showed her a path, she was not sure she could follow it. Like Alice she did not think she would ever be small enough to reach the beautiful garden. 'Even if my head did go through,' she whispered, hearing the echo of the whisper from the adjacent rock, 'it would be very little use without my shoulders.' It suddenly occurred to her she was being born again and, as this thought formed, the helix took her as if it had come alive. She was held and expelled, moved in a great vice, believing her intransigent head with its burdens of thoughts, dreams and memory must split open, and she came out somewhere into darkness. Reviving water continued to fall on her face. At last she opened her eyes to see her hand lying like a pale shell, not on sand but on fabric and, woven into the cloth on which it lay, small and clear and insignificant, the words TAM HTAB. She was in the bathroom at Janua Caeli under the tree of candles, watched by the cat with the fire in its belly, and Sorensen's little black cat whose eyes had their own green fire. She lay, like a romantic heroine in the arms of the succouring hero, her head on Sorry Carlisle's shoulder.

'Oh, Chant,' he said. 'I felt the bones of your head move, do you know that?' He looked at her with a look of wonder and dread. 'I thought you'd die.' Laura stared at him, saying nothing. Slowly his expression became more recognizable. He kissed her very briefly and said, 'The Sleeping Beauty always loves the prince who wakes her. You've had it now, Chant . . . no hope for you, I'm afraid.'

'I woke myself,' Laura said. She sat up, every joint aching as if she had indeed experienced all the things she had lived out in her dream. Her white dress was splashed with bright, clear crimson from waist to hem.

'You see – it's partly real too. It builds up pressure, like diving very deep, and you have a nose bleed,' Sorry said. 'I get them all the time in football.' He looked like no one she could ever imagine, commonplace and supernatural, the divided face he had turned to her earlier, modified, beginning, perhaps, to come together under the pressure of something new and nameless in him, as if her adventure had been his as well, and was continuing to affect him.

'Did it work?' she asked.

'See for yourself!' said Winter, who had been squeezing water over her face from a cloth. Laura climbed up Sorry like an arthritic bean climbing a stick. He turned her gently to the mirror and by candlelight she saw plainly that she was remade, had brought to life some sleeping part of herself, extending the forest in her head.

She was no longer formed simply from warring Stephen and Kate, but, through the power of charged imagination, her own and other people's, had made herself into a new kind of creature. She turned to Sorry and found he was looking, not into her eyes, eloquent with transformation but, absentmindedly almost, down at her breasts.

'You don't change,' she said to him crossly and he looked, first startled, then bewildered, and, for the first time that she could remember, ashamed.

'I d-didn't mean to,' he stammered. 'It's j-just that . . .' For a moment he appeared to be terrified, looking furiously at his grandmother kneeling and his mother standing, like a tall shadow on the rim of the pool of light. 'I'm sorry,' he said, and then suddenly laughed. Laura looked too, and saw their calm faces touched with what she thought might be a springtime change, a tentative relief, not fully developed, still at an experimental stage.

'Look!' said Winter standing beside her and holding out her hand. Laura watched as her long fingers unfolded, and there, in her palm, was a little, cheap, self-inking stamp with a perfectly circular smiling face on it that might even have been bought at Kate's own shop. Laura frowned at it for a second, and then her expression changed and she looked up at Winter who nodded once, gravely. The stamp was a ridiculous object to consider, after such a threatening journey as Laura's, yet lying in Winter's palm it became sinister in its own way.

'You must name it and instruct it,' Miryam said taking it from Winter's hand and putting it in Laura's. 'You must do it now. I know you're tired but there's very little time.'

'I don't know what to say,' Laura stammered, for her head still rang and ached, her legs trembled beneath her and she rather clung to Sorry, who took her left arm and hooked it around his shoulders, saying as he did so, 'You *do* know what you want it to do. Make up the words! Put your fingers right around it and look into the eyes of your reflection.'

'Say what you see there,' Miryam agreed. 'It's yourself reversed . . .'

'. . . made sinister . . .' said Sorry, and laughed close to her left ear. 'Be sure you really mean it!'

'I'll really mean it all right,' Laura said passionately, holding the stamp tightly. Her reflection swam in the glass. Beside her own face she could see the faces of the three witches: Winter, lacy with age, Miryam, whose lopsided smile mocked the world and herself along with it, and Sorry, watching her mouth as if he would put words into it if she faltered. Her own eyes, in spite of her weariness, were round and shining, and something in their expression made her blush all over with an involuntary fright, but she did not hesitate, holding the stamp and speaking firmly to it.

'Stamp, your name is to be Laura. I'm sharing my name with you. I'm putting my power into you and you must do my work. Don't listen to anyone but me.' She thought for what seemed like a long time, though it was really only a single second, and in that time, oddly enough, the picture of the old, whistling kettle at home came into her mind. 'You are to be my command laid on my enemy. You'll make a hole in him through which he'll drip away until he runs dry. As he drips out darkness, we'll smile together, me outside, you inside. We'll . . .' (she found her voice rising higher and growing a little hysterical) '. . . we'll crush him between our smiles.' She looked up at the reflected witches and said nervously, 'Is that enough?'

'Quite enough,' Winter said, and behind the fine lace of her age, Laura saw a reflection of Sorry's wariness.

'Terrific!' exclaimed Sorry. 'Chant, can I be on your side? I'd hate to be your enemy.' He looked at Winter with a triumph Laura could not understand. 'You've got two of us to worry about now, haven't you?' He held out, in his left hand, a handkerchief spotted with scarlet. 'It's one of Winter's,' he said. 'Pure silk – but the blood is yours. I myself blotted it off you. Wrap your mark up in here.'

Laura looked at the little stamp, frowning again. The outline had changed, but she could not quite see how.

'Shall I try it out?' she asked.

'No point!' said Sorry with a sigh. 'You've already put your mark on me, Chant. Wrap it in silk! Sleep with it under your pillow! Speak to it by name! Hold it against your heart!' Laura surrendered the stamp with reluctance, but Sorry simply wrapped it in the handkerchief and returned it to her.

'And welcome!' said Winter with her rare smile. She kissed Laura's left cheek.

'Welcome!' said Miryam kissing her right cheek. Sorry and Laura looked at each other.

'Well, why not?' Sorry asked her. 'Let's do it because *I* want to this time, Chant,' and he kissed her very gently. It reminded Laura of the soft but heavy kisses Jacko used to give when he was just learning to kiss, and found it very disturbing, for it seemed as if he kissed her for Jacko in the past, himself in the present and for another unknown child somewhere in the future. Indeed, he looked startled himself when the kiss was over, as if he too had found it haunted.

'But Jacko first!' Laura said to him, almost as if he had asked her to marry him and she was putting it off for a little.

'Of course Jacko first!' he agreed. 'We'll take a day off school tomorrow, I think. And a good sleep before anything else, I'd say.'

'You're a brave girl,' said Winter with puzzled respect. 'Sleep is certainly what you need now.'

'I'd carry you upstairs,' Sorry said, 'but you're so bloody heavy.'

'That's not what a hero would say,' Laura grumbled, 'but it's all right. I'd rather walk.'

10

Carmody Braque Brought to Bay

'There he is!' said Sorry, his eyes glued to his field-glasses, his voice affectionate. He was smiling like a huntsman who has located a notable quarry. 'Chant – he's – he's actually pruning roses!'

'What a dummy!' Laura said, taking the field-glasses, her own smile the echo of Sorry's, no less threatening, no less confident.

'I don't know,' Sorry said. 'It's a good disguise. He looks very innocent, very arcadian . . . I think that's the right expression.'

'Yes, but it's the wrong time of year,' Laura said. 'We've got a rose bush round the back and you have to prune it in July or August.'

They had found Carmody Braque quite easily by looking him up in the phone book. There he was in black print standing out on the page. CARMODY BRAQUE – Antique dealer – and three addresses. 'Antique is the operative word,' Sorry said.

They had set off on the Vespa, feeling unnatural and furtive – out on a school day without being in uniform, leaving early so that they would avoid the time when most people were on their way to school and might identify them as truants, bound on personal projects.

The home address led them to a fashionable hill suburb, every home designed by some architect, every garden the result of professional landscape design. PRIVATE ROAD said the sign, NO EXIT.

Laura enjoyed the ride. She saw and smelt the trees in handsome gardens on either side of the steep road and heard the wind among the leaves, but, as if a new sense had opened up in her overnight, she could actually feel the life in them like a green pulse against her skin, a constant, natural caress like wind or sunlight, but apart from either. High above her the gulls cried, seeing the estuary and the promise of good feeding.

'Someday I'll fly,' she cried to Sorry, daringly holding her arms wide.

'Sooner than you think if you don't hold on,' he shouted back. 'Don't be silly, Chant.'

The private road was a horseshoe of particularly stylish houses.

Rich people's houses, Laura thought, envying them gardens and garages. Sorry slowed the bike and put one foot on the ground holding them steady for a moment or two.

'Up that right-of-way,' he said. 'Very select! Look – the road ends right outside that little park. Let's spy out the land a bit. If we get up there we should be able to look down into all the gardens at the back with my field-glasses.'

'You and your birdwatching,' Laura said. 'It's just an excuse. I expect you use them mostly to watch girls sunbathing on their private lawns.'

'Don't think I haven't tried,' Sorry said.

Exploring together, they found they could look down into Carmody Braque's backyard, had seen him hanging out immaculate underwear and shirts on his washing line, and now saw him emerging once more to potter in his garden.

'By the pricking of my thumbs . . .' Sorry said. 'It is him, isn't it? You're looking doubtful.'

'It is him,' Laura replied, 'but he's changed so much.'

'He's all but sucked your brother dry,' Sorry said, his half smile becoming more of a snarl. He laughed to himself. 'It's people like him who give witchcraft a bad name.'

The glasses brought Carmody Braque within inches of Laura. His face had swelled into something much fuller, much more pouchy than it had been on Thursday last. His skin shone, pink and clear. His blotches had cleared away and his cheeks had even become rosy. Laura thought he looked an improbable cross between Dracula and Mr Pickwick. She could even see that his round dome was covered with a fine fluff of new hair, like the down on a rabbit only a few days old, little more than a mist invading a bare plateau. It was the same colour as Jacko's and for some reason this upset her almost more than anything else. Mr Braque suddenly stopped his ill-judged pruning operations and looked around.

'Right!' said Sorry. 'Stop! He'll feel us watching him in another moment. Let's go.'

It was a glittering morning, though cold for summer, for there had been a change of weather inland; snow had fallen on the distant mountains and was cooling the wind that came across the range and over the plain. Sorry in his heavy jacket, Laura in her old parka, put on their helmets once more, even though they had such a short way to go. Laura shivered a little as they went into the right-of-way.

'We'll tempt him with variety,' Sorry said, 'with the prospect of a willing sacrifice. Can you manage to look alluring and yet act as if you were constantly shrinking away from the thought of him.'

'Shall I try to look slinky?' Laura asked.

'You? That's a laugh,' Sorry replied. 'No need to make a fool of yourself. You're too young for "slinky". Be young! Young and knobbly – you know, like a foal! But you're a bit of a mixture, for all that, and that's what just might get him. Winter thought it might, and she's clever.'

'What do you mean – I'm a mixture?' Laura asked coming to a standstill.

Sorry looked back at her over his shoulder.

'You know!' he said. 'At first you look skinny, but you're quite voluptuous in your way. If anyone thinks about you, that is!'

'Voluptuous!' Laura exclaimed.

'Shhh! I'll tell you what it means later,' Sorry said. 'Don't try to put things off by starting an argument.'

'I know what it means,' Laura declared, following him again.

'Are you frightened?' Sorry asked, but not as if he cared.

'Yes, I am!' Laura admitted. 'Suppose it doesn't work?'

Sorry turned on her yet again. '*Make* it work!' he hissed in a low, urgent voice. Before her eyes his expression heightened, and he shone once more with the faint bloom of awe and, maybe, fear. 'You're just as scary as he is. Last night you were. Look, something shifted in you, do you know that? I'll never forget it. I felt your head shift, the cranial bones – I was holding you, and you remade yourself.'

'But not on my own,' Laura said, taken aback by his vehemence.

'People have died trying,' Sorry said. 'That's in our records. If Winter had been wrong . . . but she's not often wrong. Wrong about me perhaps, but not about you. She'll be right about this as well. She says you'll win.'

'I'll think of Jacko,' Laura said, and dipped into memory, where Jacko's picture had been recorded in minute detail.

'Have you got the mark?' Sorry asked.

'It's in my pocket,' Laura said, pushing her hands into her pockets as she spoke.

'Hold it ready then,' he said. 'You'll only have the one chance.'

A climbing rose grew over an arched, rustic gate.

'There's a bell,' Laura said, detecting it and holding its clapper, while Sorry opened the gate. There was a name over the gate. '"Jolidays",' Laura read. 'Who does he think he's fooling?'

'Most people, probably,' Sorry replied. 'He's got to seem like a real person.'

Carmody Braque, among his roses, turned a smiling face to meet them, but he was repelling them, not welcoming them.

'Church of England!' he cried as if we were giving a warning and then his new face changed as he recognized Laura. He looked from her to Sorry and then back again.

'My *dear!*' he cried. 'I thought you were Jehovah's Witnesses! Do forgive me!'

'Yes!' said Laura in a low voice. 'No – I'm sorry to bother you, Mr Braque.'

'I'm sure you *are!*' he cried cordially. 'I can't mistake profound sincerity. And just what do you hope to achieve, intruding on me at this early hour with your young follower?' His round eyes squinted thoughtfully at Sorry.

'Oh . . .' he cried, flinging up his hand and snipping the air with the secateurs in a peculiar, exultant gesture. 'Yes,

I see. On the right track, dear, but alas too late. And anyway, there's not a witch, young or old, can undo what I'm doing – what I have almost *done* in fact. But I'm grateful to you for bringing him. I'm intrigued to see a young male witch . . . it's years since I saw one and the last one, poor fellow, was not very young and had a harelip. Young man . . . I suppose I do call you young man . . .'

'I'm a genetic freak, I suppose, like a male tortoise-shell cat,' Sorry said amiably, 'but I'm not here to try and compel you, Mr Braque. I know my limits.'

'And how few people *do!*' exclaimed Carmody Braque, inclining his head with its nap of fine, silky down.

'I'm a sort of procurer really – a go-between,' Sorry said. 'The girl has a proposition she wants to put to you, and I'm here to watch over her and maybe negotiate on her behalf.'

'Really!' said Carmody Braque. 'I am, of course, quite intrigued. *Reeeeaally!'* he said, turning his round gaze on Laura. 'Speak on, my little spring bud.'

Roses around the gate, 'Jolidays', and all the stench of his true nature suddenly struck her like a blow, for, though the patches of his encroaching corruption had disappeared, they had only been the signs of an inner decay which a witch, or even a sensitive, could detect without hesitation. Laura thought she was going to be sick around the foot of the salmon-coloured standard rose to her left. But instead she looked up into his eyes and saw there, not the curious wolf, not the tiger that Sorry sometimes suggested, but something so insatiable that her recognition of it caused the sunlight to falter and the roses, the neat lawn and the expensive house to undergo a transformation. For a moment they became nothing more than a painted screen behind which a dreadful machinery was at work. Not only that, she recognized that this same machine operated at large in the world in mixed forms, many of them partial and largely impotent, sometimes tragically married to opposite qualities. On this occasion it was her lot to see it almost pure in the round, bird eyes, in the angle of his head, mirroring the more innocent, but none the less terrible, attitude of a hawk about to tear a live mouse in two, and all she had to combat it was an old ritual of possession which her hard-won new nature enabled her to use. But she knew she must not even think of that, and concentrated urgently on Jacko instead.

'Please, Mr Braque,' she said humbly, 'let my little brother go. Take someone else this time.'

'Oh my dear . . .' said Mr Braque. 'I'm so *sorry*. I would if I could, but your charming young friend here will tell you I am an ancient spirit. I've lived off many, many people now and I have to admit the old tides are wearing a little thin. I can't take just anyone anymore. Besides, I have become something of a *gourmet*, you might say, and why not, since I can afford it. I look – I *have* to look – for just the right one, and your little brother was *it* this time. I stalked him for weeks. I knew your movements so well and to tell you the truth I was getting very near my limit when I pounced. Very near.'

He looked at Laura, shaking his head sadly. He longed to be known, and, having the chance at last, he boasted with the most nostalgic pleasure. 'And then I've fed on so many by now I'm very very choosy. Girls like you, with rather more vitality perhaps, or sleeker, or those younger still – eight is an attractive age I think, ten is almost too old . . . But one should never make hard and fast rules. I enjoy an innocent, sucking baby, withering at its mother's breast. Dear me, no one knows what is wrong. How little medicine knows in spite of all its wonderful advances! Or I seize the mothers themselves, sometimes, just when they're happiest. Or those nice old men who never seem to run out of interest in life, retired and looking forward to golf or gardening, or women whose children have grown up and who open like flowers to the world's chances, of which I am *one!'* exclaimed Mr Braque sniggering. 'I want people who look forward without *caution,* who embrace the world . . .' He hugged himself. 'Oh, the delectable banquet of possibility all you people offer me!' Mr Braque tossed his hands into the air where his fingers fluttered like horrid butterflies. His conceit was childish, but somehow that seemed to make it more evil, not less.

'The girl's got a proposition,' Sorry said abruptly, sitting down on a white, cast-iron chair. Dimly Laura knew something had upset him in a personal way. She could not ask and he could not tell.

'Speak on,' said Mr Braque with odious courtesy.

'I thought,' Laura said, 'I thought . . .' She didn't have to act or pretend. She was shaking with fear and began to sweat a little so that the sunglasses started to slide down her nose. She jammed them back on desperately with the palm of her hand. 'I thought – if you – that is . . .'

'Do stop *snivelling,* dear,' said Carmody Braque, beginning to pick his teeth with the nail of his left-hand little finger. 'I've enjoyed talking to you. Your friend there will tell you it's rare to come across anyone who *understands.* But do bear in mind, won't you, that all this talk is making me *hungry,* my dear.'

Laura could tell, however, that Carmody Braque was enjoying himself, as a man with secret treasure might enjoy displaying it and boasting about it to someone who could never tell. In this confident and expansive mood he might put out his hand to her – he might invite her in. She hung back in hope and fear waiting, and, as if he guessed her thoughts, he added with scarcely a pause, 'It's been such a treat to be so completely myself for a little that I'll thank you for the privilege by letting you choose.'

'Choose?' Laura asked, apprehension immediately fizzing in her blood.

'Whether or not I end your brother now or spin him out over the next two or three days. While there's life there's hope (or so they say, though I wouldn't count on it) and some claim that even the last rattling moment, regardless of pain, enables us to conclude ourselves with spiritual grace. But *I* think he'll suffer the most terrible fear in his coma, shut away in the dark with only *me* for company. So I'll let *you* choose for him . . . a sort of trade discount.'

'I thought you might like to take me instead,' Laura babbled. 'You could let Jacko go and take me.'

Mr Braque looked astonished and shook his head.

'Oh, no! You just don't have the same quality of energy at all, and, though the element of self-sacrifice is interesting, curiously enough it's not particularly rare in my area of speciality.' But for all that he continued to look thoughtfully at her, his round eyes widening, his tongue caressing his teeth.

'I'd be willing, you see,' Laura whispered. 'And I'd know about you. I'd recognize you all the time.'

'I thought it might be interesting for you to have someone horrified by you, but prepared to submit,' said Sorry. 'It's its own form of speciality, isn't it?'

Carmody Braque laughed. 'What a very discerning young man you are,' he said. 'But my poor young people . . . how could you dare to put such an idea into my head? I could have both – the little brother and the big sister. Not that I necessarily will! As I told you, I'm forced to be very choosy by now.

'Not everything works any more . . . Still, show yourself, dear! You can't make an offer such as that and remain muffled up like a comic-book spy. After all, you constitute a *luxury*. So take off that jacket and those glasses and remind me just what you have to offer.'

'If you promise to let Jacko go!' Laura said obstinately.

Carmody Braque ignored her words, simply grinning and repeating, 'Show yourself!' But Laura did not move.

'Only for Jacko,' she repeated, pushing her hands into her pockets and shrugging her shoulders as if she were drawing herself in, making herself a smaller target for his darting gaze to strike.

'You are in no position to bargain,' said Carmody Braque, looking watchfully at Sorry. 'Stay your distance, you witch, don't you dare move! Besides, you are saturating her with your power. I can't recognize her at all. She might just as well be your sister.' To Laura he said, as if speaking to a stupid child, 'I must know. How promising is your life to you? Are you worthwhile? Do you anticipate love for instance, or have you . . . ?' He glanced quickly at Sorry and then back again with dreadful eagerness. Laura looked at him narrowly through the twin shadows of her sunglasses. He clicked his tongue impatiently.

'Come here!' he said, and put out his hand to bring her over the space that separated them, to know her and to take her or discard her at will. Laura heard Sorry hiss slightly with an unspoken command, but she was already moving. Her hand took on a swift life of its own, leaping from her pocket, through the air. Laura stamped her mark on Carmody Braque's outstretched palm as firmly and delicately as if she were giving him a flower.

'You've invited me in,' she said. He looked down incredulously and saw her face smiling up at him from the surface of his own skin.

Sorry, moving as quickly as his black cat, came up behind Laura, reached over her shoulder and took her sunglasses off.

'Tell him!' he commanded urgently, while Carmody Braque looked back up at her, his expansive confidence draining away from him.

'What have you done?' he cried. Laura heard, in his changed voice, the first groan of mortality. Their eyes met. She knew at once that a gate had opened for her. He could not be private from her any more. Nor could his fingers, closing spasmodically over the picture in his palm, prevent her following the chemical electricity of this nervous reaction and exploding in his head, where she was immediately powerful. Like a model man he was under her remote control and no matter where he was in the city she could either consume or nourish him. It was so easy it was hard to believe such an ability had not always been natural to her. All the same, her skin crawled and her stomach twisted with horror. She had no mercy to offer. Sorry merely laughed.

'What is it?' asked Carmody Braque again, staring at his hand with the expression of someone seeing, in his own flesh, the symptoms of a catastrophic malaise. 'What is this charade?'

'You know!' Laura said very softly. 'It's my mark.' She had not breath or strength to do more than whisper ominously, 'My mark.'

'But you're not . . . you weren't . . .' His affectation was eaten away by fear. 'I couldn't be wrong.'

'We worked a changeover,' Sorry said, and wrote his initials on to the back of Laura's neck with his forefinger. It was as if he had lost interest in anything other than her, while, for

Laura, the world suddenly altered, growing lighter and more luminous. An energy as strong and sweet as honey flowed into her, and Carmody Braque fell on his knees, just as she had once done by Jacko's bed, watching the reflection of this very man's smile play wickedly over her brother's face.

Now with shock and triumph she discerned her own ghost, looking back at her out of her victim's desperate eyes.

'Please . . .' he cried, 'my dear, young lady . . . I'm pleading with you! Is that what you want? I'll let the little brother go, of course. I'll find someone else. I didn't understand. Honour among thieves . . .' He whined and wriggled closer to her, as if he might try to touch her. 'I've never made this mistake before. There must be a way we can find common ground.' Words poured out of him. He leaked desperation. 'Now, please . . .'

'No!' said Laura and walked away, while Carmody Braque scuttled after her, still on his knees, a frantic, stunted goblin. His hands were stretched out, clutching. For a moment he looked more like a desperate crab than any sort of man.

'Please, please talk,' he cried. 'Let's discuss this like reasonable people. We have to stick together, we funny ones. Is there something else you want? Money? Perhaps you'd like to take your little brother – the boyfriend, too – on a holiday. The Gold Coast! Or even the Isles of Greece, the Isles of Greece where burning Sappho loved and sang, as Shelley says.'

'That's not a bad idea, Chant,' Sorry said. Laura turned on him angrily, and he laughed at her indignation. 'Mind you, I don't think it was Shelley who said that. I don't remember who it was but . . .'

'It doesn't matter who it was, we're not going,' Laura declared. She marched around the house, Sorry beside her, Carmody Braque following, making sounds of threat and supplication. 'Please . . .' was the only audible word.

'Jolidays!' snapped Laura over her shoulder, pushing the gate open so fiercely that the bell rang cheerfully, regardless of the anguish of its owner. Once in the right-of-way, Laura began to run, and Sorry followed her back to the Vespa. Without looking, she knew Carmody Braque had stopped at the gate and would follow no further.

'Right on, Chant!' Sorry said. 'Are your hands shaking? Would you like me to put your helmet on for you? All set? Let's blast off for Planet Earth. Does it exist? I don't think so, but we can't afford to ignore these myths, can we? Don't worry, Chant! It's all over for him. You did everything right.'

'There's still Jacko,' Laura pointed out. 'It isn't over. What shall I do next?'

'Have lunch?' suggested Sorry. 'Terror always makes me hungry.' But Laura could not imagine eating. She thought she might not eat anything ever again.

'The hospital,' she said. 'I've got to go there.'

'Oh, all right!' Sorry said, adjusting his helmet. 'Just think . . . soon you'll be able to forget all about this, and concentrate on what's really important.'

'You, I suppose!' Laura cried derisively, scrambling on to the Vespa behind him.

'Bingo!' Sorry agreed. 'Hold tight!'

Laura suddenly felt extremely fond of Sorry, who was making distance matter so little in her life, and held on to him with new confidence. In spite of his cool words he was trembling, and not just with the vibration of the bike. He had, she suddenly realized, been very frightened. The motor burst into life and they darted down the private road to be cheerfully received by the everyday rush and grumble of the city once more.

11

The Turning Point

The hospital lay, like an island of concrete cliffs and caves, overlooking a crescent of lawn to the main road. After only one visit, it felt familiar to Laura, as if it were going to be part of her life for ever. Standing in the car park, recovering from their swift progress across town, she rubbed her flattened hair with her free hand and, even without looking at him, felt this innocent act touch Sorry in a way she could not define.

'To tell you the truth, I was terrified!' he said abruptly. 'How about you?'

Laura turned to him in astonishment, for her own fear was put behind her. She had begun to think only of Jacko, while Sorry was still looking back to Carmody Braque.

'I wouldn't like to get into that state myself,' he said, looking into the air absentmindedly. 'I mean, being human isn't much, maybe, but I wouldn't want to be anything less.'

'Well, you don't have to,' Laura said, puzzled.

Sorry took her arm above the elbow as they walked through the car park.

'I don't want to *feel* too much,' he complained restlessly, more to himself than to her, but then pausing as if expecting an answer.

'It's not a thing you can choose about,' Laura said, thinking ahead to Jacko all the time.

'But I'm not like you,' Sorry said. 'You're part of a true family you *have* to love, I suppose. I mean, you just *do* love them, and that's it for you. But I need to choose, just out of ordinary self-defence.'

'So?'

'So it's more risky not to feel than I thought. I think it leaves a dangerous space. Nature hates a vacuum.'

'You'd never, ever turn into anything like him,' Laura said scornfully.

'He began somewhere,' Sorry answered. 'He wasn't always like that. He was a baby and a boy and a man, and in the beginning he probably didn't seem very different from ordinary people. Somewhere along the line he made a wrong decision – I just know it.'

'I'll bet he was an absolutely horrible baby,' Laura said, as they went between restrained flowerbeds to the main hospital door. The sun shone down on her. The lawn was springy under her feet. She felt, with vague surprise, that she was totally alive. Each fingernail, each hair on her head, seemed to be enjoying something in its own right, not simply as a piece of Laura with no existence apart from hers. She smiled at her own thoughts, just as Sorry remarked in a puzzled voice, 'It suits you, you know. You look terrific. Is all this giving you a bit of a buzz?'

Laura just shook her head, still smiling, standing on the first of the hospital steps, one step above Sorry. She turned and looked directly into his eyes, on a level with her own.

'I don't know,' she said. 'I'll tell you what, though. You can take down that poster in your room. Keep my photograph, I don't mind, but not pinned to the poster.' People came and went past them and he looked at her curiously, not so much shy as uncertain.

'What are you trying to remind me of?' he said, after a moment. 'I'll wait and see what happens. You might take off into the dim mists of the fourth form again when all this is over.'

'We're not dim,' Laura said indignantly. 'And how would you like it if I had a poster of a naked man and pinned your photo to it?' Sorry's expression became amused and slightly shamefaced.

'You can if you like,' he said. 'I'll even give you a photo.'

'I don't really want to,' Laura admitted stiffly. 'Anyhow my mother would never stop commenting if I did such a thing. It wouldn't be worth it.'

She was anxious to go, but she hesitated a moment longer and put her arms around Sorry and said, 'Thank you for helping me,' and felt, as she said them, that her words were quite inadequate.

'That's nice,' Sorry said. 'But don't look so tense. It's all right. You'll be fine. Jacko too!'

'How can you tell?' Laura asked, half-whispering.

'Because you'll *make* it come right, won't you?' he answered, in a low, intent voice. 'Your b-brother will catch survival from you. You know what you are, Chant, you're a born s-survivor.' He struggled with the last word as if it were in a foreign language, but it was the sudden feeling that was difficult for him to cope with.

'You too!' Laura told him, setting him free and retreating up the hospital steps.

'Isn't that the Lord's t-truth,' Sorry said, smiling, mocking his own intensity as he turned away towards the car park.

'Keep in touch,' he called across the widening space. Laura did not stay to watch him go, but went in at the hospital door, and gave her name at the reception desk, wondering briefly how she could have hugged a male prefect so easily, and what it would be like watching him read notices at assembly next week at school.

She reached the waiting room at last, moving past screens and a notice commanding silence. It was next to the room where Jacko lay, precious and irreplaceable, but no longer a simple child. He was a medical puzzle, a hesitant pulse, an unreliable breath, an irregular electric pattern on a little screen. But if she, Laura, could make Carmody Braque fall on his knees, she could surely find and reverse the flow of life he was draining from Jacko. The waiting room was not empty. Her father and Kate were both there, talking to a doctor. There were bright cushions on the chairs and an attempt had been made to make the little room cheerful, although those who waited there could only be anticipating despair.

'He was drifting right away,' the doctor was saying, 'but his heart beat has picked up again. He's a remarkable child to stand all this. I can't say that he's any better, but he's not worse. It's progress of a sort.' Kate saw Laura come in but did not say anything until the doctor had gone, and then she cried her name with bewildered relief.

'We've been trying to get in touch with you. They said you'd gone out with Sorry Carlisle on his motorbike.' Kate sounded both hurt and puzzled, but Laura could not explain. They exchanged a troubled glance, each recognizing something new in the other, knowing it was the wrong time to ask questions.

'Hello, Baa-lamb!' said Stephen in a kind, tired voice. 'Everytime I see you you look bigger and older and prettier than before.'

'Each time you see me I am,' said Laura a little cautiously, for she did not want to love him as much as she had once loved him, and his expression seemed to be inviting the old love back. She hugged Kate first.

'How's Jacko?' she asked, and felt her new strength falter before Kate, who was neither tearful nor distraught, but somehow without hope.

'Laura dear, the doctor doesn't think Jacko will live through the day,' she said. 'He was terribly ill early this morning. Chris has taken a few days' annual leave which was owing him, and Mr Bradley's showing him the routines of the shop. He's filling in for me, bless him, so that I can stay with Jacko until – for as long as I need to.'

'I don't think he'll die,' Laura said, but doubt had seized her at once. Her victory of less than an hour ago seemed like a fairy tale invented so that she could delay her own acceptance of a terrible reality. However, Sorry had said she was a survivor.

'I just don't believe it,' she said. 'I think he'll get better.' Kate closed her eyes as if she were controlling an intense inner pain.

'You don't understand,' she said. 'He's too weak to stand up to those convulsions any more. I think I knew when he had that first attack that he was going to die.'

She was cool and pale and tired and worn. Laura felt guilty about the rosy gold that was flooding through her at that very moment, for she thought that, in spite of eyes red from lack of sleep and old tears, in spite of the lines of thirty-five mixed years, Kate looked more wonderful than she herself could ever look, worn down and yet somehow noble, and Laura, who had often envied Kate her prettiness, yearned for something of this nobility. She also understood that her own heightened appearance hurt Kate, but only time could put the misunderstanding right. She could not explain that she had made herself shine with power because of Jacko, and not in spite of him.

'Am I allowed to sit with him?' she asked.

'We both will,' said Kate.

'We all will,' Stephen declared, but, as it happened, Stephen could not do this for long.

Jacko, in his hospital nest, looked dead already. Kate sat beside him quite calmly, wrapped in her own thoughts, but after a little while Stephen said, in a humble voice for such a confident man, that he could not stand it. As if the thought had shifted from his head to her own, Laura understood he feared not only for Jacko but for his new child coming into a dangerous world where both wickedness and blind chance might make you lose what you loved most for no real reason at all.

'I'll be back later,' he said. 'I really will.'

Kate nodded and smiled. But Laura sat very, very still and, with the patience of someone mapping by night an archipelago of tiny crowded islands, began to search for her brother.

At first Laura stared out in to the room, but with her truest gaze she looked back into her own head, not into the forests, mountains and caves of the previous evening but into a simple darkness. Nothing happened. She made herself as aware, as sensitive as she could, and sifted through the blackness until at last something moved. Suddenly Carmody Braque himself was with her, shouting that he was draining away, bombarding her with pleading, promises and abuse. His complaints fluttered around her like horrid, blighted birds, wailing and demanding so vociferously that she was dazed for a moment. Then a calm bead of light rose up out of the night and gave her something else to think about, for she had the unconscious support and companionship of Kate. If she opened her eyes she could see her mother on the other side of the bed, leaning forward towards Jacko, quite still and apparently reflective, thinking of the first time she had held Jacko and had fed him, remembering his nose pressed into her breast. Unbound, his new, creased hands had made gentle swooping gestures in the air as if he were inventing a dance. Laura's mind was so mixed with Kate's that the memory seemed entirely her own. Then Sorry crossed a corner of her thoughts in an uneasy flare of colour. She felt the ghost of last night's kiss, not the clever one of Changeover country, but the soft, heavy, unpractised one he had given her when his mother and grandmother were watching. It had reminded her of Jacko at the time, and now, through the association, she found Jacko himself, faint and frail, but unmistakable, a dwindled thread of brightness. She felt how he had closed down – how he had sealed, Sorry would have said – against the assaults of Mr Braque. There was almost nothing left.

'Jacko!' she said in a friendly, sensible voice, speaking as if he had locked himself into the bathroom at home and must now be talked into undoing the bolt and letting himself out, 'Jacko – it's me. It's Lolly.' There was no response. 'You can let me in. It's all right now! It's over!'

Carmody Braque beat against her, desperate to share the vitality with which she had begun to sustain her little brother, but Laura defended herself against him, and Jacko's frail light brightened a little. As he absorbed her love and energy, Laura opened her eyes, looked across at Kate, and smiled tentatively, but Kate did not smile back. Like Jacko, she had sealed herself, but into a powerful tranquility during which she looked at

Jacko as if she would build him back in to her and contain him safely. Shutting out this distraction by closing her eyes once more, Laura began again.

'Jacko – it's Lolly. Listen, Jacko, you've been a good boy, a wonderful boy, but you can come out now. You can let go. The wicked wolf is gone and the little pig can come out of his brick house and play.'

'What about me?' screamed Carmody Braque, fretting at the edge of her concentration. 'You can't mean to . . . you can't intend me to . . .' Laura shut herself away from him. 'Bitch! Bitch!' yelled his fading voice. 'Listen to me . . . listen . . .' He was gone again.

'Jacko!' she said. 'Would you like Ruggie?' There was a faint unfolding, a tiny brightening of assent. 'Well, listen carefully. You're safe in bed. You're in a hospital, so that shows you how important you are. You've got a locker all to yourself with a jug of orange-juice on it. Mummy is on one side of the bed and I'm on the other and Ruggie is in the locker waiting for you to wake up. Rosebud's there too, I think. They're lonely without you, so hurry up and come back, Jacko. They miss you. We all miss you. See if you can't come back a little bit more.' There was a further unfolding, nervous but definite.

'Lolly?' It was a lost echo rather than a real voice.

'Yes, it's Lolly. I promise it's me,' she said. 'Just you come towards me, Jacko.' She reached out to him with her strange power and felt him turn towards her as if she were a source of light in the darkness. But suddenly Carmody Braque was with her again, not fretting outside any more but coming at her directly through Jacko. Laura was seized by an emotion which had no name but was made up of fury and joy, quite indistinguishably smudged into each other. She met her enemy in the strengthening citadel of her brother, and he gave way before her. She engulfed and dissolved his mark, comforted Jacko with promises of stories, family meals with F. & C., all the strong, happy routines of everyday life, and as she did this she felt the psychical injury, which the mark had symbolized, heal, and knew that Jacko was safe from Carmody Braque for always. As this certainty established itself, she also felt Jacko alter in some way, felt him relax as if relieved of a persistent pain. Filled with passionate gratitude, she imagined herself as a torrent of fierce gold and let herself flood through him, giving him as much of herself as he could hold.

'Come on, Jacko,' she lured him back to the world. 'Everything's waiting. No show without Punch, you know.'

A voice spoke and it took her a moment to realize it was speaking in the outside room.

'Laura – wake up!' Kate was saying. 'Oh Laura, something's happening.'

Laura's heart was wrung by Kate's voice filled with dread rather than hope. She was panting a little as if she had run a long way. Laura could give her no convincing reassurance. Yet something was indeed happening. Jacko's eyes had opened and he was staring into the air with the newly-born look, grave and unfocused, that Kate remembered noticing in his first hours.

'It's all right!' Laura declared. 'Mum, I promise it's all right. He's getting better, that's all.'

'Go and get Dr Hayden,' Kate commanded. 'I don't know where he is, but someone will tell you. He's the nicest doctor. Or get the nurse. I don't want to leave Jacko.'

Jacko's eyes moved at the sound of her voice and found Kate, at last. At first it was hard to tell if he saw her. Then his mouth moved. He was trying to smile.

'Jacko! Jacko darling!' Kate murmured, in a voice beginning to quaver.

Laura left them and went looking for the doctor. 'What about *me*?' wailed Carmody Braque, fluttering with dreary persistence on the edge of her attention. Laura stood still, smiling. Her curving lips were closed, her eyes narrow. 'Too bad about you!' she replied, speaking aloud to the empty corridor, and her voice slid ahead of her along the immaculate white walls, slipping like a serpent across the glossy floor. 'Your turn now! Your turn Mr Carmody Bloody Braque.'

Around the corner came a tall, white figure, the very nurse she was looking for, actually on her way to check up on Jacko and his failing condition.

The nurse and Laura came back into the room to find Jacko still awake staring at Kate and holding his Ruggie which she had taken from his hospital locker.

'He said he wanted it.' Kate sounded completely distracted by now. 'He's trying to suck his thumb but I didn't like to let him with that tube in his arm.'

Shortly after, Jacko's eyes closed, but he had simply gone to sleep. The waxy stillness had quite gone from his face. He looked pale and worn but very much alive.

'Oh Lolly!' Kate said a little later. 'If only Jacko recovers!'

'Of course he'll recover,' Laura said. 'He was looking at you and smiling. It's a long time since he was able to do that.'

'Last Friday,' Kate remembered. 'Imagine, no smile from Jacko since Friday. It feels like years of real time. And as for you – you've changed, too. What have you done to yourself? I noticed, but I'm only just feeling reasonable enough to wonder about it. Is it that boy? What a time to start taking an interest in boys!'

Laura opened her mouth to reply, but Kate was too quick for her. 'Don't tell me. You didn't choose the time, the time chose you. But Sorry Carlisle's a bit ambitious isn't he, and how did he happen along in the first place?'

'I'll tell you later,' Laura said. 'It's too long to tell now,' and Kate was still too distracted by Jacko to insist on being told.

Later, the doctor talked to Stephen and Kate. 'It's too soon to say just how much of an improvement there is,' he said. 'But I must say there has been quite a dramatic alteration, and the really perplexing thing is I still can't tell you why. I'd love to be certain that it was something we did, but I can't, and even if it was, I can't be sure just *what* it was. His heart is a lot stronger – that's the main thing. There's still a bit of dehydration in spite of all we did to prevent it, but it's not critical. We'll just have to wait and see. At the moment all the signs are good.'

Laura found she was so tired the world went dim and quavering around her. She thought she might go to sleep standing.

'Laura,' Kate said, 'you look worn out. Worse than I do. Go back to the motel with Stephen. Have a good meal and a good night's sleep. Don't worry about me! I'll ring Chris as soon as I can and he'll come round and sit with me.'

Although she was arranging Laura's life so coolly, Kate looked very wild herself once again. Laura recognized in her pins and needles of frantic hope, as necessary but as agonizing as blood running into a numbed leg once more. She put her arms around Kate as if she were the protecting one, and then let her father lead her out to the car. There was no mistaking his pleasure – his passionate gratitude over Jacko's improvement – and Laura found herself forgiving him for that day of warnings long ago in the past, when she had come home to find all his favourite things gone and the house empty of his presence as if he had cut himself entirely out of her life and taken part of her with him. It no longer seemed to matter that he had loved someone else more than he had loved her or loved Kate, and in a way she felt, that, like Jacko, she had begun to recover from a secret illness no one had ever completely recognized or been able to cure.

12

Shoes Full of Leaves

Kate stayed at the hospital. Laura went to the motel with her father and Julia where, rather to her surprise, she enjoyed herself very much. She even enjoyed Julia's company for she could feel very distinctly how anxious Julia was to get on with her and how delighted she was at Jacko's recovery, partly because she was naturally glad to hear that a sick child was likely to become well again, and partly because it would set Stephen free from his previous family to belong entirely to her once again. Deep down Laura knew, perhaps better than Julia herself, that Julia had had a small fantasy in which Jacko died and that her own new baby was a boy, making her more important than ever to Stephen because she was the mother of his son. But she abandoned this secret dream without regret, hardly even knowing she had had it. Laura, astonished at the skill with which she detected it, was also astonished that she did not resent it more. Perhaps it was so remarkable to find Julia frightened that Stephen did not love her enough that there was no energy to waste on resentment. Laura thought she would never feel angry with any person again except one, and against that one she planned to turn the full force of all the fury she had ever felt.

In the morning there was a phone call from Kate to say that Jacko was still showing great improvement. Laura set off for school enjoying the magnificence of her father's car and a feeling of elation that seemed to run with her blood, pumping through her heart and out along the branching paths of her body.

'There's something going on,' Stephen said, looking ahead to a small crowd round the school gates. 'I can't think why Kate lets you go to a school like this one. I'm sure they'd take a bright girl like you in a better area.'

Laura could not be bothered reminding her father about such things as money and the difficulties of transport. She saw that the prefect at the gate arguing with some recalcitrant pupil was Sorry himself and felt the same odd lurch inside her that she had felt for the first time by the estuary on Sunday morning, and again the night before last when they had kissed in the presence of Winter and Miryam. Filled with a wonderful apprehension and excitement, she watched him for a full second before she realized that he was not arguing with a pupil but with Carmody Braque.

'I'll get out here,' she said to Stephen. 'Don't drive into that crowd. Sometimes boys try to bang on the cars as they go by.'

Stephen certainly did not want his car banged on. He drew into the side of the road. 'Have a nice day,' he said. 'And Baa-lamb, just while we're on our own for a moment – when all this is over, and supposing Jacko is safe and well again, how about coming north for Christmas? We'd love to have you.'

'Wouldn't it be better if I waited until after the baby's born?' Laura said. 'It will be a half-sister or brother and I ought to meet it.' She had started off trying to be generous to her father, but by the end of her sentence she found herself speaking a new truth. With her long anger against her father dissolving, and Jacko restored and recovering, she was prepared to be interested in a new brother or sister . . . one that would come after Jacko, not one replacing him. She even felt a little sorry for it in a kindly way, because, though it would have many advantages, like a family car that went without pushing, it would not have the adventurous life that she had in Gardendale.

Stephen let her out of the car and she waved goodbye, feeling like a good witch, but in the very act of turning to face the school gate her expression changed and with it her immediate vision of herself and her purpose.

'I shall complain to the principal,' Carmody Braque was shouting. 'I shall let him know just how uncooperative you have been.'

'His office is in the big block there,' Sorry answered, pointing. 'If you hurry you'll have time before assembly. Go on, you kids, beat it!' he added to a group of third formers standing by their bikes, watching the scene with interest. 'It's just some poor old nutter raving on.'

Some of the children moved reluctantly into school. Others proved unwilling to leave such lively entertainment.

'I know about you,' Carmody Braque shouted at Sorry. 'You and that girl! I shall let the authorities know, too, make no mistake about that.'

Laura was quite close to them by now. Sorry glanced over at the lingering group of children watching from a little distance.

'Don't you shake your finger at me,' he said in a low voice to Mr Braque. 'You're starting to look as if it might drop off.' As he spoke he was suddenly aware of Laura and turned his head. Carmody Braque turned, too, then spun around to face her, automatically holding his hand out, palm upward, in the attitude of someone asking for money. His hand was black as if the entire palm had begun to decay. Other discoloured blotches showed clearly on his skin, crawling over him like mould. His face had fallen back around his teeth once more and he grinned with the most dreadful anxiety.

'My dear,' he began, 'let's be reasonable . . .' and his voice sounded thick and muffled, choked with darkness and old time. His downfall was faster than Jacko's, and the knowledge of this, and of the heavy centuries waiting to fall on him, was the source of his panic. Over the years, thought Laura, he had gone from one quiet but horrible victory to another without opposition and had built up no ability to cope with any reversal, and here he was now, almost on his knees again before her, looking, for the first time, less than immaculate in yesterday's clothes.

Laura was glad to see him so desperate and reduced. She felt enormously strong as she suddenly became aware of the full extent of her power over him. She could make him fall down fainting at her feet, could make him last for days, weeks, even months. No one would suspect her of anything, for everyone at school knew just how ordinary she was, and from behind this ordinariness she was free to be infinitely revenged on someone who had invited her vengeance. On other occasions people she loved had hurt her savagely, but she knew they had to be forgiven because she herself hoped to be forgiven, too. It was part of a human agreement. But Carmody Braque was not human and could be punished for his wickedness. With her commands exploding in his mind he would howl like a dog, fling himself in front of the earth-moving machinery, bite pieces out of his own arm or tear off his clothes and dance naked outside the school gate, and all people would think was that he had gone mad. But even taken to a hospital and cared for by doctors, he would never, never escape her revenge. Laura was offered a unique chance to discharge her own burden of human anguish and to strike at the powers of darkness, and no one would know. So now she sent a crisp command to him, and, like a man who finds a rope tightening under his very feet, Carmody Braque sprawled before her. The first bell rang out over the playground like a huge alarm clock going off.

'What's going on?' she asked aloud, staring down at the fallen enemy and then up into the face of Sorry Carlisle, watching her from the school gate.

'Some old joker's gone round the twist,' a boy shouted.

'Yeah, he's been at Carlisle to tell him where you live,' said another. Sorry said nothing, merely looking at her with an arrested curiosity, half smiling, half wary.

'Me?' Laura cried, stepping over Carmody Braque. 'Why me?' She turned to watch as he picked himself up and retreated towards his car, wheezing and snuffling as he went.

'Everyone in! Didn't you hear first b-bell?' said Sorry with a trace of his stammer coming into his voice. He walked beside her up the concrete path that skirted the rugby field.

'Very heavy, Chant!' his light voice said, a little above her ear. 'Are you playing with your mouse a bit?'

'I want him to suffer,' Laura said. 'Jacko did. Kate did. I did. He's coming to bits anyway, isn't he?'

'You're enjoying it, aren't you?' Sorry said, without either criticism or rancour. 'I suppose that's the balance of having a heart. Perhaps I had guessed that when I decided to give mine up.' They moved across the concreted area in front of the school towards the main doors.

'I don't think it's possible to be cruel to something like him,' Laura said defensively, surprised to find herself made uneasy by the school uniform walking beside her with its seventh form blazer and prefect's badge. Somewhere behind it was the body against which she had pressed her own yesterday and which she had felt answer her embrace immediately and more generously than its owner might have wished. For a moment his face looked as if his true name was the one Chris Holly had accidentally given him – the name of Sorrow.

'I don't know what I think about power,' Sorry said at last. 'Mostly I want to go unseen. Of course, at home in my own room – that's different. Outside, well – I'd rather knit the world up than tear it apart. Knowing you is making me very jumpy, Chant, because you're making me confess to myself that I'm more set about with ideals than I ever wanted to be.'

'He's not a real person, Mr Braque isn't,' Laura said as they prepared to go their separate ways. 'He's an awful idea that's got itself a body it shouldn't have.'

'But you're real,' Sorry answered. 'It's not him I'm thinking about. It's you. It's easy for me to recognize what you're up to because I've thought of it myself sometimes – being merciless, being cruel, really. But . . .' His voice trailed away. 'I've got to go.'

'But what?' asked Laura.

'You know!' Sorry said, walking backwards for a few steps, as he moved away from her. 'There are always two people involved in cruelty, aren't there? One to be vicious and someone to suffer! And what's the use of getting rid of – of wickedness, say – in the outside world if you let it creep back into things from inside you?'

'It's justice, not cruelty,' Laura cried. 'Justice! I don't want to talk about it any more. Go away!'

'How's Jacko?' Sorry said, turning and then speaking over his shoulder.

'Getting better,' Laura shouted across the widening space between them.

'Hey – you didn't tell me you liked *him*,' said Nicky, materializing at her elbow.

'I don't,' Laura answered shortly.

'Oh sure!' Nicky said. 'Who do you think you're trying to fool?'

Laura sat in class and thought about Mr Braque and the various things Sorry had said, wondering if it was true that cruelty was the balance of a loving heart. She thought of Kate's tears, her own grief and Jacko shrivelling in his own bed. She thought of Sorry saying that cruelty took someone to suffer and someone to be vicious as if the act was the result of a collusion. A friend of Kate's had recently had a new baby and had given her older child a big, floppy doll with instructions that, if ever he felt jealous of the new baby, he was to punish the doll which could not feel. On a recent visit Laura had watched with consternation as the child punished the doll. 'I'm allowed to do this,' he said, hitting it, less, Laura felt, out of jealousy for the new baby, than because he had been given a chance to be infinitely cruel to something infinitely yielding. To Laura, the doll with its button eyes had been a feeling thing – the face had given it, at least, the appearance of feeling. She wondered if Sorry saw her in the same way as she had seen that child. Given the chance to be cruel did you get cruelty out of your system by acting on the chance, or did you invite it in?

People knew she was special today because her brother was so very ill. She was allowed to use the office phone to ring the hospital and check on Jacko's progress. He was continuing to improve.

'Medical science is baffled,' she reported to Nicky.

'Serve it right,' said Nicky. 'My mother says doctors don't really have a clue.'

'Ours has been nice,' Laura said, watching Sorry across the playground talking to Carol Bright again. All the disadvantages of being married without the advantages, she thought. She was free to be jealous, but somehow not free, at school, to go and sit with him in the way Carol was doing. But she had power over him. She watched him, and after a moment he turned his silver eyes restlessly to look at her while he continued to talk to Carol. He looked reduced and flatter, less significant than he had at home, more ordinary than he had looked to her at school last week. She looked through Nicky's notes of yesterday which she needed to copy. Out by the gate she could see Carmody Braque's black car parked and waiting for her to show herself. After the first bell, to mark the end of the lunch hour, she ran to the prefect's room and asked to speak to Sorry. This brought a certain amount of derisive and even ribald comment from within.

'What's the matter, Chant?' he asked.

'Do you really think I'm being cruel?' she asked abruptly. 'And don't you think he deserves it?'

'I don't think that's the point,' Sorry said, looking around rather furtively, but they were alone in the school passage surrounded by the faint smell of disinfectant and floor polish from the cleaner's cupboard. 'I suppose he was a real man once but he got stuck, and maybe what caught him was the same sort of choice that you've got. I don't know, but the thought of it scares me because after all, trying not to feel anything ever again is a way of sticking, too.'

'Could you take a message to him?' she asked. 'He's still out there. Tell him I'll meet him at the main gate of the Reserve. I'd go myself but I don't even want to talk to him.'

'All right,' Sorry said after a moment. 'Can I lend other support? Moral or otherwise?'

'I'll do this bit alone,' Laura said. 'Thank you very much,' she added stiffly.

'You're entirely welcome,' he replied. 'Let me know how you get on.'

'What shall I do?' Laura asked.

Sorry turned back to her. 'You've got to end him, close him off, haven't you? I don't think you're faced with any real person, just a – I don't know – a collection of appetities, say, that have managed to stay on out of their time and place. He's a sort of virus of the emotions, just managing to hold himself together.'

'Maybe if I tell him very firmly . . .' Laura hesitated.

'Try it!' Sorry agreed. 'Tell him he's already dead. Tell him in a completely confident voice. You know how. You can be really severe when you want to. But be quick or he might just wriggle away.'

'He can't. I've got him!' Laura cried.

'He thought he had Jacko,' Sorry pointed out.

'I'll try then,' said Laura and began to walk away.

'Chant!' Sorry called after her. 'I took that poster down.'

She hesitated, but did not look back again.

After school Laura did not go home the usual way. There was no reason why she should. Mrs Fangboner's house had no Jacko in it. Mrs Fangboner herself had sent grapes to the hospital (and very expensive ones, too) and had telephoned to find out how Jacko was getting on. Kate and Laura had eaten her grapes and now Laura felt she was not entitled to make fun of her any more. In the Mall the bookshop was still open, but the assistant behind the counter was Chris Holly, and from Wednesday he would be replaced by a cousin of

Mr Bradley. It was strange to think that, if for any reason she and Kate vanished, the Gardendale Shopping Complex would barely notice their absence. Instead of turning towards this familiar area, which Laura sometimes felt to be an extended back yard of the house in Kingsford Drive, she turned towards the Gardendale Reserve.

She was not thinking of Mr Braque directly but about Stephen and Julia, Kate and Chris, letting them tumble over and over in her mind, as if she were watching them through the round, glass window found in the doors of certain washing machines. She thought about the tendency the world had to form pairs and then shake every one up like dice and encourage them to fall into new arrangements. She thought about love and sex and wondered which one came first and if there was much difference between them in the long run. Were they separate but interchangeable, or did they run into each other? Many people spoke of sex as if it were rather unfortunate but could not be avoided. Some people, like Mrs Fangboner, complete with a husband and children, never mentioned sex, but did not hesitate to discuss her digestion and its troubles which seemed every bit as personal. Kate believed in true love which Laura should wait to attain, yet true love had brought Kate unhappiness, and she herself had turned to a man she had known for only two days for consolation and escape. Somewhere, she thought, there must be a single, unifying principle that would make sense of all this rich variety, and would explain, too, why suddenly the sight of Sorry standing at the school gate that morning had filled her with a soft electricity, exciting but not totally amiable. Laura clasped her arms across her breast as she walked, but whether she was protecting herself, rehearsing an embrace, or holding some memory close to her, she could not tell. Reluctantly she must now think of Mr Braque whose car stood outside the Reserve gates.

He was out of it before she came up to him, holding out his hand. He snarled at her like a cat confronted with a particularly unnatural dog, but when he spoke it was to beg.

'Please . . .' he said. 'Please . . .'

Laura, who had started the day highly elated, now found she could feel very little. It was as if all the tension had gone out of her feeling. The thought of behaving wickedly to Carmody Braque had had its own excitement, but now her heart was full of nothing but insubstantial ghosts of horror, hope, love, fear and hatred, all grown thin, with no power to move her. She knew, as she looked at him, that Carmody Braque was horrifying but she could not be horrified. His ancient substance was breached and he could not heal himself. Terrified and furious, he was seeping into extinction and all she could feel was a weary almost absentminded distaste, nothing like the shrinking horror his first and less desperate appearance had aroused in her. He could not seal as Jacko had sealed. One of the dark patches on his face had burst into bubbling sores.

His clothes, bought perhaps in the pleasant expectation of a continued, virile existence, hung on him, loose and dirty, his teeth had become a neglected goblin cemetery. Catching her eye, his smile stretched itself wide with anxiety. Behind him the Gardendale Reserve stood with its rather grimly determined commitment to recreation. It was land which had been held in the original subdivision and bulldozed flat for tennis courts, grounds for netball, cricket, rugby and soccer. There was a track around it where people went jogging. But from the gateway a short, paved path led to a memorial for a civic-minded councillor who had died while the Reserve was being bulldozed, and it was for this that Laura headed, with Mr Braque sidling and querulous, coming behind, alternately abusing her and supplicating. In the distance a man on a mowing-machine looked strangely archaic, as if he were driving some sort of mechanical chariot, and a team of miniscule marching girls stepped in fairly straight lines, moving and gesturing to blasts of their instructor's whistle. Laura turned at last to face Carmody Braque.

'Go back!' she said abruptly.

'Go back?' he cried. 'Go back? You've made me walk all this way and now you tell me . . .'

'Listen,' said Laura. 'You're already dead. Admit it. You're just left-over bits and not the best bits either.' She made her voice as severe as she could. 'Stop pretending to be human. Be what you truly are.'

'Oh, no!' screamed Mr Braque. 'No . . . I was invited . . . I was called in . . .'

'I'm uninviting you,' Laura said. 'You've overstayed your welcome. OK? I was going to punish you slowly, but Sorry Carlisle says it might not be good for me. So go back and let's get it over and done with.'

As if her words had an immediate force, running like a disintegrating shock through the figure so barely held together, stretched thin by many, many years of ignoble survival, something horrifying began to happen to Carmody Braque. His voice was raised in shrill, whining expostulation.

'Oh, don't make me – if only you knew – if only you knew . . . I fell in love with the idea of human sensation, you see. I couldn't, no I couldn't give it up. And, you can't imagine, you take it all for granted – it's yours by right so you never think: the pleasures of touch and taste. Your skin alone – your skin affords you such – *rapture!*' cried Mr Braque, clawing at her. What remained of his face twitched all over, a tiny, violent quivering as if he had just been killed. 'To eat a peach, picked straight from the tree and warmed by the autumn sun, to bite a crisp apple – the first juice – a revelation – or to feel the sun on bare skin. Salt! Salt!' cried Mr Braque writhing, 'Salt on a fresh-laid egg, boiled for four minutes, or to lick fresh, human sweat.' His face was slipping to bits, the right side rather more quickly than the left. His voice wavered, as if it were being played at the wrong speed.

'Go back!' Laura whispered, trying to look away. 'You're not going to do to anyone again what you did to Jacko – never!' But she could not take her eyes from her victim. She forced her gaze into ruthlessness and used it as a goad to drive Mr Braque back toward his beginning, murmuring his despairing catalogue of sensual pleasures. His face changed and changed again and bits of many faces looked out of it – men, women and little children, all of whom had taken various pleasures in being alive, and had fallen victim to the ravenous spirit pleading before her.

'Let me feel – let me go on feeling . . .' Mr Braque pleaded. His voice grew more bubbling. 'Let me . . .' he said, and choked. His protruding tongue was now quite black and round, a parrot's tongue in a man's mouth. His mouth did not close properly again, as if the jaw had begun to dislocate, and his voice squealed on, increasingly incoherent. 'To feel . . . to feeeel . . .'

But Laura had feelings as part of her human right and did not need to steal other people's. 'Feel . . .' said the hateful voice grown thick and churning, and Laura could only tell what was said because of what had been said before, and he continued to change back through the centuries of stolen life until his clothes collapsed around what at first appeared to be a rotting, heaving mass which lay still, at last, and was nothing but dead leaves.

Mr Braque's clothes, which had recently looked grubby and limp on him, looked immaculate again when folded around the leaves – extended more or less in the shape of a man, a little damp, smelling of melancholy, but in the end not in the least horrible. Laura sat down beside them. She looked up at the sky which had nothing to say to her . . . it just went on being blue in its implacable fashion.

She thought she would never move again but would sit there until she turned to stone and became part of the monument. Jacko was saved. Her enemy was gone. She had come to a stop at last. Laura felt wet all over and looked up with surprise although she knew the sky overhead was clear and there was no rain. She was dripping with perspiration, and very cold inside her head. A moment later she realized that the cold actually belonged to the stone against which her head was leaning. She was grateful for the discomfort which brought her back to life. A school shoe came into her line of vision.

'There, you see . . .' said Sorry's voice. 'I couldn't keep away. Forget him and come away with me. It's nothing horrible, is it? Only dead leaves!' As he spoke he was feeling gingerly in the pocket of the jacket on the ground.

'What are you looking for?' Laura asked.

'Car keys!' he said. 'If I leave the keys in his car there's a good chance that someone will steal it and drive it away. It's not impossible, and the more confused things are, the better for us. Why did you come here, of all places? It's so public you could have sold tickets.'

'But it's the loneliest place I know,' Laura said at last, in a puzzled voice. 'On week days there's great spaces and nowhere for anyone to creep up behind you.' The marching girls in the distance formed fours and saluted an imaginary dignitary. The mowing-machine clattered savagely.

'It's certainly surrealistic,' Sorry said, beginning to move back towards the road.

'Don't let anyone see you at the car,' Laura warned him.

'School prefect arrested for car conversion,' sighed Sorry, turning it into a newspaper headline. He walked across the grass to the bushes and trees that had been planted around the Reserve. Laura watched him and then blinked as he vanished. Five minutes later he reappeared, laughing. 'The marching girls might think I went in there for a pee if they happen to be glancing this way,' he said. 'There's an old bloke in there with a bottle of wine – two bottles, I think. When I reappeared he said to one of his bottles, 'Don't worry, Dorothy. It's just the good witch of the North.' Who'd have thought that any one who'd read *The Wizard of Oz* would wind up as a wino in the Gardendale Reserve!'

'Perhaps he just saw the picture,' Laura said, and Sorry laughed.

'It's over, Chant!' he said. Laura nodded, but did not move. Sorry squatted down in front of her.

'Chant?' he said. 'Didn't your mother ever tell you you get piles from sitting on cold concrete? Don't go all limp now! Get up. Be a man!'

'I can be just as good not being one,' Laura said, but she was glad to have an order to follow at that moment. She stood up beside him.

'It's over,' he repeated. 'All over!' and stared down at the shoes, worn to match particular feet and a particular way of walking and now filled with dead leaves. For the second time that day he looked as if his true name was Sorrow. Then he laughed, hooked her arm through his and led her down the narrow path back towards the road.

'Come back to my place,' he tempted her. 'I'll show you that space on my wall and make you a cup of – I don't know . . .' He looked around vaguely. 'Of cocoa, perhaps. That sounds homely and comforting. Don't look so deadly. You've won. Jacko's getting better, the bad spirits are flown and I think you've got beautiful legs. What more could you ask for?'

Laura began to cry. She was puzzled by her own tears, for she was not feeling unhappy. Still, it seemed she had been saving them up for a long time and had to spend them freely at last. Once begun they would not stop coming. She trembled as if she was cold with a chill or burning with a fever. Her tears fell on and on like warm rain. Sorry looked at her with dismay.

'Here, no crying!' he said. 'I can't stand crying.'

'I know!' Laura agreed, weeping generously. 'All the disadvantages of being married and . . .'

But Sorry turned on her abruptly. 'Shut up, will you?' he exclaimed. 'I say stupid things at times. Don't bother remembering them! It's just that tears are catching.'

They were almost on the road, crossing the narrow belt of shrubs and trees that ran around the recreation ground.

'Come in here for a moment!' he said. 'Not that side! The old wino's in there.' In the shadow of the summer leaves he began to kiss first her wet cheeks and then her mouth so that she tasted her own salt tears on him. 'Go on – put your arms around me,' he told her. 'There – you hold me tight and I'll do the same for you. Forget Mr Braque – forget Jacko even – just think about this, Laura . . . Laura . . .'

'I wasn't even sure you knew my first name,' Laura said at last.

'I save it for best,' he told her, looking thoughtfully around the narrow, green room of leaves within which they stood. 'We'd better go, though. Don't get me wrong, but I think you should go to bed for a little bit and sleep everything off.'

'I feel better than I did,' Laura said. She half wanted Sorry to kiss her again.

Later, Laura woke up lying on the old settee in Sorry's study, a patchwork cushion under her cheek, and a rug over her. Sorry sat, not at his desk but beside her, doing some unspecified homework. Laura watched his hand move over the paper. It was brown and slightly angular and had a smear of grease from the Vespa across the back.

Sorry wrote steadily on, then suddenly said, without looking at her, 'Chant, I rang your mother and either she or your father will be along to relocate you soon. She sounded very suspicious, I must say. Maybe you'd better start waking up and putting your shoes on. No sense in behaving impeccably and not getting the credit for it, is there?'

'Is it dark?' asked Laura.

'Twilight only,' Sorry said. 'Summer twilight, and I'm deep into parliamentary development under the Stuarts. Exams for me soon. Bursary exams and the end of school. It's quite a remarkable thought.'

Out in the Reserve, unseen by either of them, a breeze blew around the base of the memorial to Councillor Carroll and set a few leaves scudding before it. The old man who had been observed by Sorry earlier, having drunk his wine and slept off some of its effects, picked himself up and began to go home. He was astonished to see a perfectly good suit of clothes lying on the edge of the paving around the memorial. He did not wonder why the shirt was inside the jacket and the shoes full of leaves. He gathered the clothes into a bundle and went on his way, ignoring a sudden gust that blew impotently against him, whining sadly as he stalked on through it and across the Reserve, laying a temporary trail of restless leaves behind him as he went.

13

Gooseberry Fool

'Here's Lolly,' cried Jacko, as Laura came across the lawn. He bounced across to her and Laura fell on her knees to meet him for he was like a large, bounding puppy, expecting to be welcomed all over.

'How's your mother?' asked Mrs Fangboner tolerantly, bringing Jacko's basket, Ruggie neatly folded, and Rosebud smiling on top of everything else. 'Getting on well with her new friend? I was round there the other day and he was cooking the dinner. That's nice, I thought. All home comforts.'

'He's a wonderful cook,' Laura said, exaggerating a little in order to irritate Mrs Fangboner. 'But we still have fish and chips on Thursday. Ready, Jacko?'

'I'm all ready, and Rosebud's all ready,' Jacko declared. 'Off we go with Sorry.'

'I see the Carlisle boy's got a car.' Mrs Fangboner directed a sharp glance over the hedge to where the curved top of the Volkswagon showed from the road beyond. 'All right to be some people, isn't it?' But her voice, though critical, was not unkind.

'It's his mother's,' Laura said. 'Now his exams are over, he's not going to school like the rest of us. He's doing work for the school community service, weeding old people's gardens, and things like that.'

She picked Jacko up, though he was quite able to walk by himself.

'You carry me and I carry Rosebud,' Jacko said. 'That's fair, isn't it, Lolly?'

They said goodbye to Mrs Fangboner and went out to the car. Sorry was reading the afternoon paper. Laura put Jacko's basket into the back seat beside her school pack.

'All right! Off we go!' cried Jacko, for Miryam's car had come to seem like another family car where he was allowed to give orders.

'Seat belts on!' Sorry said, and they moved off, driving through Gardendale in moderate glory.

'Nothing at all about our departed friend in the newspaper, these days,' Sorry said. 'He's vanished off the face of the earth. How baffling!' A few minutes later he drew up outside Laura's house. 'There you are. It's not so very far, is it?'

'It is if you have to walk with Jacko and carry a pack,' Laura replied. She looked at him doubtfully. 'Are you coming in?' Sorry was particularly colourful in an old, red shirt and blue jeans. He suddenly looked like a man and not a boy, and would look like a boy only once more in his entire life, when he put on his school uniform to attend the school break-up. In some ways he seemed a very different person from the one who, only six weeks ago, had pushed her against the wall in his study and touched her and asked her to invite him in, yet the memory of that occasion and of other less arrogant embraces lay constantly between them.

Something about the quality of the afternoon sunlight on his skin made Laura ask curiously, 'Do you shave?'

Sorry, passing Jacko's basket from the back seat, gave her an amused and vaguely puzzled glance as he replied, 'What do you think? I was a seventh former and old in my class, remember. Besides, how do you think I keep that satin finish?'

'It just seems strange,' explained Laura.

'Yes, it is strange,' Sorry agreed. 'However, one thing Winter and Miryam forget when they talk about feminine mystery is that being a man is very mysterious too, and I suppose shaving's part of it.'

'I'll shave when I'm grown up,' boasted Jacko, and ran his hand over his face, buzzing to himself. There had been a new morning sound in the house sometimes recently, the sound of Chris's electric razor, and Jacko had been very excited by it. Laura was filled with a sudden melancholy at the thought of Jacko shaving.

'Wouldn't it be nice to stay three for ever and ever?' she asked in a sentimental voice.

'He very nearly did,' Sorry replied ominously. 'Come on, Chant! Snap out of it! I'll carry your pack in.'

'I can carry it myself,' Laura declared immediately.

'I know you can,' said Sorry. 'But why not take advantage of me while I'm around. I'm not going to be here always. That's what I want to talk to you about.'

'You want me to make you a cup of tea and whip up a batch of scones,' Laura grumbled, as she and Jacko went up the path.

'And a fruit cake,' Sorry shouted after her. 'Let's indulge in a few traditional values while we've got the chance.'

Laura did make tea, and cheese sandwiches. The old, whistling kettle with its slow leak had gone. Chris had bought Kate a shiny electric kettle which made life simpler, though

Laura rather missed the frantic scream of the old one. When she entered the living room Sorry and Jacko were absorbed by a game on the floor. Laura put the pottery mugs down on the table, studying Jacko's soft, shining, golden-brown curls and Sorry's rougher, paler hair, bleached by the summer sun. Tonight, in his study, he would put on his black dressing-gown and his rings and become something different, a creature of the imagination, the enchanter of the dark tower, but either way he was a difficulty in her life, sometimes seeming to hurry her towards a conclusion when she wanted to go slowly, sometimes hesitating when she got impatient with mystery and wanted everything understood.

Now she saw with nervous pleasure that he had constructed a little farm on the carpet to entertain Jacko. His hands curved in the air, grassy hills grew under them, arched like the backs of green kittens as he stroked them into existence. There were little cows, little sheep, and pink and black pigs. There was a farmhouse with a flower garden in front of it and vegetables at the back, its cabbages the size of pin heads.

'Tell him it's not a toy,' Laura said rather anxiously. 'It's just a game, Jacko. It will melt away like an iceblock.' But she kneeled down beside Sorry and watched over his shoulder as he drew a line with his finger and set a little river flowing from one worn place on the carpet to another one where it vanished into the weave and soaked away to nothing.

'You've missed something out,' she said and leaned against his back as she stretched her own hand down to the river. An image formed in her mind and she let it flow through her, and take on its own reality in the farm. 'Pink crocodiles.'

Five or six pink crocodiles as long as darning needles basked on the river bank. Jacko flung up his arms, clasping them across his head with delight, but Laura and Sorry now became absolutely still, like people under a spell. She could feel the warmth of his skin against her own through her dress and his red shirt.

'I don't know,' said Sorry at last. 'It's *my* mother that ought to worry, not yours. I try to mean well, but you give me a hard time, Chant.' Jacko now went to get Rosebud so that he could show her the little crocodiles, and Sorry and Laura kissed each other behind his back.

'Did you make that cup of tea?' Sorry asked, and Laura gave him his tea and put the plate of sandwiches on the floor between them.

'Picnic!' said Jacko, and it really was rather like a picnic by the little farm on the carpet.

'Miryam and Winter have conned you a bit,' Sorry said. 'They've been a lot easier since you came along. Until a few weeks ago Miryam was sorry she'd given me away, Winter was sorry she'd ever let Miryam have a child to save their old farm . . .' He gestured at the farm on the floor between them.

'Aren't they still sorry?' Laura asked.

'Well, they think I've improved,' he said. 'I suppose they think there's hope for me, and that makes them happier. I saw Miryam looking at me this morning and she was almost complacent, instead of looking as if she had a dangerous pet on the end of a piece of rotten string.' He smiled to himself. 'I suppose I *have* kept them anxious on purpose, getting my own back, but suddenly I can't be bothered. It's like a dream of childhood. Yet only a few weeks ago I was quite certain I didn't want to feel fond of anyone ever again.'

'I didn't want to have anything to do with my father,' Laura told him, 'but I don't mind now.'

'Remember, I told you about the psychotherapist in Sydney?' Sorry asked. 'She told them I was severely alienated. I looked it up in a dictionary and it said 'estranged' and 'diverted to a different purpose'. Well, we're both alienated now, Chant. I'm estranged and you're diverted to a different purpose. They thought of me as a sort of – say an uncontrolled charge of electricity, and you as a way of earthing the charge – bringing it back into line.'

'What are you telling me all this for?' Laura said at last. 'I know it already.'

'I'm going away,' Sorry said. 'Not immediately, but soon – early in January. I've been chosen as a trainee for the Wildlife Division. They only take on five people every two years so I'm really lucky. I went along with my bird photographs and, well, I know a lot about birds, and I've done a bit of tramping, and the long and short of it is I'm in.'

Laura stared at him blankly. 'You're leaving me on my own?' she cried incredulously.

'On your own!' exclaimed Sorry. 'Yes, quite on your own, except for your mother, your mother's friend, your brother, my mother, my grandmother, your friend Sally, your friend Nicky, not to mention bloody Barry Hamilton and Lord knows who else.'

'You know what I mean,' Laura said. Sorry, who had been watching Jacko bent over his pink crocodiles, looked up smiling.

'I think it's just as well though, don't you?' he said. 'I keep wanting to go to bed with you. At first it seemed simple. I knew I could make you want to. But it's not simple at all.' Jacko was getting a little bored.

'My Rosebud likes those little crocodiles,' he said. 'Are there any tigers on this farm?'

'Tigers would eat the pigs,' Sorry said.

'One tiger,' said Jacko holding up his forefinger. 'He can eat cabbage.'

'Get your tiger book, Jacko,' Laura said, for she knew it would take him a little while to find it. 'We could have the tiger story.' Jacko went off into his own room cheerfully enough.

'How could you be sure you could make me want to?' Laura asked, half curious, half scornful.

'How did you know I was a witch?' Sorry said with a shrug. 'That was such an intimate thing to know about me, it made me feel we'd been lovers already. I felt you'd seen me naked. Winter and Miryam were delighted when I told them I'd been recognized by a girl, but they told me to wait until you were older, and I would have done, but you came walking in. Chant, I promise that when I looked up and saw you standing in the doorway I nearly melted away with astonishment. She's come to get me, I thought. My hour has come.'

'It had, too,' Laura agreed.

'Well, I don't think so – not quite!' Sorry said discontentedly. 'You really are too young. It's not even legal, not that that matters so much, but you and Kate get on well together and I don't want to cause any more family rows. And besides, all the time I saw you at school, I thought you looked older than fourteen, but when you went to sleep on the sofa in my study you looked a lot younger. I wanted to protect you, and by then you only needed protecting from me.'

'So you gave up all your other ideas!' Laura exclaimed scornfully.

'I haven't given them up,' Sorry said. 'They've just got mixed up with a lot of other things. You've got at least three years of school ahead of you, and I've got four years of training. Round about then we might, oh . . .' he suddenly sounded irritated, 'get married, I suppose. Live together somehow.'

'You'll meet some other, older girl,' Laura said resentfully.

'Give over, Chant!' Sorry commanded. 'We're both on the same side, you and me, remember? And anyhow you're as likely to meet someone else as I am.'

'Serve you right if I did!' Laura cried.

'It would, wouldn't it?' Sorry agreed unexpectedly, thumping his knee with his fist. 'Half the time I think I'm stupid. I don't know what's wrong with me. I don't want to be like this.'

'Lolly, I can't find it,' Jacko called.

Laura began to get up to go and help him, but Sorry took her arm and said, 'Hang on a moment, Chant,' and kissed her again. 'I'm sickening for something dreadful,' he complained. 'Maturity or some other social disease!'

Laura felt his left hand, his sinister hand, between her dress and her skin. 'You probably won't get a very bad attack,' she said, nervous but enchanted. 'Not a fatal one.'

'Let's go through to your room now,' Sorry suggested. 'Come on, Chant! Invite me. If you think I'm doing the wrong thing, tell me what you want and I'll do what you say.'

'There's Jacko,' Laura said, 'and Kate will be home in a minute.' She could not see Sorry's face for he had hidden it in her neck and shoulder but she felt him smile.

'You're more anxious than you let on,' he told her in a muffled voice. 'You're more interested in romance than sex, and why not?'

'Lolly!' called Jacko plaintively, but Sorry still would not let her go. 'The difficulty is I'm unreliable,' he said.

'Do you love me?' Laura asked him. It was something she had wondered about a lot in recent days.

'How do I know a thing like that?' he answered restlessly. 'It might be wicked lust. I might be a villain, not a hero.'

'Well, I think I love you,' said Laura. 'So maybe that's what makes the difference.'

'Lolly!' said Jacko again and sounded as if he were coming to look for her, so she struggled away from Sorry and found the tiger book almost at once, because she knew it was not with Jacko's other books, but hidden under his pillow.

When she and Jacko came back, Sorry was in the kitchen hurriedly scraping and scrubbing potatoes, a job Laura was supposed to do, and singing to himself under his breath.

'I go to Wellington first,' he called out to her, 'and then – I don't know where – fisheries in the Southern Lakes Acclimatization District, or somewhere around Rotorua-Taupo. I get to Mount Bruce Reserve somewhere along the line. I'll enjoy that. I love birds. I'm not so sure how I'll feel about fish, but no doubt I'll love them too when I get to know them well. I do get holidays, of course . . . work a lot of weekends but get other days off instead. I'm really looking forward to it.'

Laura, too, felt the beginning of an unexpected relief. Life would settle down again and she would have a little longer to be Kate's daughter and Jacko's sister. Something Sorry had said reminded her of a past puzzle that still remained to be asked about.

'Sorry!' she called.

'Right here!' he answered.

'I want to ask you something.'

'Ask away!'

'I want to see you when I ask you.'

There was silence, then Sorry appeared in the doorway of the kitchen.

'Do your damndest!' he said. 'My strength is as the strength of ten because, unfortunately, my heart is pure.'

'Fancy you accusing me of romance!' Laura told him severely. 'You read romances yourself.'

'And you want to know why?' he guessed.

'Why?' Laura asked.

Sorry gave a deep sigh. 'It's a treacherous question,' he remarked. 'Well! All right! My mother used to read them. One or two a week. Supermarket love stories bought along with the soap powder.'

'Miryam?' Laura cried disbelievingly, almost laughing. Sorry had a scrubbed potato in his hand. He tossed it up in the air and caught it again. Then he shook his head.

'My other mother,' he said. 'I missed her for ages. I still miss her. Many times I've wished I could see her again, but there you are – she loved babies, not grown-up, shaving men, and besides it all got so terrible. There's no way she can ever think of me except as something that didn't work out and filled her life with trouble. So I used to read romances just to – to keep in touch with her, I suppose. And they're quite interesting in their way. I know they're awful, but they're so very popular there must be something in them that women find irresistible. Something like catnip. If I could work out exactly what it was, and isolate it, I'd be irresistible too.'

'You might have to give up books like those,' Laura remarked darkly.

'That's right! You've taken my poster and you're threatening my romances,' Sorry said after a pause. 'You'd better have something pretty good to offer me in their place, Chant.'

He went back to the kitchen, and Laura read Jacko a few pages of his tiger book. The little farm on the floor faded away. There was the sound of footsteps outside and the sound of a car door slamming. Jacko forgot the story and leaped to his feet.

'It's my mummy,' he said. 'Mummy's home.'

'Give me one hug,' said Laura. She felt so much affection towards the world she had to use it up somehow.

'Chant!' hissed Sorry, appearing at the kitchen door. 'Chant, your dress is done up crookedly. No one wears a school uniform like that.' He began unbuttoning and then buttoning her dress. 'This is one of my last duties as a school prefect.' Jacko bounced by the door, and as the handle turned, Laura put her arms around Sorry.

'You'll get me shot, Chant,' he hissed.

'They can get used to it,' Laura said as the door opened and Kate came in, Chris Holly behind her, gathering Jacko into her arms and squeezing him until he squeaked with protest and laughter. Kate saw Laura and Sorry over Jacko's head and her smile certainly wavered.

'I hope you've scrubbed the potatoes,' she said. 'Are you staying for dinner, Sorry?'

'No, I've got to be going,' Sorry said. 'My mother's expecting me to turn up with her car. Besides we're having my favourite pudding for dinner tonight – gooseberry fool.'

'Come for fish and chips tomorrow,' Laura suggested. 'Come to tea with F. & C.' Sorry, looking at Kate cautiously, said that he might, if it was all right.

'Of course it is,' said Laura, and Kate agreed, amiable but without true enthusiasm, and then, perhaps feeling her own coolness, added almost at once, 'You seem to be seeing more of Laura these days than I am.'

Sorry looked sidways at Laura, and she could feel, almost as if she were thinking them herself, various answers cross his mind.

'Yes, well, don't look on it as losing a fourth former, Mrs Chant,' he said at last. 'Look on it as gaining a prefect!'

'Or a Wild Life officer,' suggested Laura, opening the door to let him out.

'So long for now, Chant,' he said, vanishing down the path. 'Look after yourself.' A moment later she heard his mother's car start and drive away. She could tell its motor from all others.

'That was a bit cheeky,' Kate said, frowning after him. 'Lolly, why on earth did you ask him to come tomorrow? Thursday's our special, family night.'

'Chris comes,' Laura pointed out, at the exact moment Chris said, 'Wake up, Kate. Why do you think she asked him?' and putting his hand on her shoulder, shook her gently. Kate gave Jacko a little extra hug and put him down again.

'He was having his tiger story,' Laura said, 'but he stopped listening when he heard you coming. Chris can read it. I've read it thousands of times before.'

'I'm cooking dinner,' Chris said. 'Jacko can come and give me a hand if he wants to. Or he can read his tiger book to me in the kitchen.'

'You can't compare Sorensen Carlisle with Chris,' Kate said half indignantly, still thinking of Sorry and F. & C. and Thursday night.

'Kate!' said Chris. 'You and Laura don't look much alike, but I couldn't help noticing you looked at young Carlisle in just the way Laura looked at me the first time I came in here, also on a Thursday night I seem to recall.'

Laura heard the voices talking on as she went to her room to change her clothes. She put on jeans and a T shirt, looked in the mirror to do her hair and – there it was – the very face she had been promised weeks earlier on the day of the warnings. Was it possible to be in love with someone who was trying not to have a true heart? And was it wise of him to think of coming back to the world of feeling when feeling could tear people to bits? Maybe he had chosen estrangement wisely and should stay estranged, even though he could see in her the possibility of consolation and escape.

'Laura!' shouted Kate. 'Laura, I'm sorry to have nagged as soon as I got home. Come out and talk to me.' Laura took another moment to make herself sociable again and then went out. Kate sat on the edge of the table counting money.

'Forty-two cents!' she said. 'That's all the real money I've got left in the world. I'll have to go to the bank tomorrow. I've actually got a cheque to pay in. Stephen paid for the hospital, and sent a little extra to go with it.'

'Big deal!' said Laura, but smiling as she spoke. 'It mightn't last.'

'I don't expect it will,' Kate said. 'But it's nice while it does. I can understand him being slow to pay. You see, in a way the man who married me doesn't exist any more. I must just seem like a long-ago fairy tale to him, whereas money in hand is always real. After a while it must seem as if he's paying off ghosts.'

'You weren't very old when you got married, were you?' Laura enquired casually. Kate's eyes shifted sideways to look at her.

'I was eighteen, as you very well know,' she said. 'Don't you get any ideas. I'll never let you make that sort of mistake.'

'I'll have to make my own then, won't I?' Laura answered.

'Very slick!' Kate exclaimed. 'Very smart! I wonder where you're getting that from?'

'I've always been smart in my own way,' Laura said. 'Mum, being married at eighteen wasn't a total disaster. You got Jacko and me.'

'I know,' Kate said. 'I think of that over and over again. My worst mistake and my two best people! How can you make judgements when things are so mixed. But you've got to make them, all the same.' It seemed to Laura that Kate was saying the same thing that Sorry had said a little earlier.

'I'll admit,' said Kate thoughtfully, 'that this thing you've got going with Sorensen Carlisle does worry me. He's too knowing, too – too serious. He should have a girlfriend of his own age – and someone else's daughter,' she added, grinning rather shamefacedly. 'I'd be really tolerant over that. "Oh well, girls will be girls," I'd say. But Lolly – for the life of me, I can't be easygoing over you. And you're just too young.'

'That's what Sorry says,' Laura agreed, but did not add that he also confessed to being unreliable.

'Does he say that?' Kate asked, swinging her legs as if she were fourteen herself, jingling her family fortune between her hands. 'Watch out for him, Lolly, that's all! It sounds like a line to me. Watch out for him! But since we're on the subject – would you mind, Laura – would it be very awful for you, of course I don't see how it could be, but would you mind, if somewhere along the line, Chris and I thought about getting married?'

'I don't mind you thinking about it,' Laura said as cunningly as Sorry himself. 'Are you going to?'

'We've hinted at it once or twice,' Kate said. 'I nearly asked him last week but then I thought it wasn't fair, three of us to one of him. However, he came across with a direct suggestion about ten minutes ago. He said we were going to need a good, clear head somewhere in the family. He said we'd grown too exclusive to each other – you and me that is – and he just might be right.' Kate laughed as she spoke, and threw up her arms sending her forty-two cents flying around the room.

Laura was thrilled. 'Don't pick it up!' she cried. 'Leave it! Our family fortune thrown to the winds!'

Chris came in, wearing an apron that Kate never bothered to wear, holding the tiger book like a tray with four glasses on it, with a carton of apple-juice beside them. Jacko followed proudly, holding a green bottle with a gold top.

'Champagne – or as good as!' Chris declared.

'Let me see!' demanded Kate taking it, and reading the label. 'Oh yes, a very good, fizzy year! On an occasion like this, it's bubbles we need more than actual wine.'

'And music!' agreed Chris. 'Where's our string quartet?' He wrestled with the cork, and it came out at last, with a pop, releasing a pale, hissing fountain of wine which leaped up joyously, splashing all four of them. Jacko shouted with excitement, bending his knees as though he were going to jump very high in the air, but when he did jump he rose only about an inch off the ground. 'May we all go like that when our time comes!' said Chris, pouring what wine was left into the long glasses which had once held peanut-butter.

'Oh dear,' said Kate to Laura, 'suddenly I feel so happy I can't bear it. Yet it doesn't feel unnatural. It feels like a true human condition.' Chris turned the radio on and began searching for acceptable music.

'On with the dance,' he said, 'let joy be unconfined.' Music flooded the room. He turned to Laura. 'Will you dance with me, oh beauteous one?'

'I will in a minute,' Laura said. 'I'll dance with Jacko first. You dance with Kate.' Chris did not object. He and Kate began to dance, Kate holding her glass of wine, Chris still wearing the kitchen apron.

Quite suddenly Laura knew that what Sorry had once said was true. Like a holograph, every piece of the world contained the whole of the world if you stood at the right angle to it. Quite clearly, in the room, she saw herself and Sorry walking around the estuary, the grey herons flying, the kingfisher clicking its beak, the crabs scuttling and semaphoring messages of invitation and threat to one another. She looked up and saw the ceiling complete with cobwebs, but she also saw a troubled moon buffeted by nor'west clouds, and when she looked back into the room she could see the wall, and somehow, through the wall, a city street and a hurrying figure which she knew to be her own, set in past time to move eternally to Janua Caeli, a name which, Sorry had told her, meant 'the door of heaven'.

To her surprise Sorry's voice spoke to her, as clearly as if he were standing beside her.

'Chant, what are you doing wandering around in my head? Do stay in your own, there's a good girl.'

'I was thinking about the estuary,' she said.

'That's it then,' he answered. 'So was I. You know what this means?'

'Yes,' said Laura, 'you'll be able to help me with my answers when I do School Certificate next year. I'll get one hundred percent and be top of all New Zealand.'

Jacko came over to Laura and leaned against her. 'Sorry made a little farm,' he whispered.

'Yes,' Laura agreed.

'With little pigs and crocodiles!' said Jacko. He was holding his Ruggie and now began to suck his thumb.

'I made the crocodiles,' Laura pointed out, and lifted him on to her knee. She could smell the family shampoo in his hair and see his mouth turning up on either side of his thumb as he smiled.

'Are you thinking of me, Chant?' Sorry said. 'You feel very affectionate.'

'I'm cuddling Jacko,' Laura replied. 'You feel affectionate, too. Are you thinking of me?'

'I was thinking of the pudding we're having for supper, actually,' he said. 'Gooseberry fool! Still, it's not so different, really.'

'You think I'm like a pudding?' Laura exclaimed indignantly.

'It's my *favourite* pudding!' Sorry reassured her. 'It's creamy and sharp at the same time. Chant, four years is a hell of a long time to wait, isn't it? Even three!'

'The first hour's already gone,' Laura answered.

Kate and Chris danced almost in time to the music. Jacko leaned his head against Laura and watched them dreamily. Suddenly he thought of something and sat up, turning to face her.

'Hold on a bit longer!' he said, remembering something strange, and looking at her face as if he were seeing it almost for the first time. 'That's what you said to me, isn't it, Lolly? 'Hold on!' you said, and *I did* hold on. I held on like this . . .' He clenched his hands into fists and screwed up his face. 'I held on, and you came and got me out.'

'Out from where?' Laura asked him in a whisper.

'Out of the dark,' he said uncertainly. 'I didn't like it, Lolly. I held on, didn't I?'

'You held on beautifully,' Laura said, and he put his head back against her, nodding to himself and beginning to suck his thumb again, so he did not see her cry a little, head bent, in the room full of wine and dancing and music.

In the darkroom, at the end of his garage, Sorry worked, developing photographs. He whistled softly to himself in the dark, then turned on a red light to watch his chosen images magically swim back out of the past, darkening on the photographic paper. The red light cast a demoniac glow over his face, his expression bright but unusually gentle. Laura slowly formed on the paper, reading, walking, laughing. Sorry washed the photographs in water.

'You're a wonderfully developed girl, Chant,' he told her, right across Gardendale.

'Are you doing those photographs?' Laura asked him, and he groaned and said, 'The romance is going out of my life before it ever got properly into it. I'm becoming an open book to you. Never mind. I'll fix you, see if I don't!' and he put the photographs in the fixing solution.

'I know something you don't,' Laura said, unexpectedly triumphant, for a certainty, as clear and sparkling as a sea wave, burst over her. 'You're the one that's fixed, poor Sorry, fixed by love no matter how scared you are of it. You can't twist out of it. At least, I'm clever enough to know that.'

'An ever-fixed mark,' Sorry said uncertainly, 'looking on t-tempests and never b-being shaken, and all that? You might b-be right, but only time will tell. Time t-tells everything, given time.'

Outside in the city, traffic lights changed colours, casting quick spells of prohibition and release. Cars hesitated, then set off again, roaring with urgency through the maze of the Gardendale subdivision, a labyrinth in which one could, after all, find a firebird's feather, or a glass slipper or the footprints of the minotaur quite as readily as in fairy tales, or the infinitely dividing paths of Looking-Glass land. Kate and Chris danced, the potatoes over-cooked gently, Sorry carefully hung his pictures out to dry while his cat watched him, purring for no reason, Laura dreamed of many things, and Jacko, pleased and puzzled by other people's lives, fell asleep on her knee while the strands of wool along the edge of his Ruggie swayed backwards and forwards on the small tide of his even breath.

Read on for an extract of Margaret Mahy's Carnegie Medal-winning novel, *The Haunting*.

1

Barnaby's Dead

When, suddenly, on an ordinary Wednesday, it seemed to Barney that the world tilted and ran downhill in all directions, he knew he was about to be haunted again. It had happened when he was younger but he had thought that being haunted was a babyish thing that you grew out of, like crying when you fell over, or not having a bike.

'Remember Barney's imaginary friends, Mantis, Bigbuzz and Ghost?' Claire – his stepmother – sometimes said. 'The garden seems empty now that they've gone. I quite miss them.'

But she was really pleased perhaps because, being so very real to Barney, they had become too real for her to laugh over. Barney had been sorry to lose them, but he wanted Claire to feel comfortable living with him. He could not remember his own mother and Claire had come as a wonderful surprise, giving him a hug when he came home from school, asking him about his day, telling him about hers, arranging picnics and unexpected parties and helping him with hard homework. It seemed worth losing Mantis, Bigbuzz and Ghost and the other kind phantoms that had been his friends for so many days before Claire came.

Yet here it was beginning again . . . the faint dizzy twist in the world around him, the thin singing drone as if some tiny insect were trapped in the curling mazes of his ear. Barney looked up at the sky searching for a ghost but there was only a great blueness like a weight pressing down on him. He looked away quickly, half expecting to be crushed into a sort of rolled-out gingerbread boy in an enormous stretched-out school uniform. Then he saw his ghost on the footpath beside him.

A figure was slowly forming out of the air: a child – quite a little one, only about four or five – struggling to be real. A curious pale face grew clearer against a halo of shining hair, silver gold hair that curled and crinkled, fading into the air like bright smoke. The child was smiling. It seemed to be having some difficulty in seeing Barney so that he felt that *he* might be the one who was not quite real. Well, he was used to feeling that. In the days before Claire he had often felt that he himself couldn't be properly heard or seen. But then Mantis had taken time to become solid and Ghost had always been dim and smoky. So Barney was not too surprised to see the ghost looking like a flat paper doll stuck against the air by some magician's glue. Then it became round and real, looking alive, but old-fashioned and strange, in its blue velvet suit and lace collar. A soft husky voice came out of it.

'Barnaby's dead!' it said. 'Barnaby's dead! I'm going to be very lonely.'

Barney stood absolutely still, feeling more tilted and dizzy than ever. His head rang as if it were strung like a bead on the thin humming that ran, like electricity, from ear to ear.

The ghost seemed to be announcing his death by his proper christened name of Barnaby – not just telling him he was going to die, but telling him that he was actually dead already. Now it spoke again.

'Barnaby's dead!' it said in exactly the same soft husky voice. 'Barnaby's dead! I'm going to be very lonely.' It wasn't just that it said the same words that it had said earlier. Its very tone – the lifts and falls and flutterings of its voice – was exactly the same. If it had added, 'This is a recorded message,' it would not have seemed very out of place. Barney wanted to say something back to it, but what can you say to a ghost? You can't joke with it. Perhaps you could ask it questions, but Barney was afraid of the answers this ghost might give him. He would have to believe what it told him, and it might tell him something terrible.

As it turned out this ghost was not one that would answer questions anyway. It had only one thing to say, and it had said it. It began to swing from side to side, like an absent-minded compass needle searching for some lost North. Its shape did not change but it swung widely and lay crossways in the air looking silly, but also very frightening.

'Barnaby's dead!' it said, 'Barnaby's dead! And I'm going to be very lonely.' Then it spun like a propeller, slowly at first then faster and faster until it was only a blur of silver-gold in the air. It spun faster still until even the colours vanished and there was nothing but a faint clear flicker. Then it stopped and the ordinary air closed over it. The humming in Barney's ears stopped, the world straightened out; time began again, the wind blew, trees moved, cars droned and tooted. Down through the air from the point where the ghost had disappeared fluttered a cloud of blue flakes. Barney caught a few of them in his hand. For a moment he held nothing but scraps of paper from a torn-up picture! He caught a glimpse of a blue velvet sleeve, a piece of lace cuff and a pink thumb and finger. Then the paper turned into quicksilver beads of colour that ran through his fingers and were lost before they fell on to the footpath.

Barney wanted to be at home at once. He did not want the in-between time of going down streets and around corners. There were no short cuts. He had to run all the way, fearing that at any moment he might be struck by lightning, or a truck, or by some terrible dissolving sickness that would eat him away as he ran. Little stumbles in his running made him think he might have been struck by bullets. His hair felt prickly and he wondered if it was turning white. He could imagine arriving at home and seeing his face in the hall mirror staring out under hair like cotton wool. He could imagine Claire saying, 'Barney, what on earth have you been up to? Look at the state of your hair.' How could he say, 'Well, there was this ghost telling me that I was dead.' Claire would just say sternly, 'Barney, have you been reading horror comics again?'

As it happened it was not Claire who met him when he got home but his two sisters, one on either side of the doorway – his thin knobbly sister Troy, stormy in her black cloud of hair, her black eyebrows almost meeting over her long nose, and brown, round Tabitha, ready to talk and talk as she always did.

'Where have you been?' she asked. 'You're late and have missed out on family news. But it's ok – the family novelist will now bring you up to date.' By 'the family novelist' Tabitha meant herself. She was writing the world's greatest novel, but no one was allowed to read it until she was twenty-one and it was published. However, she talked about it all the time and showed off by taking pages and pages of notes and talking about those, too.

'I stopped to . . .' Barney began. He felt his voice quaver and die out. He couldn't tell Tabitha about his ghost, particularly in front of Troy who was five years older than he was and silent and scornful. But anyway – Tabitha was not interested in his explanations. She was too busy telling him the family news in her own way.

'We are a house of mourning,' she said in an important voice. 'One of our dear relations has died. It's really good material for my novel and I'm taking notes like anything. No one I know has ever died before.'

Barney stared at her in horror.

'Not Claire!' he began to say because he was always afraid that they would lose Claire in some way, particularly now that she was expecting a baby which Barney knew was dangerous work. But Tabitha was not upset enough for it to be Claire.

'Great-Uncle Barnaby . . . a Scholar relation,' she went on and then, as Barney's face stiffened and became blank she added, sarcastically, 'You do remember him don't you? You're named after him.'

'I'm going to be very lonely,' said a soft, husky voice in Barney's ear. He felt the world begin to slide away.

'Hey!' Troy's voice spoke on his other side. 'You don't have to be upset. He was old . . . and he'd been ill – very ill, for a while.'

'It's not that!' Barney stammered. 'I – I thought it might be me.'

'Lonely!' said the echo in his haunted ear.

'I thought it *was* me,' Barney said, and suddenly the world made up its mind and shrank away from him, grown to tennis ball size, then walnut size, then a pinhead of brightness in whirling darkness. On the steps of his own home Barney had fainted.

Margaret Mahy (1936–2012) is one of New Zealand's most celebrated children's writers. She is the author of more than 150 titles, which have been translated into many different languages and sold around the world. Appointed to the Order of New Zealand in 1993, Mahy also won many global prizes for children's writers, including the Carnegie Medal and the prestigious Hans Christian Andersen Award.

Also by Margaret Mahy

The Haunting

The Tricksters

Memory

The Catalogue of the Universe